BLOSSOM
ON THE WIND

BY

L TAYLOR

To John & Liz

So lovely to see you here in Edinburgh — here's to more visits.

Enjoy the book

Much love

Lea

Copyright @ L Taylor
First published in 2022

For all press and enquiries contact us at:
leataylor@thebookwhisperers.com

DEDICATION

Dedicated to those loved and lost along the way

ACKNOWLEDGEMENTS

I'm indebted to Andy and Cameron who have come to know what it is to live with a writer; thanks for your patience, understanding and willingness to put up with my eccentricities. Andy in particular, for editing and reading early drafts – including the bloopers which shall not be mentioned further.

My dogs, Rex and Rufie, the heart and soul of the house, always up for walks to blow cobwebs or find inspiration.

Mary Turner Thomson, couldn't have done this without you, your amazing skillset (too numerous to list here) or your infectious sense of humour. Oh, the Giff-offs we have had!

Claire Steele, for your support and guidance; essentially the catalyst to all my writing.

Friends who have graciously read or listened to excerpts or deigned to beta-read for me: Sophie Devereux, Nix Hindle, Mandy O'Connor, Yasmin Neale – your feedback has been invaluable.

Much love and a grateful nod to those who are an integral part of the tapestry of this book – you know who you are.

And finally, all the incredibly hard-working team at The Book Whisperers – you utterly rock!

Chapter One

March 1977

I must get this flat, I must get this flat - my breath came in short bursts as my feet pounded the pavement. I heard the chimes for twelve noon and my stomach lurched. Being ten minutes late and barely seventeen wasn't going to help. Especially as I needed to present myself as reliable and grownup.

I quick-stepped past a long row of Georgian terraced houses with their rich swags, luxurious curtains and, I bet, afternoon tea - with little finger extended, naturally.

Across the road the view changed to squashed up terraces; multi-coloured peeling fronts a riot of greens, yellows, blues; discarded mattresses nestling among weeds; and rusted bikes in unkempt gardens. One really stood out, it had old tyres piled in the corners and a long line of dirty, empty milk bottles leading down into the street from its front door.

Number three. I'd written it on the back of my hand. Number three was the house with the milk bottles. On the street directly outside, a couple of motorbikes were parked on patches of oil stains. I stopped momentarily taking it all in, my heart stepping up its pace.

A soft breeze blew, like a whispered promise, picking up the cherry blossoms from a tree two doors down. I watched the pink petals, tender as a puppy's belly, spiralling and fluttering in the air. They chased and swirled in the doorway like small tornados; some lay bruised and brown on the step as though crushed in battle. Maybe, just maybe, I thought, this is the beginning of the change I'm looking for.

I rang the doorbell. Within, a dog barked and dog paws pattered down the stairs alongside the thump of a pair of human feet. The door opened and before me stood Mr Meagher, the landlord. I recognised him as the owner of a flat I had stayed in. He had found me kipping on the sofa in a sleeping bag. Apparently, he owned several flats around town. Beneath his bushy eyebrows, a pair of squinty brown eyes peered at me as he smoothed back his thinning hairline. He stood before me in his blue workman's overalls, a screwdriver jauntily perched in his top pocket. Beside him, panting, sat a huge Alsatian.

I looked from him to the dog.

'It's alright, he only bites when he's hungry.' Mr Meagher gave an impish grin, clearly relishing the fact that the dog made people feel uncomfortable. 'Frankie, isn't it?' His voice was kindly. He smiled and held out his hand.

I shook it, feeling the strength of his grip. My hand felt tiny in his.

'I'm Mr Meagher, the landlord. If you'd like to follow me.'

He led me up a flight of grubby carpeted stairs stopping on the first landing to indicate a bathroom and toilet. Then we climbed another set of stairs leading to the main living areas. Our last stop was the sitting room. All the windows were open, suspiciously so. The room smelled of polish and cigarettes. On the sofa were two young people, their bodies sprawled as though they'd been hastily scattered there.

I guessed they were at least a couple of years older than me. I hadn't met any people my age living away from home. They appeared confident, speaking before being spoken to and giving direct eye contact, something I'd not yet mastered. Their eyes washed over me. Was I giving the right impression? I clutched my bag closer to my chest. What if they don't like me or have someone else they like better lined up?

The room was a decent size, with a black faux leather two-seater sofa, two matching armchairs and a television perched on top of an old sideboard opposite a small sash cased window. A huge poster dominated the wall with its alien landscape of misshaped stalagmites. Above the electric fire staring down with militant intent was a poster of Che Guevara with a jaunty pair of John Lennon glasses hastily drawn in felt tip. In the far corner, a stereo with an impressive stack of LPs. It all appeared very grown up in a hip, sort of way.

'So, this is it,' said Mr Meagher, 'take your time, have a look around. Oh, and this is … sorry, I've forgotten your names.' He nodded at the couple and then cleared his throat as if giving a cue to say something.

'Hi, I'm Tonk,' said the skinny youth who looked as if he hadn't quite grown into himself. His arms and legs were gangly, like they couldn't decide whether they had stopped growing or where to put themselves without looking awkward. His smile exposed an uneven set of teeth temporarily hidden by a bum-fluffed lip. He wore an earring and a striking Mohican hairstyle and, if I wasn't mistaken, black eyeliner that made the whites of his eyes stand out. I shifted from one foot to the other.

Next to him sat a girl. Fresh and clean looking. Her dark, short, permed hair framed her face perfectly. She wore a white cheese-cloth shirt, flared jeans with hand-sewn flairs and had the largest bluest eyes I'd ever seen.

'Hi, I'm Barbara.' She shot up from her seat. 'We'll be sharing a room. Come on, I'll show you.' Giggling, she took me by the arm and led the way.

Sunlight streamed through the curtains showing a pale copy of what the room had once been in its heyday. Still, it was serviceable and represented a much-needed roof over my head. From the window I watched a long-haired young man clad in denim start up his motorbike. He revved the engine as it spluttered then growled noisily into life, puffs of smoke escaping and popping from the exhaust. She followed my gaze.

'Oh, that's Bean, he lives next door.' And having seen me shiver she added 'He's quite harmless, they all are. They're just into bikes, heavy metal and don't like washing.'

'Oh,' I half smiled, recoiling at the idea of living next door to someone who didn't like to wash. I looked around the room, its dressing table piled with make-up, eyeliner, mascara, hairbands, bangles, hippy beads, and an array of perfume bottles. There were two single beds either side of the room and a tall chest of drawers, with one drawer open stuffed to the gunnels with clothes.

'You get the bed with the closet behind it; you'll be able to hang your clothes up there.' I almost laughed out loud, clothes? *You mean a pair of jeans, a skirt, and a shirt.*

'Oh, and by the way, call me Barb. Barbara sounds like I'm in trouble.' She flashed me a warm smile.

I dumped my bag on my appointed bed.

'I'm Frankie. Just Frankie, not Frances, Frank, or anything else.' I smiled back.

Mr Meagher popped his head into the room. 'Are you staying then?'

'Yes,' the word shot out of my mouth before I'd even thought about it.

'Ok, I'll need you sign the agreement and its £20 deposit and your rent, up front.'

I emptied my purse out on the bed and counted out the notes and coins, leaving myself with £2.60 for the rest of the week. Then followed him into the living room, signed the agreement and handed over the money.

'I bet you'll be glad to have a bed of your own after kipping on that sofa with that boa constrictor on the loose, eh?'

I shifted from one foot to the other half expecting Barb and Tonk to say something, but they just sat there quite unperturbed.

'Yes. This is much better. Thank you.' The memory of waking up to find a huge ten-foot snake coiling its way around my legs made me shudder. Mr Meagher arrived just as the screaming started, me still in the sleeping bag trying to scoot across the living room like I was in some weird sack race with a bloody great reptile writhing after me in hot pursuit.

Mr Meagher and his dog had barely disappeared through the front door when Tonk reached beneath the sofa and slid out a Bad Company LP. On it was a larger than normal hand-rolled cigarette.

'This calls for a celebration,' he chuckled, lighting it with a flourish. His face disappearing for a moment behind a plume of smoke.

'Welcome to the flat.' He took a long puff and handed it to me. I hesitated.

'What is it?'

He blew out a column of smoke. 'What, you've never …?' He shook his head and tutted, half smiling. 'It's a joint. It's not addictive if that's what you're worried about,' he proffered it to me.

It didn't feel like pressure, more an act of kindness. I guess I didn't want to offend or appear too green, so I took it and had a small puff. I coughed until my eyes streamed, my body doubled over on itself in protest. Tonk looked on bemused and Barb leapt up and left the room.

'You'll get used to it,' said Tonk.

I tried to apologise between stifled coughs and wiping my streaming eyes, my body all bunched up as though trying to disappear. I imagined Tonk could feel the heat from my face, and maybe if he did, he didn't show it. When I'd finished coughing, he carried on like nothing had happened.

'So, what's your name?'

'She's Frankie,' said Barb entering the room with three mugs of tea on a tray. 'Do you take sugar?'

'Mmmnn, yes please,' I said reaching for the tea, glad of the distraction. I dropped three spoons of sugar in my cup, a moment passed before I realised Barb and Tonk were staring at me.

I shrugged, 'I like sugar.'

'Yeah, I can see that,' said Tonk, eyebrows raised but his eyes were smiling. 'Tate and Lyle'll be happy.'

I smiled and supped my tea, sneaking quick looks at Tonk and Barb when I thought they weren't aware. Tonk was busy constructing something on the LP cover and Barb was riffling through the stack of LP's trying to decide on what to listen to next.

In profile Tonk's hairstyle reminded me of a dinosaur, a spiked red Mohican, typical punk style. It took me back to a moment in my childhood, my little brother and me playing on the front room floor. Danny had sunk his plastic stegosaurus into his lumpy porridge making stegosaurus grunts as he did so. He looked back at me with rebellious glee, eyes shining behind long lashes, snotty nose oozing towards his top lip and sticky fingers covered in porridge. The thought of him caught in my throat as I pushed the grief aside. After all these years the thought of Danny and how he died still haunted me.

Tonk's dinosaur spikes gave me a distinct urge to laugh though. The more I tried not to, the worse it got. First it was a small titter bubbling up from the back of my throat. I clamped my hand over my mouth, my whole-body coiling like a spring, but the sound seemed determined to find a release and escaped through my nose in strangled snorts. Then a laugh broke free like an explosion of noise until I ended up bent double laughing, tears rolling down my cheeks. Helpless.

Tonk looked up, a grin spreading across his face. 'Looks like our Frankie is stoned.'

I loved that moment, I loved how Tonk had used the possessive pronoun, 'our.' It made me feel claimed, like I belonged, accepted, and as I rolled about in kinks of laughter, I wrapped that word around me like a huge luxurious hug.

Barb giggled in agreement, the mirth escaping from her mouth like rising bubbles. Then Tonk joined in, slapping his knee and thumping the arm of the sofa, his laugh like an explosion of long, loud haaa haaa's reminding me of a braying donkey. After what seemed like an age of laughter, our breaths settled and Barb put on what I was to later learn was her 'now let's get down to business,' sensible face.

'So: house rules,' she said, folding her hands in her lap. 'We share the bills equally,'

'When Barb says we, that also includes Jerry, the bathroom resident.'

I opened my mouth to say something but was lost for words. Why should I find that unusual? After all I had had a spell of staying in someone's bathroom. I closed my mouth.

'And we all pay the same amount towards food. We shop together so everyone gets what they want,' Barb nodded encouragingly.

Then Tonk chipped in, 'But it's best we don't go when we're stoned because we only come back with sweets and biscuits.'

I gulped. 'Oh. When do you need the money by and how much do you need?' I felt my stomach squeeze. 'I don't get paid till Friday. I've got ...'

'That's okay, we'll sort something out,' soothed Barb. You didn't have much left after paying Mr Meagher, did you?'

I shook my head and looked down at my shoes.

'We usually put in a fiver each and anything left over goes towards fish and chips on a Saturday. If Sam's working there, we usually get a discount.'

'Yeah, but that's only because he's into you. Being Saturday today we are planning to get some tonight. Are you a tomato sauce or brown sauce girl?' said Tonk.

'I don't know, I've never tried brown sauce,' I replied.

'Well, we can sort that when the chippy opens,' he looked at his watch, 'in just two and a half hours.'

The chippy was a ten-minute saunter down the road. The chip shop owner knew Barb and Tonk by name. When we got back to the flat, we were ravenous and tore into the chips. As it turned out I liked both tomato sauce and brown and mixed the two. A travesty according to Tonk who was utterly appalled.

Later that afternoon Colin, a friend of Tonk and Barb, turned up with a couple of his friends in tow and was welcomed with much fuss and fanfare. Colin was a frequent visitor. He drove a Morris Roma which, Jerry later reliably informed me, had mushrooms growing on the inside. Jerry emphasized the word mushrooms, but it was lost on me.

Colin, I was to learn later, was the dealer. The hash man. He challenged my assumptions of what a dealer was. Not that I really had an assumption. I thought of dealers as people who stuck needles in their arms or snorted things up their noses and listened to Jimi Hendrix while wearing bandanas and copious strings of love beads. Colin seemed pleasant enough, well-spoken and groomed, the kind of young man you'd take home and introduce to your parents. And, considering the amount of cannabis he smoked, quite articulate. He sat with an LP on his lap and rolled joint after joint until the room was suffused in thick smoke. By the time I was partially comatose Tonk shouted. 'Damn.' He stood up, looking around. 'I've lost my blim.'

'Blim?' I didn't know what he was talking about.

'A little piece of cannabis,' hissed Barb.

Everyone sat up. The main light was switched on and eyes blinked and squinted as they adjusted to the light.

'Maybe it's fallen down the back of the sofa,' offered Barb.

Tonk, joint hanging precariously out the side of his mouth, removed the cushions but still couldn't see well enough and so lit his lighter.

'Ah, yes, there it is.' He held the lighter perilously close to the sofa, its flame positively licking the plastic. I held my breath, could feel words rushing to the front of my mouth, dancing on my tongue, but daren't speak up. Suddenly there was a flash of light and thick smoke. The sofa was alight, rapidly melting before us.

'Fire!' Barb shrieked. Everyone got to their feet. Tonk tried stamping the fire out, saving his blim first, obviously. Bodies moved to gather milk bottles from the kitchen and fill them with water to fling over the sofa. We created an unruly line, passing bottles back and forth. Soon water was everywhere, and the fire quickly, but well and truly doused.

Barb threw open the window, the smell inside was rank and overpowering. She shoved a cushion over the melted, wet spot and Tonk, still with joint in mouth, retrieved some air freshener from the loo and proceeded to liberally spray the room. We retired to the kitchen and sat in a huddle around the table and on the floor looking quite shocked in a stoned sort of way.

'Such a distressing situation,' announced Colin. 'This calls for an emergency joint!'

His edict broke the ice. Everyone started talking at once regaling the event, who did what, how quickly it went up, congratulating themselves for having all those milk bottles to hand. It was as if ice had been broken and the tension released.

'What about Mr Meagher?' I piped up. 'Won't he get cross and chuck us out?'

'He doesn't have to if he doesn't know,' said Tonk.

'We'll cover it up with a cushion' Barb grinned.

'Or you'll have to sit on it when Meagher comes round,' said Tonk.

I was horrified, the thought of Mr Meagher finding me hiding the melted hole in the sofa and blaming me. I had visions of being slung out on the street, dragging my few possessions behind me.

'Don't listen to him. He talks a load of shite sometimes,' Barb had obviously clocked my concern.

My ears pricked up when I heard Tonk regale a time when someone had fallen asleep with his feet next to a fire and the soles of his shoes had melted, the memory offsetting other bizarre and funny tales, raising voices and laughter.

I felt obliquely distanced, listening to those shared histories that obviously bound them together. There was so much verve and fun about them. To me, they seized life by the throat and squeezed every drop of possible fun they could out of it. Even more so when their capers bordered on dangerous activities. I was drawn to them, thrilled by them but at the same time my toes squirmed, and hands gripped, I faltered and questioned, should I - could I - let go and really become part of them?

Soon everyone had settled back down like nothing of any consequence had happened and within the hour we were back in the sitting room smoking again. Gradually the volume on the sound system got louder and louder. After a while, I noticed a dull thump that developed into an insistent banging. It pierced through the music – Steve Miller had been playing on the turntable for what seemed like an age, but no-one seemed capable of getting out of their seat to change it. The room was wreathed in ribbons of smoke as if the mist had come down from the hills and made its home there.

I wondered whether the neighbour below was having some work done, the banging had been going on for quite a while. Thump, thump, thump. If only he could match it with the beat of the music. Then another spliff came my way and the banging drifted into an altogether dreamy domain.

Chapter Two

As the day merged into early evening a stranger entered the room bringing fresh air and a pocketful of sweets. His long dark hair hung over his face partially covering his cheeky grin.

'And this,' said Tonk, 'is Jerry. Jerry this is Frankie.'

Jerry obliged by giving a long low bow. 'At your servile,' his eyebrows danced as he spoke, showing anything but deference.

'He came to visit someone at the flat and just never left,' offered Barb. 'Took up residence in the bathroom,'

'He does oblige by moving out when the bath's needed,' said Tonk, as though he could hear my thoughts.

Jerry interrupted, 'Hey, look what I found.' We all turned our heads. 'Munchies.' His eyes lit up with glee as he waved the sweetie bag before us and then he emptied it on to the floor. It broke us out of our torpor. Bodies dived, hands grabbed; space-dust, bars of chocolate and boiled sweets.

'And guess what else?' He made a thing of slowly pulling what looked like a wodge of blotting paper stamped with pink and yellow smileys from his pocket.

A ripple of excitement went round the room. 'Acid' came the hushed whisperers from smiling lips, as though some religious icon had just entered the room.

'Looks like we're all going tripping this weekend.' He laughed raucously; mouth open showing all his fillings. It had a mirthful but wicked edge to it, like a jester gone wild. Then he stopped and lifted his nose in the air. 'What is that fucking awful smell? It's rank!'

'We've been smoking plastic,' said Tonk.

On profile Jerry reminded me of Will Shakespeare, pointy beard, long hair but not the high forehead as shown in the line drawings I'd seen in the schoolbooks. Jerry wore a denim jacket and topped the look off with frayed jeans and pointy black cowboy boots. He was your typical high jinks, wild child biker with an eye for mischief and a willingness to follow it through.

The music stopped momentarily as it changed track. The banging started up again.

'What is that?' Tonk muttered, mouth full of chocolate.

'Oh, I think it's the guy downstairs, he's been at it all afternoon,' said Barb.

'Oh yeah, that reminds me,' said Jerry. He stood awkwardly in the middle of the room, as if a thought had just occurred to him. 'He asked me to tell you to turn the music down.'

'Oh,' said Tonk, still evidently enjoying his chocolate. 'Was that all?'

'Milk bottles,' mumbled Jerry.

'Milk bottles? What about them?'

'He wants you to clear them off the steps.'

'Oh, okay. But they're not all ours!'

'Now come on, love thy neighbour,' joked Barb.

Then everyone started cracking up and still nobody moved. There must have been about 30 empty bottles sitting on the steps next door.

Shortly after, there came a hammering on the front door. Jerry went to the bedroom window to investigate. He came back with a mischievous grin.

'It's our neighbour. I told you ... '

'Yeah, but you only told us about it five minutes ago,' said Tonk mildly annoyed.

'Don't you think he's being a little impatient?' said Barb. She looked to Jerry and matched his grin.

I watched the two of them; they were hatching something.

'Hmmn,' said Jerry, stroking his beard in an exaggerated manner. 'I think we need to show him the Eye of Sauron, what do you think?'

'Yes. The Eye of Sauron,' chanted Barb and Tonk gleefully.

'The Eye of Sauron?' They all nodded their heads in unison. Following Jerry, we all trooped into the bedroom where he lifted up the window then dropped his trousers and hung his arse out the window shouting, 'Oi you! Bugger off.'

The banging stopped.

Barb and Tonk corpsed with laughter, tears rolling down their cheeks. Jerry was busy taking a bow in front of our guests. I wasn't sure what to make of it. Barb clocked my quizzical look, 'Have you read Lord of the Rings?'

I shook my head.

'It's a brilliant book. I read it to a bunch of us over Christmas. In the book *The Eye of Sauran* relates to the bad wizard. We've made our own interpretation of it as you can see.'

The banging stopped and we returned to the living room. Colin and friends left shortly after leaving a mess of bits of tobacco and Rizla paper all over the floor.

'Will I get the hoover and clean that up?' I was trying to impress and also show my gratitude for them choosing me as their new flatmate. It was still my first day and despite all the chaos I was still trying to figure out how the land lay.

'No,' the rest shouted in unison.

The vociferous response rather took me aback.

Tonk laid a hand on my arm. 'Colin leaves enough to make several joints with his mess.'

It took me a few moments to translate what he meant, to me it was just well, a mess. 'Anyone else, fine, but not with Colin,' said Tonk gently.

Jerry left the room to make another round of tea.

I settled into the chair. What sounded like a shuffling noise was coming from above, as though someone was walking about in the roof space. To my horror, the loft hatch opened slowly and down dropped a pair of denim-clad legs and deftly jumped to the floor. Then another set and another. Soon four bodies were standing in our front room.

'Nice of you to drop in,' said Tonk not in the least bit phased. I sat wide-eyed, and open jawed.

'We're from next door,' said one of the lads addressing me with a slight nod.

'More commonly known as *The Mad House*,' added Barb.' This is Bean, that's Bob, he's Dezzy and he's Mike.'

I smiled rather bemused, my eyebrows knitting furiously. As if in response, Mike said jocularly, 'We're just popping in.' The lads sniggered.

'Another raid is it?' said Tonk.

'Yeah, 'fraid so,' said the one I recognised as Bean.

'Raid?' I ventured to ask.

'Yeah, a drugs raid. They can't touch us in here.' Mike caught the fringe of fine blond hair that covered his face with his tattoed forefinger and tucked it behind his ear.

'No wa… w… w…'

'Warrant,' offered Mike. 'Don't mind Dezzy, he speaks better when he's stoned.'

Dezzy gave him a shy punch on the arm, his face flushing pink.

'But we love you anyway, Dezzy,' said Barb giving him a wink. He smiled, a bashful pink smile that spoke of crushes and the warmth that kindness brings.

Jerry came back into the room. 'The wagon's still parked up the street.'

'They'll be gone soon. You don't mind if we stop till then, do you?' said Mike who had already plonked himself on the floor.

'Yeah, that's fine,' shrugged Tonk. 'Come in, make yourself at home.'

The rest of the lads found places to sit, all boots and dirty denims and made busy with rizla papers and random album covers. They bantered back and forth as if nothing at all strange was happening next door. Tea was made and distributed and the only thing that punctuated the conversation was the occasional thump on the floor from the neighbour downstairs.

Mike stood up and left the room returning five minutes later saying, 'Looks like they've gone.' He rubbed his hands together with glee. 'So, who's up for going to the Pav tonight?' A chorus of voices replied, 'Me!'

'You'll love the Pav,' said Barb.

'Pav?' I queried.

'Yeah, The Pavillion. You have to come,' chimed Tonk.

Not having any money and feeling uncomfortable about borrowing I protested. 'Oh, I don't think so. Thanks, maybe another time?'

'Nonsense,' said Barb. 'It's our treat. We can't go out and leave you on your tod.'

Automatically I put my little finger in my mouth and started to bite, a habit that had become second nature.

'It's done,' said Tonk. 'We'll get you in for free and you'll not need to worry about drinks ...'

'But ...'

Tonk held the flat of his hand up. 'Not another word, okay!'

That night we headed out en masse to witness all the denim and black leather-jacket-clad creatures came out to dance at the Pav. It was an ordinary looking prefab building containing one huge room, toilets, entrance and a bar. The lights were so low they were virtually non existent, to dramatic effect. It throbbed with deafening rock music and drew a sea of young rockers from all around the county.

The Pav was situated away from any residential or commercial buildings, right smack bang in the middle of Montpellier Park next to an old bandstand. Which to me seemed like a contradiction in and of itself, brass bands and heavy rock didn't sit well together. The music at the Pav was played so loud that we could hear it as we came up the street and into the park. My heart was thumping with anticipation and excitement. Outside the entrance was a throng of bodies gathering in the dark, waiting to be let in. And against that backdrop, the sound of numerous motorbikes approaching; the roar of the wide-open throttles as they cruised up The Promenade or the Gloucester Road. Rows of bikes all lined up one after the other just outside the entrance, their bodywork gleaming under the streetlights.

Inside the air was filled with the scent of patchouli, cannabis, and spilt beer. Bodies heaved, swathed in sweat from frantic dancing and hair swinging, especially when Deep Purple came on the turntable. I felt too shy to dance at first, too self-conscious. From the shadows I watched the figures writhe and jerk to the music, anything seemed acceptable, but head banging appeared to be the most favoured mode of expression and I marvelled that they didn't throw up from the excesses of drink and violent head jerking.

Barb and I staggered home that night locked arm in arm surrounded by the rest of group from the terrace.

Chapter Three

As the weeks passed, I settled into my new home and all the chaos and laughter it represented. But other things I had managed to maintain slipped. My cleaning job fell by the wayside, it wasn't conducive to staying up late or not even going to bed at all.

I signed on. It was quite a revelation to be given money for nothing. I took my place in the dole queue down the lower end of the High Street, filled in the relevant form, signed and took my cheque. We would then make our way to the Post Office to cash the cheques and head back home to blow it all on smokes. It seemed like a glorious existence. But spending the dole cheque sensibly was something that all of us needed to work on.

On one such occasion, when the last of the dole cheques had been spent and all that remained was one sprouting potato in the cupboard, Barb looked at me from across the kitchen table and pulled a face.

'We're £5 short on the rent this week. Meagher's not going to be happy.'

Tonk dealt with the situation like he always did. He pulled out his Rizlas and started to roll a joint at the kitchen table, scattering most of the tobacco on the floor as he did so.

'This requires some heavy thinking,' he said as he lit it up and became engulfed by a cloud of thick smoke.

'We could try pawning the telly?' suggested Jerry, but that was greeted with a collective 'Naaaaa.' We sat about with long faces, the spectre of Mr Meagher's wrath hanging over us. Then

Barb got up and left slamming the front door behind her. She reappeared ten minutes later with the local newspaper in her hand.

'Looks like one of us should get a job.' She threw the paper on the table. Jerry leaned forward, mocking horror, holding his head in his hands.

'Steady on!' said Tonk. 'Don't you think it a bit drastic?'

'Well, someone's got to do something or else we'll all be out on our ear,' said Barb. She sat down at the table, opened the paper at the jobs section and began scanning diligently. Before long, her eyes lit up.

'Ha! Look at this. It's perfect.' She started to read, 'Temporary Demonstration Ladies wanted; prior experience preferred but not essential. Full training given. Start ASAP. Competitive rates of pay.' She stood up. 'Come on Frankie, let's go get us an interview!' I followed her down to the phone box out of curiosity and watched in awe as she worked her magic.

The following Monday, after a morning's training, we found ourselves standing in the aisle of a well-known supermarket wearing the mandatory silk sash emblazoned with the words 'Butterball Turkeys.' It wasn't what you'd call the nicest of areas, most of the customers being unemployed or unemployable. I'd hardly get my sales patter out, 'Can I interest you in a butterba…' before I'd get told to fuck off. Needless to say, to do the job required quite a number of ciggy breaks outside the back of the store to steel us for the next customer. We didn't sell a single turkey and got rammed several times by customers and their trolleys for our troubles. Not that we really minded, the pay was excellent, and being stoned made things bearable.

Barb taught me the rudiments of cooking. 'You can't live on cornflakes!' Her exasperation was palpable as she caught me tucking into my third bowl one evening.

'Didn't your mother teach you how to cook?'

I shook my head resolutely. 'No. And I'm glad she didn't, her boiled eggs could kill from fifty paces.'

'Right,' she rubbed her hands together. 'Well, we'll get that one sorted for a start.'

Under Barb's careful tutelage I learned how to make soup, cooked breakfast, shortcrust pastry and Sunday roast with all the trimmings. Her reputation for Sunday roasts at the terrace was renowned. Sometimes, as many as twenty bodies piled into the sitting room waiting for food to be served. Some brought offerings to add to the meal, potatoes, greens, sometimes even a shoulder of lamb or beef. Cutlery and plates were borrowed from The Mad House and food was served and eaten in shifts. On the odd occasion we would use The Mad House's oven and hob too but only if there was no other option. Oven cleaning wasn't a priority for the Mad House.

During one such session, just after I'd mopped up the last of my gravy off the plate, the doorbell went. I listened as a body charged down the stairs to answer it. Shortly after, Jerry popped his head round the door, 'Frankie, it's someone for you.' His voice had taken on a serious, measured tone. I put my plate down, wiped my mouth with the back of my hand and descended the stairs two at a time.

My Dad was standing on the doorstep staring at the medley of milk bottles lined down the steps, a sheepish grin on his face. Seeing him made all the air escape from my lungs. I flung my arms around him and hugged him tight.

'Dad! It's so good to see you.'

He released himself from the hug and held me at arm's length.

I babbled with excitement, 'Do you want to come in? It's a bit busy in the flat just now, though.' As if on cue, a roar of laughter came from within. 'We seem to be feeding the whole neighbourhood,' I beamed.

'No,' he smiled weakly, and half turned his head away, 'I don't want to disturb you if you're busy.'

'Disturb? Dad, don't be silly! Come on, I've not seen you in months.'

'I know, I'm sorry. Things have been a bit ... Here, let me look at you again.' He stepped back to look me up and down once more.

He had lost weight I could tell. He didn't quite fill out his coat like he had before. There were dark circles around his tired eyes.

His face was grey and gaunt and there appeared to be a stoop about his stance.

'Are you okay Dad?'

'Me? Sure,' he pulled himself upright forcing a smile that might have fooled everyone else, but not me.

He had on his usual tie and old worn Marks and Spencer's shirt beneath the blue anorak that he normally wore, but there was something amiss. Something so subtle I couldn't quite put my finger on it. But I sensed it, like that feeling you get when someone's standing very close, but not quite touching.

'How did you find me?'

'It wasn't easy. I started with Patsy's mum ... '

'Ah, that makes sense. I did try to find you Dad but the number you gave me didn't work.'

'I know, I'm sorry. That's another long story.' He looked awkward. 'Shall we take a walk?'

We decided to walk along the cutting path next to the railway line. As we ambled we talked, the conversation light and casual. I told him all about the flat, the friends I had made, how happy and settled I was there and how the only thing I really missed about home was our dog, Bonzo. At one point we stopped; he leaned heavily on the railings looking over the railway track trying to catch his breath. He turned his head to look at me sideways.

'You do look happy. I can see it in your face.'

Then, uncharacteristicly for Dad, he cupped my face in his hands and said 'My most precious girl ... I'm so sorry I let you down ... ' The rims of his eyes had pinked up, as if he was going to cry.

'Dad, what do you mean? You weren't to blame. You couldn't help how things turned out. It's just the way Mum ... the way she behaves.'

He stood, looking into my eyes.

'But I can't forgive myself. I should have tried harder.'

'You did what you could Dad. We both did.'

He hesitated, dropped his hands, and looked away. I could see the muscles working at the side of his jaw. They always did that when he was struggling with something, particularly something that bothered him.

'Your mother wants you to visit.'

I felt the heat rise in my cheeks, a spike of anger. There it is, I thought; Mum had got to him. Instinctively I stepped away.

'Why would I want to do that?' I spat the words out like they burned my mouth. I didn't need to tell him how betrayed I felt. He winced, searching for the right words, ones that would soothe and placate.

Hooding his eyes with the span of his hand, 'I know she can be a nightmare, but she does care.'

I didn't answer, it was taking all my might not to walk away from him.

Taking his hand away from his eyes he looked at me directly. 'Give her a chance. She's your mother after all. Despite what you think Frankie, she does care.'

I turned my face away and gritted my teeth. The number of times I'd been fed those lines. And here I was again, being asked to put my head in a lion's mouth, one that you knew would snap it off without a backward glance. 'Care! What does she know about caring? I'd love to know how she would define it, because it's nowhere near my understanding of the word.'

I didn't want to see her. I couldn't fathom why she treated me so badly and it always left me feeling bad about myself. I didn't want to try patching things up or figuring it out anymore. It hurt too much.

'For me, Love. Would you do it for me?' The moment stilled and telescoped down. A cloud passed over the sun as though someone had dimmed the light or blown a candle out on a summer's evening.

'I don't understand, Dad, why do you still champion her. After all she's done to you?'

He shrugged, 'You can't help who you fall in love with I suppose.'

Bloody typical I thought gritting my teeth. He can't help himself despite everything that had passed between them. I loved him for it, but it also exasperated me.

Before he left, he made me promise to visit Mum and in exchange he promised to keep in touch more regularly. The prospect of having Dad back in my life on a regular basis made me incredibly happy. Seeing him had grounded me, left me with some semblance of hope, with a sense of being loved. I didn't relish the prospect of reconnecting with Mum, but a promise was a promise.

I phoned her late that afternoon to arrange a visit. She insisted I visit on Friday evening, 'it's the only night that suits me.' Yeah, really. It was the start of the weekend conveniently picked to be inconvenient. Barb and I were due to go to a party then. When I told Barb of my predicament she laughed lightly. 'It's no problem, the party will still be going on into the early hours and we can turn up at any time. Go and see the horrendous ogre and get it over with.'

That Friday I got someone from the Mad House to give me a lift. I was planning to take the bus into town after 'the meeting' and catch up with Barb. Pitching up at the back door I hesitated and then knocked softly. My eye was drawn to the browning blossoms cowering in the crevices of the doorstep and I wondered if I could still make good an escape. Then I heard Bonzo's bark and his paws skittering about on the kitchen floor – it made me smile before I saw my mother's figure looming large in the backdoor's frizzled glass. She opened it just a crack, barring Bonzo the opportunity to come out and do his elaborate hello dance.

She looked me up and down through slitted eyes.

'What DO you think you look like?' she sniffed pointedly, 'and you smell awful too. Bloody hippy oil. Go round the front. You don't live here anymore so you've lost the privilege of using the backdoor.'

Here we bloody go, I thought as I trudged round to the front door. I rang the bell and waited. I could hear Bonzo's frenzied barks in the background. She snatched open the door, 'You didn't need to ring the bell I already knew you were here. And you're late.'

Late? By two minutes, but who's counting? I sighed, That's three things wrong and I'm not even across the threshold. I lifted a foot to step in.

'Wait.' She held flat of her hand in front of my face. 'Do you think it's respectful to call round to see your mother while you're wearing that tat on your face and you're not even wearing a skirt.' Her lip had curled up at the side. She was in one of those moods.

I stood on that doorstep dumbfounded. Obviously, I didn't meet all the unwritten rules. I should have known, shouldn't I? It was tempting to be haughty, I wanted to say something like *Well, perhaps you should have sent me an RSVP stating as such* or, *Oh no, the witches telegraph didn't reach my house* or better still, *Fuck You*. But instead, I held my tongue and let my head swim in her bile.

'No, I'm afraid you can't come in until you arrive here appropriately dressed and have at least a bunch of flowers for me. Go home, get changed and do this properly. It's all about respect and manners.' Then she slammed the door, leaving Bonzo barking at the window, his tail wagging so fast it looked like he would take off at any moment. He didn't understand either.

'Bollocks,' I muttered under my breath and turned to head home, feeling all the anger and frustration welling up as I walked. I hadn't got far when I heard a motorbike pull up beside me.

'That was a quick visit. Hop on I'll take you back.' Bean handed me the spare lid at which point I burst into floods of tears.

'She wouldn't even let me in.'

'Why ever not?' Bean looked perplexed.

'Because I was wearing make-up, because I wasn't wearing a skirt, and because I hadn't taken her any flowers.'

'Oh shit, not cool.' Then, surprising for Bean, he produced a handkerchief. 'Here, your mascara's run. Now you look like a panda!'

I raised a weak smile.

'Hop on, we'll get some flowers from the petrol station and drop back home. You get your face cleaned up and shove on your work skirt. I'll drop you back at your Mum's and wait about for you, how does that sound?'

'Really, you'd do that for me Bean?'

'Yeah, of course. And don't let her get to you. She's just trying to fuck with your head. You must show her that you're better than that. Be cool. Alright?' He pinched my cheek and then I put on the lid and hopped on the back of the bike.

On the return trip I held on tight, wind funnelling up my skirt making me shiver. I pursed my lips against the cold and shut my eyes, it felt like I was being dragged back into some ugly vortex. I knew then how it was going to be and braced myself.

When I got to the door it all seemed rather farcical. As I pressed the bell, I felt indifferent, or was it because I was stoned? Prior to leaving, Bean insisted I had a toke 'to take the edge off.' It did. It loosened me, took away the rattles and nervousness. I fought to keep the smile off my face.

Seeing Bonzo made the whole visit worthwhile. His greeting was extravagant even by Bonzo's standards. He cried, he danced, he knocked me over and licked me putting his paws on my shoulders, wagging and licking, deliberately disobeying Mum's orders. He stayed at my side during the whole visit looking up from time to time to check I was still there. And my hand kept straying down to find his head, his ears, his muzzle for the reassurance I knew he would give.

Mum was sullen, her face set to angry. I could tell by the hint of a sneer on her lips and the way she pulled on her cigarette. Short quick pulls, ripping it from her mouth and blowing out quickly.

'In there.' Her finger jabbed in the direction of the living room. 'Sit.' Nodding at the smaller chair opposite hers.

I sat.

She made a point of switching the television off as if to give more gravitas to the situation, a ploy that she used to great effect when I was a child.

Here it comes. My body tensed, I felt the rush and pulse of blood in my ears.

She sat, hands resting on the chair arms, ashtray, and cigarettes to the ready, looking imperious, firing a battery of questions and not giving me time to finish my sentence before the next question came. I wanted to giggle. In my head the words *No one expects the Spanish Inquisition* played over and over, daring me, goading me to laugh. Lecture after lecture came: my failure to be a good daughter, my failure to get a job or what she considered to be a job. My choice of friends, what I wore, my make-up. I sat through the diatribe sipping my milky tea from a bone china cup and saucer clock-watching. When the chimes struck nine pm I put my cup down, ruffled Bonzo on the head and made my excuses.

'But I'm not finished with you yet. You haven't even asked me how I am.'

'No, I haven't have I?' I shot her a bold look. 'You haven't really given me the opportunity.'

With that she threw what was left in her teacup over me.

'Get out, you insolent bitch and don't come back until you have found your manners.'

I ran out of the house before she had the chance to change her mind, or worse, physically set about me. Bean was sitting on his motorbike waiting at the end of the road.

'Duty done then?'

'After a fashion.'

'Right then, let's get you home, changed and off to the party, Cinderella!'

Chapter Four

Late September 1977

I first time I met Blake was after one of the Pavllion sessions. He came back to the flat with the rest of the crew, an acquaintance of one of The Mad House occupants. He sat quietly in the corner of the room, smoking a joint, not saying much. Observing. I don't recall exchanging a single word with him but could sense a presence. Everyone seemed to tip-toe around him, even Tonk.

He was still there in the morning, asleep in the chair in the corner, big hands splayed across the arm rests, head drooping, his long hair covering his face like a curtain. Tonk kicked the bottom of his shoe, he awoke with a start. We fed him tea and buttered toast, and then he left. I didn't think much more of it, a lot of people stayed over in the flat. It was no big deal.

It just so happened that Barb was off to visit her parents that Sunday, her mum's birthday. She bustled about fussing over her wardrobe, her makeup, how she wore her hair and, for the first time ever, she snapped at me over something trivial. She had been off-key all week. Subtle little things like being less patient, smoking more than usual, seeming preoccupied. I figured it might have been her monthlies – but after her outburst I wasn't so sure, after all she'd never been that bad before. I wondered if she was getting uptight about the visit home as she had been stressing over what to buy her mum. Yes, that must have been it.

In the back of my head I felt a little envious to have a mum that you loved so much that you worried about what to buy her.

Tonk had plans too and was due to leave late-morning to catch a bus somewhere. It meant I'd have had the flat to myself. Normally I wouldn't have minded, but Tonk seemed a little on edge about me being there alone and persuaded me to come out with him. Had he not sworn me to secrecy about where we were going, I might not have gone. But curiosity got the better of me. We met at one of his friend's flats – where a small fellowship of punks met on a monthly basis to play something called *Dungeons and Dragons*. How Tonk managed to inveigle his way into it I'll never know, but we whiled away the best of the day with it. Walking through the Sunday streets on our way home he spoke of all the people we knew who visited the flat. Who was funny, who was kind, who was loopy, adding little anecdotes about each. Then he mentioned Blake, the guy who'd stayed overnight - said something like 'he's unpredictable,' which I read as 'spontaneous.'

'He doesn't say much, does he? And his eyes, black as coal. It's like they can see right through you.'

Tonk dropped his gaze to the floor and kicked at an empty beer can lying on the pavement. 'Mind yourself with that one, he's trouble.'

It never occurred to me to ask why.

Tonk touched on the magic of the friendships at the flat and laughing nervously referred to us all as the Lost Boys.

'We're all estranged, haven't you noticed?'

I didn't quite understand, not being one for big words. 'You're going to have to explain that one,' I said looking at him sideways.

'We don't exactly fit with society, do we? Like we're none of us normal. And look at you and me, estranged from our families.'

'I s'pose …' We walked in silence for a while, watching the shadows grow short and long beneath the streetlights. I was hoping he wouldn't ask me my story as I didn't know how to frame it, just that Mum was 'difficult'. Did that sound like enough of a reason to be kicked out of home? Can you really admit to someone else that your mother didn't like you without them questioning you? So, I took the lead and posed a question. 'So how come you left home?'

He wrinkled his nose and sniffed, like he was summoning the words he needed to talk about it. 'My mum's boyfriend. He was an arse.'

'Ahh. What about your dad?'

'He was an arse too. Left home when I was ten. He ...' Tonk cut the sentence abruptly. 'Anyway, I'm better off without them. No more hassle.' I saw a grimace cross his face. I changed the subject. 'But Barb's not a Lost Boy or should I say Girl, is she?'

'No, not that I can tell but she keeps her cards close to her chest. Her folks seem great though, always sending parcels of grub – no problem. Barb's just Barb. Although she did go to a private boarding school.'

'That's interesting. I thought she had rather a posh accent.'

'You can run into anyone in Cheltenham with a posh accent though, can't you?'

'I s'pose.'

'Maybe the posh school was a bit of a head-fuck though.'

'How do you mean?'

'Well,' Tonk slowed his pace and bit his lip, 'Imagine being shipped off away from your parents at the age of seven and only seeing them over the holidays, and even then, that didn't always happen from what I can make out.'

'So, she is a Lost Boy then. Just a posh one'

'Yeah, when you put it like that.'

'Barb has kept me right though. Taken me under her wing and shown me how to make my way without too much hassle. She's taught me how to cook, how to hitch-hike and a load of other stuff.'

Tonk nodded, catching my drift.

'We went all the way to London and back in a day just so's she could pick up some boots at Camden Market, dessie wellies. I'd never been to London before.' I chuckled, 'and she took me to some of the coolest second-hand shops. Got me some clothes suitable for the temp jobs I've done lately.' The thought of the temp job pulled me up short. I remembered that bad tempered office manager barking at me, calling me useless for not knowing how to work the Gestetener. That was the final straw and I told her to shove her bloody gesteteer where the sun doesn't shine.

I snivelled all the way home like a child, angry with myself and even more angry with that horrible bloody woman. Barb was home when I got in and looking me up and down with a wry smile on her face saying, 'Go on then, tell me. What happened?' I sobbed and hitched as I told her, only half expecting her to take my side. Her response surprised me.

'Frankie, at times you can be such a child. Don't let her get to you. You give her and all people like her, power over you when you react like that. Now, come on, dust yourself off and pick yourself up.'

I smiled to myself just thinking about it.

'And see this jacket, we share it. I'd never have been able to afford something like this if I bought it new.'

'She's got a kind heart has Barb.'

A motorbike roared up the road towards us, its pillion passenger barely hanging on, swaying from side to side, waving and shouting wildly as he went past. We stopped and waved back, Tonk putting his fingers in his mouth and whistling. We watched as the tail light disappeared round the corner at the end of the road, the sound of the baffles slowly fading into the night air.

'Bloody nutters,' sniggered Tonk.

'The Madhouse?'

'Yeah.'

'More Lost Boys, eh? And what about Jerry?'

Tonk looked at me sidelong. 'Ah Jerry. Yep, he's a Lost Boy for sure. He never talks about his family, I know he's not from round here. Cirencester, I think he once said. But for all his wildness, he has a heart of gold and would do anything for anyone. Did I tell you about how we got our TV? It was Jerry. Barb had been ill, had to stay home for about ten days so he took it upon himself to get us a TV. Nicked it from Tescos, bold as brass. Just picked it up and walked out the wrong way down the escalators with it under his arm.'

'And you were okay with that?'

'He didn't tell us that part until about a month later. Too late to do anything about it at that point.'

'He's always the life and soul of the party isn't he?' Tonk chuckled and thrust his hands deep in his pockets. 'Yeah, something like that. Mind, he does have his black moods. Just give him space when he's like that. Okay?' He looked at me pointedly and raised his eyebrows. 'Okay?'

'Okay.'

'Good.'

We walked in silence for a while, shoulders bumping like shadows boxing.

'You know, I'm glad I found you lot. I don't care if we are at odds or, what was that word you used? Estranged, from normal families Tonk because you lot, the flat and the madhouse, are all the family I need. You might all be nutters, but at least I know where I stand.'

'Yeah. We all look out for each other.' A smile spread across his face making the corners of his eyes crease. 'It's where I feel I belong, don't you?'

'Yeah,' I smiled.

We talked about music. Tonk told me of the concerts he had been to see and named his top five – the ones he wanted to see. His stride stretched and bounced as he talked about his favourites. He convinced me to hitch-hike together to the next Reading Festival to see the headliners: The Police, The Tourists, The Cure and Motorhead, but he couldn't persuade me to go to a punk concert. All the spitting, pogo-ing and bottle throwing just wasn't my style.

We walked home, all the way from the other end of town, the cold nipping our ears and fingers, our breaths making funnels of smoke like human dragons. The conversation ranged wide and wild. At one point Tonk talked about a run-in with one of his old landlords, a letting agent that overcharged for a pokey flat with broken windows and floorboards, where the heating didn't work and 50p in the meter seemed to last five minutes. He complained bitterly about the state of the flat, but they did nothing about it. Even worse, they refused to refund his deposit on spurious grounds. 'Fucking capitalist bastards!' he spat. 'They did the same to poor guy that took the flat after me too.'

I looked at him, his face set to anger, eyes blazing and that twitch he had with his nose when emotion overspilled.

When we reached the well-off area of Montpellier, the streets were slumber empty. The night sky began to lose its darkness, giving over to a soft pink blush. A lone blackbird sang out into the stillness, as if bringing down the morning with every single note. As we crossed the road, we passed the Estate Agents, his old landlords.

'Bastards,' Tonk muttered under his breath.

'Yeah, bastards,' I said in support. Then he bent over and picked up a half brick lying at the kerb and lobbed it through their plate glass window. There was a spectacularly loud crash, glass shattering and scattering, followed by an alarm going off.

'Shit, run!'

We legged it, disappearing into Suffolk Square and the streets beyond. Running for a good ten minutes until our breath gave way and gales of laughter overcame us. When we got home, Blake was there, waiting on the doorstep.

'Alright?' said Tonk, but his voice was flat. He climbed the steps and stood with his back to Blake as he put his key in the door.

'Aren't you going to invite me in? I've brought you some smokes.'

Tonk stiffened, 'Aw mate, we were just going to pass out. I've got work in the morning.'

I flicked him a quizzical look and managed to stop myself spouting but you don't have a job do you?

Blake was insistent, 'Come on. It's not like you to pass up the opportunity for some good gear and you'll not want to miss out on this,' he pulled out a little bag, the type banks use for coins and waved it under Tonk's nose, 'Red Leb.' Even though his words were friendly there was something about his tone that said otherwise. He stood just a little too close, his leather jacket creaking with every move. An awkward moment passed between them, Blake, his right thumb rapidly twisting the ring on his pinkie finger as he looked directly at Tonk.

I watched Tonk's shoulders drop, his voice resigned. 'Alright then.' He dithered with the key as if hoping it wouldn't fit or he'd find the door jammed. He opened it and we all trooped in. When I looked at him briefly, I could see that his smile was set as if there was a bad smell beneath his nose.

I took myself off to bed leaving Tonk and Blake to it. I felt relieved when I heard the front door slam some twenty minutes later and Blake's bike start up and drive away. Curious I dragged myself out of bed and popped my head round the living room door. 'Everything alright?' He looked up, his mouth forced a tired smile. 'You sure?' He nodded his head and pinched the top of his nose between his eyebrows. 'Yeah, nothing for you to worry about. Go back to bed. Go on.' He shooed me away with his hand. 'Go on.' I was tired so didn't put up much resistance but went back to bed with a sense that something wasn't quite right with Tonk

Barb didn't come home that night. I imagined she had stayed over with Sam; their romance seemed to be blossoming. I assumed Tonk and Jerry had gone out early the next morning too, as the flat was quiet. Jerry was always one for making noise, singing tunelessly, or crashing about in the kitchen, radio blaring. Peeping through the bedroom curtains I noticed all the bikes outside were gone, only the oil stains remained, glinting in the light like magpie's wings.

The flat seemed airless and eerie. I went to the kitchen and made myself a brew. Throwing open the window I stood looking out to the view over the allotments supping my tea. Then I heard something, a movement come from the other end of the flat.

'Hello?' No one responded. I turned back to the window then heard what sounded like a muffled sob.

'Hello?' I called again. I put my cup down and went to investigate. I peeked into the living room. The curtains were closed, it was enveloped in darkness. Crossing the room I drew back the curtains. Then did a double take. 'Jerry, what are you doing? He was sitting in the corner of the room folded in on himself almost afraid to look me in the eye.

'I dunno really.' His eyes seemed vacant, like his thoughts weren't quite getting through. 'Trying to think I s'pose.'

At first, I wondered whether he was stoned, but there was something about him that made me think otherwise. 'Oh. What's that?'

A tatty piece of paper lay on the arm of the sofa. I could just make out the scrawled words 'Dear Mum and Dad.' I looked at him, noting his red swollen eyes. His face looked flushed. He swept the page with his outstretched palm as if to brush something invisible away. His discomfort was palpable, a shoulder turned slightly away from me, the downward tilt of his head and slight furrowing of his brow.

'Do you need a hand?' I ventured nearer. He looked awkward; his mouth was saying no but its tone was saying yes. It was a difficult thing to balance, his dignity, and his pain. I sat in the chair next to him and offered him a cigarette.

'Tell you what, I've got some much better writing paper than that. Are you stuck for words? Do you want me to give you a hand?' I watched the subtle tension in his shoulders drop as if someone had let a gasp of air out of a balloon.

'I dunno, yeah. Yeah.'

'Tell you what, I'll write it, then you can copy it out in your hand.' He hesitated as though checking to see if it were safe to speak.

'That'd help,' he turned his attention to the tip of the cigarette deliberately knocking bits of ash off into the ashtray as if it were some important intricate job. 'I can't read Frankie. I've never been able to read.'

'I don't think Jesus could either but that didn't seem to stop him. Now, sit tight, I'll fetch the paper and you think about what you want to say.' I was determined not to react, not to let him think that I thought any lesser of him because he couldn't read. When I got back to the room, he had switched a lamp on in the corner but was still troubled I could tell. He was gripping the biro so that the whites of his knuckles showed as if he was willing it to write the words he needed to say.

'Okay,' I sat down breezily, 'so let's start at the beginning. What do you want to say to your folks?'

He bowed his head and barely shook it and in that moment I saw the child in this grown hard-man, one that was afraid and ashamed but wanted, no needed, to connect with his roots, to find an anchor.

'That's just it. I don't know where to start.'

'When did you last see them?' He shook his head and tears began to well up in his eyes. 'I dunno,' he whispered, 'years.'

'The first step is always the hardest, Jerrington Cutums,' I gave him an encouraging wink then opened the pad and started to compose. 'So, let's tell them where you are, that you're okay and you hope the same for them. Shall we give them the phone number in case they want to get in touch?'

He nodded meekly. When I finished writing the note, he looked brighter but not bright enough for me to think he was in the clear. He was not alright, and I resolved to keep a close eye on him. Tonk's words went round in my head 'He's a Lost Boy … we all look out for each other here.'

Chapter Five

December 1977 onwards

I never intended going out with Blake. He wasn't my type. There wasn't the chemistry, not that I had any real experience in those matters – perhaps a snog and a fumble at the school disco but nothing to really write home about. My undertaking of love and romance was of childish infatuations that you advertised on your schoolbooks or carved into school desks: *Frankie 4 Mark, forever.* But, it didn't mean anything. Not the real heart stopping, stomach flipping, full blushing love that takes you unawares and turns you upside-down.

This was different. Insidious even. I hadn't seen it coming being so enamoured with my new-found friends. He was a biker of sorts, a bit of a loner but he also came with a reputation. One you didn't mess with. A man of few words who spoke with his fists. Most of his communications were one-word grunted sentences. Everyone was on edge when he was around. To some extent I found it interesting watching the dynamics as people became less of themselves when he was about. There was a respect there, but a respect I later learned that came from fear. He was a bit like a grenade with a loose pin.

He started hanging round the flat, turning up each night, seating himself in the corner until he just became part of that corner. After a while it became more unusual to see him 'not there.' If I tried to ensure that I wasn't left alone with him, it wasn't because I felt unsafe around him, I didn't. His interactions with me were almost animated, smiling and making odd facial expressions that caught me unawares and made me laugh, but often those cautionary words of Tonk's chimed in the back of my head.

It got to the stage that every time I went out, he was there, like my shadow, watching me. If I happened to speak with another guy he'd sidle up and just stand there, letting his presence be known until they just moved away like there was this silent hand moving them on. I wasn't quite sure what to do.

And then it happened, I woke up after dropping a tab of acid the night before to find him in my bed. A great cheesy grin on his face. I felt sick. I had no real recollection of what I had done and all I could think was, Christ, how am I going to get out of this? But the thought of turning this 'crazy' down would be like being a Kamikaze pilot. It would end in tears. So, stupidly I went along with it until I became so embroiled, I couldn't find a way of getting out of it.

My occasional visits home served to make me cleave to him even more. It was the same each visit, a lecture on how disappointed Mum was with me, how her friend's and work colleagues' children were so wonderful whereas I, in contrast was a waste of space. The flat, the job, the boyfriend, my lifestyle, none of it came up to par. I always left feeling deflated and emotionally battered.

Blake couldn't give a toss about what my mother thought and given the opportunity, probably would have said as much to her face – with both barrels. His attitude made me feel bolstered against her negativity, the hard man that took no shit, not even from my mother. But that kind of flattery and protection came with a price.

Nevertheless, there were moments, when I almost convinced myself, I was happy. That spring, being a case in point where I felt invincible and alive. He'd picked me up from the end of the road near my mother's house after a visit. The sun was melting into the horizon like a great orange lozenge. Blossom drifted from the trees and caught in my hair as I climbed on the back of the bike. I got a whiff of patchouli as I snuggled into his jacket. 'The colours on his leathers didn't scare me, nor did his tattoos. I relished the image and the message it gave out – all the neighbours along the street peeping out from behind the nets curtains, tutting.

He clocked them and winked at me as he started up the engine. The Triumph burst into life, a loud throaty roar, then pulled away from the curb, majestic and haughty. We cruised up the main road until we hit the winding country roads, I felt wild, untouchable, and defiant. Led Zep playing in my head, I wanted more. Holding tight, my arms wrapped around his waist, pressing into him, my head tucked over his shoulder. I could feel his heat, the suppleness of his body - he could have driven me anywhere.

We arrived at a run-down pub, his favourite. It was situated in the back of beyond with droves of impressive looking bikes parked outside. A Cotswold cider house, a drinking den stowed out with leather clad bikers and old yokels with red noses. We took our pints of cider to a quiet corner and sat people watching and supping until my lips and fingers grew numb – such was the alcohol.

He kissed me tenderly to bring back some sensation. When the kissing got more intense, he took me by the hand and led me beyond the pub garden to the hayfields. Afterwards, still tangled together, we watched the rabbits forage, nervous and jittery, witnessed dragonflies manoeuvring their way around, all spark and light. We stayed there until the ground grew cold and damp, slumbering like something from A Midnight's Dream. Eventually we threaded our way back to the bike. The moon in full splendour, kept the shadows behind us as we flew through the Cotswold lanes home again.

His temper first reared its ugly head early one evening. We were on the bike heading out to a pub near the top of Cleeve Hill. Blake liked to run the gauntlet and weave the bike in and out of the cars. The bike was heavy but held the road well. Up ahead a car pulled out. It's acceleration was slow and we caught up with it quicker than anticipated. I suspect the driver didn't see us as he was turning, it was a close-run thing and we narrowly missed collision. A simple mistake to make and really, to my mind Blake was in the wrong, he could have pulled back a bit. But he was having none of it. He put his head down closer to the handlebars,

I felt his shoulders tense, the muscles on his arms went almost rigid. Pulling back the throttle, he chased the car up the hill, narrowly missing an on-coming car on the bend. Up ahead, the car turned into the petrol station. That was the driver's biggest mistake. We pulled up the other side of the pump next to the car. Blake turned off the engine, got off the bike and punched the bewildered driver who was busy filling up his tank, to the ground. The attack was vicious, Blake's eyes were temporarily dead as his fists flailed, stopping only when another car pulled up, then he jumped on the bike, started it up and headed off. All I could see was his bloodied knuckles as they gripped the steering. His anger continued to smoulder even when we arrived at our destination. He turned on me, grabbing me by the throat and putting me up against a wall, 'Not a word, you understand?'

It didn't feel like fun anymore. For a moment there I wanted out but then he bombarded me with tenderness and apologies, he fed me an excuse I was willing to accept – too naïve to question.

One Saturday morning while we were lying in bed Blake propped up on his elbow and smiling sweetly said 'How 'bout we get our own place? C'mon, you know I'm really into you. Me and you, we're good together.'

I smiled, flattered but I felt my stomach lurch. I was happy where I was with Barb, Tonk and Jerry, they were family.

'I'll take care of you.' He reached up and tucked a strand of hair behind my ear. 'You won't regret it. C'mon, what do you say?' His dark eyes crinkled at the corners as his mouth curved, a half smile.

He read my expression as tacit acceptance.

'Let's smoke this to celebrate.' He leaned over, reaching his arm down and retrieved a joint from beneath the bed, 'I've been saving this especially for this occasion,' and then he put it into my mouth and fired it up, watching me closely as I exhaled. 'I love you, Frankie Miller.' And then he kissed me tenderly.

A part of me swelled with pride and excitement. I felt claimed, like someone had shone a light on me, showed me that they cared, was willing and wanted to take a risk on me. A flush of defiance flared within, 'this'll show my mother, now she won't mess with me.'

If I were to be really honest, I wanted to say no. Within, every fibre of my being was telling me not to do this. I knew that his sweet smile could turn in a split second. However, I had seen what those fists could do, so I kept my counsel.

Within the month he had found a flat on the other side of town. When we first moved in with no furniture but a decent sound system, I danced wildly to our favourite tunes. We lived on sardines on toast and slept on the floor under a mound of blankets. I got caught up with what I thought was the romantic, living with my boyfriend, getting a flat together, making a nest.

After about a year the relationship lost its sparkle, the cracks started to show earlier than that if I'm honest. What once seemed fun and edgy became boring and monotonous. At first, I was happy to go to work, after all it was for us. Blake would rise with me and take me to work, weaving through the busy morning traffic on the bike. It was all smiles and I love yous. When the honeymoon period wore off the real Blake began to appear.

He didn't bother to try – with anything. Our first Christmas set the bar for things to come.

I placed his present, a metal triumph badge for his leathers, on the armchair and stood back, smiling.

'What's this?' Barely taking his eyes off the TV screen he took a long pull on his joint and casually flicked ash on the floor.

'Go on, open it.'

He ripped off the packaging, raised his eyebrows then flicked his eyes back to the TV. The badge lay discarded on the arm of the chair, its pin in the air like an upturned insect. 'Didn't get you anything, didn't see the point. I hate Christmas.' I stood still for a moment fighting to keep my trembling lip under control. I fled from the room and stifled my sobs in the kitchen. 'Stupid cow,' I muttered to myself, 'really, what did you expect? Bloody chestnuts on an open fire and Frank Sinatra singing Christmas songs?' It began to dawn on me that there might never be any happy ever afters. Perhaps I wasn't trying hard enough?

Christmases passed with no presents under the proverbial tree, birthdays went by unacknowledged. Days melded into each other without much fanfare. I tried my best to make light of things but to very little effect.

As the bills mounted, I took on extra work at a pub. Five evenings a week on top of my day job. But nothing pissed me off more than coming home to find zilch had been done. Dirty dishes from the night before still in the sink, no food in the fridge, mess everywhere. I'd get in from work and he'd be sitting there like an ugly baby bird squawking 'Tea!' Or 'I'm hungry?'

Sometimes there'd be company, his friends drunk on beer and smoking. More mess, noise and bad behaviour, sometimes fights and things getting broken. Then he brought the motorbike into the flat, dismantling it in our small living room. It leaked oil everywhere, ruined the carpet – that's the deposit gone. I got fed up with finding bits of engine, pistons and spark plugs in the kitchen, even in the oven.

Riding on the back of the bike in the depths of winter meant nothing but being cold and wet and not being able to feel my fingers. My life seemed caught in an endless round of working while he sat at around getting stoned with whomever dropped by. He never worked, couldn't find anything legal that suited him. I'd come home cook, clean, shop, then go back out to work again.

Tonk called round out of the blue one Sunday afternoon. I was in the middle of doing the washing, struggling with the mangle at the old twin-tub when he peeked in through the kitchen window. I caught the look on his face as his eyes skirted the room. Blake was lying still drunk from the night before in the corner. I invited him in for a cuppa, and while he was there Blake stirred and lit a cigarette but then went back to sleep with it in his hand. The tip fell off and started to burn a hole in the carpet. I went to deal with it and accidently disturbed Blake. He sat up, wild and bewildered, took a random swing at me and told me in no uncertain terms where to go before slumping back down again.

'Hey, that's enough.' Tonk said sharply, but Blake was too far gone to hear.

'It's okay, honestly. Just leave it. He's grumpy because he's got a hangover. Best you go now, eh?'

'Are you sure?' a perplexed look crossed his face, eyebrows knitting.

'It's fine,' I soothed, casually pulling my sleeves down over my bruises.

Chapter Six

Perhaps I'd realised before then that this relationship wasn't going to go the distance, the biggest indication was that I'd made sure that my contraception was sorted. The last thing I wanted was to get pregnant. The pill didn't suit me, gave me horrendous headaches so my doctor persuaded me to have a coil fitted instead.

If lying sprawled on the doctor's couch with him strong arming the device into my body wasn't bad enough, the pain most certainly made up for it. I writhed in agony; legs splayed as he commanded me to 'keep still.' I saw stars as I left the surgery clutching onto the wall to steady myself. I couldn't face the cycle home so took a taxi that I could ill afford, and went straight to bed.

'Aren't you going into work tonight?' Blake turned the main light on and loomed over me.

Half dazed with sleep and pain I replied. 'No, I'm not feeling well.'

'But I need your pay packet tonight for a deal. Get up!'

'No,' I replied weakly, 'you'll have to wait. I'll pick it up tomorrow.'

He kicked the bed snarling 'You're a selfish lazy cow.'

I was too much in pain to even consider fighting back and perhaps, in hindsight, that wasn't a bad thing.

I knew it was all going wrong when we went back to his favourite pub about fifteen months after I'd first visited. It was driving rain on the way there. We were wet through. Wet leather has a way of chilling you to the marrow. I was so cold I couldn't stop shivering; so, I took a seat by the fire. The heat helped somewhat but a strange gnawing pain had begun to niggle around my pelvic area. All I wanted to do was go home and curl up with a hot water bottle. Blake had other designs on the day which entailed spending our money, playing pool and drinking with his cronies.

When I hinted that I was feeling unwell his face set to thunder, 'You always fucking ruin things, get over it and stop whining.' Then he turned his back to me.

That was it, chapter closed.

I went back to huddling by the fire, tired and in too much pain to even want to engage with anything else. Things got ugly when someone paid me attention and bought me a hot toddy. It was purely an act of kindness, nothing else.

Blake clocked it. 'What do you think you're doing? Are you after fucking my Mrs?

He was up in the guy's face, growling, making a show of himself in front of everyone else. The room went quiet and all I could hear was the crackle and hiss of the fire in the grate. To me it sounded like unspent tension.

The barman, white tea towel round his neck, bellowed, 'Get him out of here. I'll have no trouble in my pub.' A couple of burly bikers wrestled Blake outside. He struggled and snarled like an animal gone wild. I mouthed apologies to the man who bought the toddy and followed meekly, stumbling past the two bikers standing at the door barring Blake's way back in. He was still swearing and threatening all sorts when we got to the bike, at which point he turned his rage on me. I was past the point of caring. Spasms of pain were pulsing through my body to the extent that my hands automatically curled into a grip, while beads of sweat had gathered on my brow.

The last thing I remember was stepping through the door into the front room and seeing my ashen grey face reflected back at me in the mirror. Blake's voice was droning in the background, he was still angry from the scene at the pub that I – of course - had caused.

Another acute wave of pain ran through me, so intense that I passed out. I doubt Blake would have had the where-with-all to call the emergency services, he was too annoyed. More than likely he would have left me where I lay. It was pure luck that Barb happened to call round and it was her who called an ambulance.

I was kept in hospital for a couple of weeks. I had an operation to have the coil removed, was given a blood transfusion and a battery of intravenous antibiotics. The coil had perforated my uterus. I was told a lot of things that I didn't really understand. The doctor used big medical words and I felt too embarrassed and stupid to ask him to explain what it meant.

'Why did you have a coil fitted?' he rose up on the tips of his toes asking pointedly. His retinue of students hanging on his every word. The words stuck in my mouth, I couldn't say in front of all those people that I didn't want to get pregnant by my boyfriend. I thought they would think me stupid.

'Generally doctors only fit the coil to women who have had children.' He gave me a stern, discerning look then he turned and addressed his audience. I felt their eyes on me and shrank further down the bed.

Mum deigned to visit during my stay but left me feeling worse. She was unwilling to discuss or indeed tell family or friends that I had any form of problem down there. Automatically she assumed that the problem had come about as a result of having sex. Perhaps it was, but the coil should never have done that to me, I knew that. Mum was insistent that by way of the fact that I was in the hospital with women's problems, I had brought shame upon the family. She gave me no sympathy and left after off-loading a barrel-load of guilt and the parting remark, 'Well, at least it means I won't have to worry about becoming a grandmother.'

I wept all afternoon until a kindly nurse bought me sweet tea and tried to settle my concerns.

Blake only managed to visit the once – not that I minded, it proved to be something of a break. It also meant I didn't have to worry about him running into Barb, Tonk or Jerry who always made an effort to turn up. Jerry, often worse for wear and giggling at the sight of women in nighties.

One time he turned up with a handful of flowers which he gleefully admitted to nicking from peoples' gardens. He handed them over and pulled up a chair, his face beaming. 'I got a letter. Look.' He pulled it from his pocket and thrust it at me. 'Would you read it to me?'

'Sure.'

The paper was still warm from where it had been nestling in his breast pocket. The handwriting on the envelope was neat and small with curly tails on the g's f's and y's. The letter read:

> *My dearest Jeremy, I hope this finds you well. Regretfully I have to inform you that your father died a fortnight before your letter arrived. Fortunately, it was quick, and he didn't suffer but I must tell you that you broke your father's heart. Too much time has been wasted now to worry about what was done and said back then, I'm only glad to have contact with you again.*
>
> *Please come home and see me when you can.*
>
> *Love always, Mum.*

The smile fell from Jerry's face before he dropped his head in his hands and sat motionless.

'Jerry,' I whispered. 'You okay?' It took an age before he lifted his head.

'You want to talk about it?' I put my hand on his shoulder.

'I, I'm not sure …'

'Well, you have a captive audience. I'm not going anywhere.'

'My dad was … Me and Dad didn't get on. I was never his favourite, not like Geoffrey. He was always comparing me to him. Always Geoffrey this, Geoffrey that. You'd have thought he was a bloody saint the way he carried on,' he paused, pulling out a pouch of tobacco from his pocket and proceeded to roll a cigarette. 'When I was 16, I borrowed Geoffrey's bike from the garage, I took it without asking permission and it got stolen.' Jerry looked up, his eyes seemingly seeking forgiveness. 'It's not like I wanted that to happen. Anyway, when I got home, I got such a hiding I could hardly sit down. It didn't make sense to me.

Even though Geoffrey had died six years before, he had a bike, and I didn't.'

'Jerry, that's awful on so many levels. How come Geoffrey had a bike and you didn't. Was the bike the cause of his death?'

Jerry shook his head, 'No, it was leukaemia that took him.' He paused for a moment and then came back to himself.

'That night it all went round and round in my head until it grew out of proportion, and I couldn't make any sense of it. I was so angry. The hiding was the last straw. So, I packed some things and tried running away.'

'Jerry, I'm so sorry.'

'I got caught about a week later and returned home. Dad didn't really speak to me after that. We lived under the same roof but just didn't talk. Not until I was seventeen. I'd got a part time job helping out on one of the local farms, Tom Patton paid me well. He even showed me how to fix up the old tractor and tinker about with engine.' Jerry's face warmed with the hint of a smile as he recalled his friend. 'I saved up and bought a motorbike. A C15, BSA lovely old thing it was, not too reliable until Tom helped me work on it. We spent hours rebuilding the engine, respraying the tank, making it look shiny and new. God I loved that bike.'

'So, what happened then?'

'I drove it home to show Mum, I'd told her all about it. I'd barely pulled up onto the drive when Dad came out and pulled me off the bike. Kicked it over and was bawling and shouting about me looking like a hooligan and what was I thinking ... Mum came out and tried to calm him down. She was crying. While Dad was distracted, screaming for her to get back inside, I picked the bike up, started up and just drove off.'

'What, you never went back?'

'No.'

'What about your mum?'

'There was nothing I could do. I stayed at Tom's for a while but then decided it was best I leave completely.'

'So why did you come here?'

'Why do you think? I met a girl ...' distracted, he fished in his pocket for some matches, like he was rummaging about in his mind.

'I just wish I confronted Dad, told him how I felt, cleared the air. He was such an arrogant bastard, always right. A bully too. He bullied Mum – she didn't dare disagree in case he set about her.'

'He beat her up too?'

'No, not physically, but he had a vicious tongue.'

'Was he angry all the time?'

'To be fair, he wasn't, not all the time. Sometimes, when Geoffrey was alive, he could be quite a laugh. But you didn't want to cross him. He used to be in the army or 'the regiment' as he called it. Made it as far as Captain then bailed out to join the Civil Service. We tiptoed around our lives hardly daring to squeak without the threat of it coming to the Civil Service's attention – or that's what dad would tell us. God how I hated the fucking Civil Service. Of course, I never lived up to Geoffrey's standards at school. He won cups for everything whereas I could hardly spell my name. Used to drive dad mad. He'd call me lazy and stupid, tried to embarrass me into sorting it but I just couldn't, it was just a jumble of wriggly lines to me. How could I read that?'

I nodded and reached out to touch his hand.

'I was nothing but one great big disappointment to him – and that was far worse to me than being beaten.' Jerry sat for a while turning the match box over and over in his hand

'Are you planning to go and see your mum?'

'Dunno, the weekend maybe?'

'Okay, but keep me posted. I might be back home by then.'

'The end of your holiday. You're going to miss your all-inclusive meals, hot baths and not having to do the domestic stuff.'

I drew in a sharp breath. 'I dread to think what sort of state he's left the flat in by now. Can't say I'm relishing going back to Blake.'

'You know you can always come back to ours don't you.'

'Yeah, thanks. But you know what Blake's like. He'd throw a fit and go for all of us. I'll be alright, I'll manage somehow.'

Jerry rose from his chair and stuck his rollie in his mouth. Best I get home and have something to eat. I'll see you Frankie, you take care? He made to walk away then turned and looked back, 'And thanks Frankie. Really, thanks.'

Blake had a subtle way of playing on my fears. Had a well-oiled, silver-tongued way of making me think it was all my fault, that I wasn't good enough, that I needed to try harder. When I got home still weak and unsteady from the hospital his whittling away at me started. He complained about the mess that he had created but had left for me to clear up when I got back. He threw my food back at me and worse, ignored my pleas to leave me be at night.

As the months passed the harrying and goading came and went. I felt myself slowly ebbing away and, with it all, my friends. I knew they didn't like him; they'd said as much. It got to the stage I felt too embarrassed to tell them of the damage his fists did or the cruel words he'd used, or that we'd fallen out again.

He made the atmosphere unpleasant if anyone called round, they stopped dropping by and gradually, it felt that there was nothing left but him and me. By the time I was twenty I felt old. Old and tired and going nowhere with brittle nerves and little confidence.

Why was I so gullible? Why did I stay? Maybe I'd become addicted to the highs and lows. It was toxic and intoxicating. Maybe it was all I knew. Afterall, wasn't it like that when I was at home?

They say it takes a woman seven attempts to leave an abusive relationship. At the time I didn't know the meaning of the term and certainly didn't recognise myself in that context. I'd been so conditioned by my upbringing that I felt I deserved it.

Blake began to drink heavily. The more he drank the more violent and unpredictable he became. Sometimes he acted like a cornered animal, attacking for no apparent reason. It wasn't just me. I'd witnessed him launch at his friends, for little or no provocation. His favourite was to wrestle them into a strangle hold headlock, feeding off fear, making them submit then mocking them for being such a wuss afterwards.

He had this look, a hard stare, like a warning shot, a snake before it strikes. It was possibly a behaviour learned from his dad. I'd only met his dad twice and both times were unpleasant. He was a sour man with a broken face; silver lines across his flattened nose, looking every bit like a bad tempered pit-bull.

The first time I met him, he didn't acknowledge me and barely spoke to his son. It was the middle of the afternoon, he was still in his vest and boxers, sat in this filthy armchair positioned squarely in front of the TV, volume turned up loud, and surrounded by empty cans and an overflowing ashtray.

Blake was trying to communicate something. 'Dad,' he'd called, shouting above the TV. I don't recall what was said exactly. But then it came, that killer stare, a look of pure evil. He held Blake in it for a few seconds, his upper lip curling slightly. I watched as Blake swallowed hard, his face whitening. Then it happened.

His father leapt on him punching and swearing. 'You little fucker. You don't come in here shouting the odds at me to impress your little tart!'

Blake just took it, all meek and compliant, his head bent as his father taunted and punched him.

'What a useless push-over you are. A pussy.' His father bellowed in his ear, pacing round him, jabbing.

In another context I might have laughed, this overweight pot-bellied man with greasy hair and repulsive yellowing toenails looked ridiculous but his actions, his swagger, spoke of a savagery I did not want to know.

I felt sorry for Blake. No doubt that had been the landscape of his growing up. Where was his mother? Miles away if she had any sense. Blake hardly ever spoke of her. I knew that she had left when he was young. No prizes for guessing why. I suspected she was battered black and blue along with the usual barrage of insults, and yet Blake had no compassion or forgiveness for her. On the rare occasion he mentioned her, he virtually spat her name, often referring to her as an 'effing C'. It was shocking –

bordering on pathological hate. His father had obviously fed him a pack of lies until Blake believed it.

In the early days, I once naively asked if he had any pictures of her and he snapped, 'No, why would I? Dad and me burned all pictures of the bitch. In fact, we burned everything.' In an oblique way I understood, some family relationships are complex; the one I have with my mother being a prime example. But despite all the vitriol and tantrums she's still my flesh and blood. I may dislike her behaviour, but I do love her in a weird messed up way.

I found it odd that he could act so dispassionately towards the woman that bore him and yet could be utterly charming when it suited him. Oh yes, he knew exactly how to work his charm, especially with me. Playing with me like I was something to be conquered and coerced. Keeping me confused, and controlled, for his pleasure and convenience.

I came home once to find him, and his cronies installed in the kitchen with an air rifle taking pot shots at the neighbour's cat. When I complained he turned the gun on me and chased me through the house. I locked myself in the toilet where he shot me in the thigh through the keyhole.

'But babe, we were just having a laugh. You're overreacting. It's just a scratch!'

Little things set him off. He'd turn on me with his vitriol or worse, his fists. I couldn't sing in the kitchen. I couldn't leave the flat without giving a full account of where I was going or how long I'd be. The noose was tightening.

It started with a slap, the surprise more shocking than the physical act of being hit. Then it became slapping and shoving and ultimately escalating to full on punching and kicking. I forget the number of times I spent at the Accident and Emergency department dealing with my unaccountable falls and bumps. The threats became more menacing, it got to the stage where he didn't bother to try and hide his anger. It was a case of 'No more Mr Nice Guy,' following the same pattern as his father no doubt.

I found myself paying closer attention, trying to read his moods. His body language, the slope of his shoulders, the way he looked at me, that cocked half smile that didn't match his eyes. If he sat forward, if his fists were clenched. It didn't take much to set him off, send him over the edge. The harder I worked to appease him the less effect it seemed to have and yet, if I acted skittish, he would come at me more asking 'what's wrong?' or 'why are you behaving like this?'

Oh, I had thought of leaving, a thousand times or more. But he'd apologise, promise never to do it again, give excuses that seemed plausible, leave me feeling guilty, more and more he would even convince me that it was my fault. So I'd end up not just forgiving but actually apologising, as I'd try to start again with another dent in my armour.

Then the day came when I walked out of work. It was a job I'd managed to hold down for over two years but lately it had become increasingly oppressive. My boss, a married middle-aged man who should have known better, had been giving me a hard time. I'd been working as a typist for a company that made typesetters. I put up with him leaning across me, invading my personal space, undressing me with his eyes and all the lewd suggestions. But the day he stood behind me in the lunch queue and pressed his semi-hard cock against me I picked up my bag and walked. Something just snapped.

Why was it that men felt entitled to take and do what they want? Where was it going to end? Some of the other men in the queue witnessed what had happened and just sniggered. It was just a joke to them - watching a woman being humiliated, kept in her place. It made me want to hurl.

I didn't see the point in taking it to anyone in the company, it would probably be a man I spoke to, more than likely one of his cronies. I was dispensable and knew I'd be told to put up and shut up. I was done with the place and couldn't bear to go on anymore.

I left a note in the typewriter as a parting gift. It had one word, emboldened and all in capitals. ARSEHOLE.

Feeling quite smug with myself I headed into town hoping to meet up with friends. Home was not the place to go for solace, not this time. I went to an old watering hole favoured by the Mad House and was greeted by some friendly faces. It felt like quite an occasion, being out, like old times. That was when the trouble started.

Blake turned up with his biker cronies. He saw me from across the room and the smile dropped like a stone from his face. Before I knew it, he was at my side and grabbed me roughly. His eyes were half closed, and his breath reeked of alcohol. My heart sank.

'Why aren't you at work?' He jutted out his chin and raised himself up as he gripped my shoulder.

I sensed what was coming and tried hard to swallow but my mouth had gone dry. 'I ... I...' but the words wouldn't come.

His grip got tighter. He was hurting my shoulder

I swallowed hard. I knew I couldn't lie. 'I walked out. I'm sorry. I walked out because my boss kept coming on to me.' I was hoping that for once he would understand, take my side, reassure me, and say, 'There, there. Never mind.' But who was I kidding.

He inched closer, his voice low and threatening as he levelled deft punches to my gut. 'You silly bitch! What the fuck are we going to do for money now?' He stood in a way that no-one could see what he was doing.

I heard myself pleading, apologising over and over, fighting to keep the tears from my voice but my fear just fed him more. The insults and punches, mingled with beer breath, kept coming.

Squeezing my eyes shut, I tried to bend my body away yet still look as if I was standing, ending up like a human question mark. My feet betrayed me, standing rooted as my body quailed. If only I could run, but panic made me clumsy. I knew that if he caught me, if I tripped, I would get a hiding there and then. Would anyone dare stop him before he caved my head in or worse? I tasted the fear in my mouth, like chewing on silver paper, giving tiny shocks, my teeth clenched so hard it felt as though they would crash through my jaw at any moment.

I just wanted out. Away. For a great big hole to appear and swallow me whole. The embarrassment and shame I felt paralysed me.

My breath was shallow, slight like a butterfly's wing.

Distract him, said a voice in my head. Then I heard the words 'Take me home and do it.' They were my words, my voice, soft but clear, like waking from a coma. I moved dreamlike, registering how low I'd fallen - it's what you do to survive isn't it?

Just as Blake gripped my coat collar another hand grabbed him from behind and swung him round. The guy was bigger than Blake, both broader and taller. They squared up, hardly a hairs breadth between them.

'I can see what you're up to, you pathetic little man. You touch one hair on her head, and you'll have me to answer to.'

Blake seemed to shrink at the confrontation. I could hear it in his voice, just a tone higher, a tad too light to sound genuine.

'Graham! It was just a little disagreement wasn't it babe?'

I looked away, dumbstruck, my white mouth pursed into a small thin line. Inside everything was being taken on board in slow time.

'Are you okay?' A pair of kind brown eyes looked at me. My head indicated a feeble no as fat tears rolled down my cheeks.

'Come on, let's get you away from here.' His touch was solicitous as he put his hand on the small of my back and led me away. When we got round the corner my knees buckled and the shaking kicked in.

Graham took me to a mutual friend's house. He was a friend of Tonk's and took the time to get a message to him. At the time I was more worried about how Graham's girlfriend would react, her man bothering to look out for me. I twisted the button on my coat until finally it came off leaving a big crater in the material, my fingers fiddling with it like a tongue with a broken tooth. I couldn't recall the journey but remember looking at my palms and pulsing fingers and thinking these small hands, not even fully grown, didn't stand a chance. They've never stood a chance.

An hour later both Tonk and Barb appeared. We gathered in a hug, heads together, me shaking as I looked at our shoes. We were all wearing Dessie Wellies, like we were part of a special tribe.

'Frankie, what the fuck! How long has this been going on?' Tonk pursed his mouth as if trying to hold on to his words, his cheeks bulging he was so full of them.

'Why didn't you say anything?' Barb looked perplexed but her voice soothed as her hand gently rubbed my back.

I tried to find the words, my mouth dry, it's tongue sticking to the roof, rendering it incapable of formulating and synchronising consonants and syllables with the sounds.

'Well, that's it. You're coming home with us tonight.' Tonk stuck his hands into his pockets, his frown lines so deep you could have stuck pennies in them.

'I'm not having any of your *'no I can't*' nonsense.' He was talking more to himself than he was to us. I felt a warmth flood through me, Barb and Tonk looking out for me and using the word home like they were my parents.

'He's right Frankie, you'll have to come home. You'll be safer with us and we'll take care of you.'

It made sense but I was so shaken I didn't want think about it – all the what ifs. I couldn't face it. All I wanted to do was blot it from my mind.

Tonk got us fish and chips from the local chippy, came back with it stinking the room out with the smell of vinegar. We sat and ate them as we watched a video. The plan was for me to go back to the flat with Tonk and Barb after we'd watched the film.

At 9pm someone was hammering at the door, a loud insistent battering, rattling the door on its hinges, making the letterbox flap hiccup. The lights in the sitting room went on, the video was stopped and we all sat there petrified. The hammering continued. From behind the curtain Barb peeked out the window.

'It's him,' she whispered. 'How did he know you were here?'

We waited in silence not knowing what to do.

There was a loud bang from downstairs followed by the sound of heavy boots thundering up the stairs.

The living room door burst open. I felt wooden, didn't dare turn my head but felt his black eyes boring into me. He stood behind the sofa and placed his hands around my neck. I felt his hair tickle my face as he leaned down to whisper in my ear.

'Come home with me now or I'll smash this place up too.'

My heart sank, beating loudly in my chest. I knew he meant it. My eyes took in the room, wide with fear.

Discreetly Tonk put his hand over mine. It felt warm and clammy with a hint of a tremor. He was out of his depth. He looked directly at Blake. 'Leave it out mate.'

Blake was having none of it. As he loomed over Tonk I felt Tonk's hand squeeze mine tighter like he was filling me with his own fear.

When Blake spoke, it was more like a growl than an utterance, even his upper lip peeled back to show his teeth. 'Shut the fuck up. Was I speaking to you? Was I?' Spittle gathered at the corners of his mouth; little flecks of ranting foam.

It reminded me of the old men you'd find in the pub on Sundays after church; pint and a chaser, talking politics and getting more and more agitated until someone throws a punch. Everything about Blake screamed he was beyond reason, from the intensity of his stare to pace of his breath and the curl of his clenched hand.

He grabbed my hair and winding it slowly around his fist, pulled hard, twisting my head back at an awkward angle, his eyes still fastened on Tonk. His menacing voice in a low whisper.

'Now you,' he jabbed his finger in my back, 'you're coming home with me. Right now. Understand?'

As soon as we got outside the cool air hit us and Blake calmed somewhat. We walked the three miles home in silence with me trailing slightly behind toying with the idea of making a run for it. But I had nowhere to run to. If he caught me, it would be so much worse. The cold night air wrapped around us while the long shadows seemed like ugly creatures feasting on our misery. My steps were small and clipped, my body folded in on itself like a telescope. I was dreading what awaited me.

When we entered the flat the smell hit me. A stench like putrid steak mixed with something acrid and burnt. It was so strong that I could virtually taste it. The urge to wretch was overpowering. I fought to keep my mouth clenched and wondered what the hell had possessed him to take things so far.

He pushed me into the room. Heaped in the middle was the charred stinking mess of what were once my clothes. The urge to scream rose and curdled in the back of my throat.

That night he raped me. Dribbling in my ear 'You are mine. If I can't have you then no one can. I will never let you leave.'

I didn't struggle, didn't put up a fight. There was no point. I just had to lie there and take it. Try and get away in my mind's eye. It wasn't difficult. I'd been there before. Shards of images bobbed up; his body heaving on top of me, a quickened foul breath, 'Keep still, keep STILL.' I lay there, detached, hiding up in the corners of the ceiling, looking down into the shadows thinking of where I would go once this was all over. All the lovely places in the world I'd not seen, yet.

When he was done, I turned on my side and curled up, crying softly. I lay there thinking I should have listened to Tonk.

I thought about Danny, my little brother whose face I could no longer remember. After he died nobody really spoke about him again. It was as if he had been erased. For years I had blamed myself. The image of me trying to open the front door and not being able to reach, taking up precious time haunted me. His head in my lap on the way to the hospital and Mum wailing in the car. I thought about how things might have been if he had lived. Would I have left home when I did? Would he have been there for me, could he somehow have stopped things spiralling? What would he make of this situation? He loved playing the hero, was obsessed with the cowboy films, especially the ones with John Wayne coming to the damsel's rescue. But he wasn't here, he was away, gone to a safer, happier place.

This was not the life I wanted to live – and I was damned if I wasn't going to live it. How many times had I had this conversation with myself, more than I could count on my fingers and toes that was for sure. Then somehow the drama slipped by, promises were made and I'd convince myself that all would be well. It was easier to stay. I knew I had nowhere to go. I didn't want to go back to my mother with my tail between my legs it was just as suffocating with her crowing over me. Couldn't impose myself on everyone at the old flat - Blake would have made it a nightmare for everyone.

So each time it happened, I became that extra bit more vigilant, closing off the light to my true self, feeling more and more cut off from friends and the outside world until I'd reached a point where I just felt pathetic and was just too tired to consider anything else.

I had learned from an early age how to not talk, not speak of the unspeakable. It was as though my mind had created a shield for me to hide behind, ignore what was happening. I'd tell myself there were others out there who had it much worse. Even though I'd never met them. I was caught in a similar kind of trap to when I was a kid, not saying, putting up, feeling isolated, blaming myself. There was an allure at first with Blake, I had seen the respect he got from others just by the threat of his fists – I thought that threat, that fear, he created would protect me from my mother. I assumed that being with him would bring me respect and empathy, but the price I had to pay for it became more expensive every day. It was as though I'd been drawn unwittingly to something I knew, like my DNA had recognised it, 'Here, here's the pattern you're used to.' It had commanded and I responded like some sad moth to a flame.

The next morning, I opened my eyes, still swollen and red from crying. I was lying on my side, my wrists hurt where reddish bruises bloomed. Everywhere was tender, extremely tender. My body felt like a cracked, broken shell. It wouldn't have taken much, one punch more perhaps, and I'd have been crushed completely.

I looked at him lying beside me, utterly relaxed, mouth open, snoring softly, not a care in the world. He would never comprehend the damage he had wrought. His standards were different from mine. Even if I'd confronted him, he'd have laughed in my face like he always did and tell me I was over exaggerating or imagining it.

'It's all in your head just like your mad fucking mother.'

Every time his words cut to the quick, taking what little strength I had, it was a deliberate ploy to undermine, particularly when he'd say, 'Oh babe, I didn't mean it.'

Finally I realised he had power over me only because I gave him it. I hadn't known what I was doing at first - too eager to please and frightened of the pay back. Then I had actively began doing things to avoid the fall out, the punches and verbal tirades. I had been putty in his hands.

In that moment I hated him with every fibre of my being. I would have loved to have smashed something heavy over his head and have done with him – but I didn't have the strength, mentally, physically, or morally. I knew, to get through this I had to find another means. I had to hold it in, hide how I felt. Present a front that everything was all right and I was okay. If not, he would find a way to use it against me – expose my weakness and choke me slowly with it. I knew with an abstracted certainty that next time he would kill me.

This was the turning point though, the moment that I started to plan. I WAS going to get away – or die trying.

Chapter Seven

December 1979

I needed a plan. I needed to go somewhere where Blake couldn't find me. Three years I'd been with this guy. Three years of drudge and fear. Poverty and pride had been my enemies, I kept them close and fed them with my bitterness and broken dreams.

In my head I made a list of possibilities then crossed them out as I went down them, desperation mounting with each one. Even the people he didn't know on the list, like Nanny, the woman who had shown me something of a mother's love all those years ago. She was an anchor point I carried in my heart, that beacon in the dark to remind me that not everyone is bad. I worried about what might happen if I went to her and he tracked me down. Nanny was too old to cope with that kind of trouble and she didn't live far enough away. He was sure to find me.

I discounted going home – not that Mum would have taken me back anyhow, but she would have relished the 'I told you so's'. As for Dad, he was working away somewhere up north. Mum seemed to know more about his whereabouts than I did - so much for keeping in touch.

Graham? Perhaps he might step up, but I knew he wouldn't have been able to look out for me twenty-four seven. Blake would probably go to his place first given the history.

The flat? I didn't want to put Barb, Tonk, and Jerry through it even though I knew they would have done anything to help. Just the thought of the potential repercussions made me sick to my stomach. The Madhouse would probably get involved and then, all hell would be let loose. Bikers fighting bikers and the whole thing getting completely out of hand. No, I didn't want anyone getting hurt on my account. I had got myself into this mess, and no-one else should have to suffer for that.

And then I remembered, Kirstie, a friend I'd made working at the pub. The first time we met I wasn't sure of her. She seemed so self-assured and had a handle on everything, could even bring the difficult customers round with her easy banter. She was also a magician with figures. Could tot the price of three beers, a vodka and tonic and a packet of crisps in the blink of an eye whereas I'd be counting on my fingers and toes. She also had this strange habit of wrinkling her nose when presented with bullshit. A great roar would go up in the bar if anyone spotted it and we'd all look on at the person standing before her waiting to see what happened next. It was legendary. Best of all, Kirstie was a great mimic. I would beg her to do a 'take' on the pub manager - Pathetic Pete as we called him behind his back. He had this tendency of combing his hand through his thinning hair and making his eyes pop. Kirstie would take it to another level which had me howling with laughter. It got to the stage where all she had to do was lift her hand to her head – which she made a point of doing, standing behind Pete when he was talking to me and revelling in my squirming as I tried to keep some composure.

I miscalculated and got it wrong with our first introduction I got defensive and over reacted. 'So, what if I've got a ladder in my tights. No one's going to see it from behind the bar and it won't affect my work. So keep your nose out of my business.' I stormed into the kitchen for a smoke which was rather pathetic given I'd only been at the job ten minutes. She gave me five minutes to cool down and followed me.

'Here hothead!' she threw a new packet of tights down in front of me at the table. My cheeks burned. 'Oh what a beamer,' she chided, grinning from ear to ear. 'You're going to have to work to live that one down.' As the weeks passed, I grew to know that there wasn't a malicious bone in her body, her 'slagging,' as she called it, was friendly banter with huge dollops of humour thrown in. Any opportunity she'd subtly remind me 'not to get up-tights,' or 'run that one past me again,' winking or nudging me as she did so. She nicknamed me *Frankie The Ladder* but never let on to any curious punter who asked why I'd got such a strange name. As our friendship grew, we became quite a team behind the bar entertaining the punters and winding up the manager who could never keep up with our antics.

It was the quieter moments on the walk home after work where all the secrets were shared. Our footsteps echoing on the pavement and shadows rising and falling under the orange glow of the streetlights. This was where our friendship was cemented. I learned that Kirstie had been adopted by a well-to-do family who paid for her education but kept her at arm's reach both emotionally and physically. She told me how her father was warm and giving but hen-pecked by his cold and demanding wife. She was mother in name only and Kirstie felt the weight of her rejection until she met Joe and the two of them ran away together. As relationships went, to me Kirstie and Joe were perfection personified, utterly devoted to each other. Poor as church mice but it didn't take much for them to be happy. Joe could spin a yarn out of anything and make it entertaining and hilarious, right down to losing a bus ticket.

Fortunately, I had the nous to keep the friendship under wraps. I never mentioned it at home or referred to Kirstie and Joe. Instinctively I didn't want Blake to know about them, they were my best kept secret.

It was a short-lived friendship, six months maybe, but we totally got each other, like looking into the mirror. Perhaps it was because, as it turned out, our mothers seemed to be cut from the same cloth – not that we exchanged that much but from the little we did share there were a lot of similarities.

Kirstie hadn't liked Blake one bit. 'He's a plank,' she'd hiss, having witnessed him behaving badly on numerous occasions when he came into the pub with his friends. 'What the fuck are you doing with him?' Her look was one of total incomprehension, but she never pressed for a response. We understood each other on an instinctive level.

I felt bereft when she told me she was leaving. I thought of all the memories we weren't going to make, all the laughter we weren't going to share in each other's company. The decision to move to Ireland had been made quickly, within the space of a couple of days. Joe, her boyfriend's dad was ill and that was it, they were going to up-sticks and leave on Friday, payday.

Just before she left the job to go back to Ireland, she pointedly took me aside. 'Keep it safe,' she whispered as she folded my fingers around the note she placed in my hand. 'You never know when you might need it.' I had it hidden beneath the cutlery tray at the flat - feeling quite smug that Blake would never think to check there; it was right in front of him every day. He scrutinized everything else to the minutest detail, even went through my pockets on a regular basis but I suspect that was more looking for money than anything else.

Finally, realising I had a way out gave me a little sense of power, excitement even. I could leave if I wanted to. My secret weapon.

Blake would never think to look for me in Ireland, why would he? He had never been introduced to Kirstie. I did worry about what I would do if she had moved on or wasn't able to put me up, even for a short while, but then I countered that by thinking that it couldn't be any worse than the situation I was in.

I hadn't factored in never having enough money to do the deed. How to get there? I was due some pay from my job, that would be a start, especially if I held back on the rent. The landlord didn't usually moan until it was a month late at least, so Blake wouldn't notice.

I slipped out of bed and pulled my clothes on, still mulling over my half-formulated plan and slipped out of the flat. I ran to the phone box before I changed my mind.

It was Graham I turned to initially. He'd said if I needed anything to let him know. It was a brief call, Nix, his girlfriend answered. Although we'd never met, from the few words we exchanged I could sense a gentle kindness. Perhaps Graham had told her what had happened. I suspect he had been waiting for me to get in contact - he seemed prepared, his response measured - and he knew exactly what to do. Everything necessary was covered. I just had to wait two weeks. Tell no one and bide my time.

The days ticked by – one by one - as if I was walking on eggshells. Looking beaten and keeping my head down.

When the time came, I left the house early. I told Blake we were out of milk and was just popping to the shops. Graham was waiting in his car at the end of the road, engine running. I took nothing but the clothes I stood up in. When I got to the passenger door and pulled it open, Jerry popped up from his hiding place in the back seat.

'Surprise!'

I had to catch my breath as I dropped myself into the passenger seat. It was indeed a lovely surprise but I was jittery, terrified of Blake waking up and realising I was running out on him. My hands were still trembling as I fastened my seat belt, Jerry babbling excitedly from the back seat.

'Did you think I was going to let you do this on your own? Besides, I fancied a day trip, we could even see if we could find that pub the Beatles played in after we've dropped you off couldn't we Graham?'

Graham flicked his eyes to the rear-view mirror and inclined his head in a manner that said, maybe.

Jerry's eyebrows shot up as he looked back at him in the mirror, a hint of mischief in the glint of his eyes. Then, almost as an afterthought, he leaned forward and squeezing my shoulder softly uttered, 'You're going to be fine, Frankie.'

I turned, looking behind me and gave him a wan smile. Graham revved the engine and manoeuvred into the traffic. After a while I ventured. 'I didn't know you two knew each other.'

'Yeah,' Jerry chuckled.

'It's all on account of my sister,' Graham offered, a smile playing on his lips. 'She enticed him up to Cheltenham then dumped him two weeks later because he'd run out of money.'

'Heartless hussie,' piped Jerry.

'So how come you know Tonk then Graham?'

'You want the long story or the short?' he stepped up a gear as the traffic moved off from the lights.

'Short.'

'No, long.' Jerry wedged himself between the two seats like I used to do as a kid in the back of Dad's car.

'Okay,' Graham sighed, 'I'll give you both versions.'

'Go on then, get on with it. I'm all ears.'

Graham chucked at Jerry's bold insistence. 'We were at school together. I was in the year above. I first met him outside the headmaster's office after he blew up the science lab.'

'And what were you doing outside his office?'

'God Jerry, you're really nosey.'

'I was caught smoking.'

'Ooh, such bad boy.'

'Okay then, so what did you get up to then? ... '

I heard their voices, the banter going back and forth but hardly registered what was said. In the normal course of things I would have revelled in it but was too preoccupied checking the side mirror for sight of Blake's bike and the tell-tale thrum of the engine. It was only when we got way past Birmingham and had stopped off at a motorway café for a cup of tea that I settled somewhat. I still insisted on sitting in a seat so I could see everyone coming and going. Just the sight of a biker made me jumpy.

From there we drove non-stop to Liverpool docks, singing songs like *Crazy Little Thing Called Love* at the top of our lungs, which was funny because neither Graham or Jerry could hold a note. The more distance we put between us and Blake, the lighter I felt, like the yoke was being lifted as each mile passed. The fear was still there but more contained, boxed in with the lid tightly secured.

I wondered how he would be reacting, had he realised that I had gone? Probably not. It would be evening when the penny dropped and by that time, I'd be safely on the boat making my way to Dublin and he wouldn't have a clue. It was the furthest I'd ever been away from home. Day trips to Campden and hitch-hiking didn't count.

At one point during the journey when the excitement lulled, and conversation faded Jerry tapped me on the shoulder. 'Frankie, I've been thinking ... about this ... what you're doing now.' He stroked his beard as he tried to pull the thoughts into the open, 'My Mum, I'd always thought of her as being weak the way she let Dad treat her. But now that I come to think of it, I see it as a strength.'

'How do you make that out Jerry?'

'Well, she could have tried to fight back but it would have been pointless. Instead she had to think strategically, kind of manoeuvre Dad into thinking it all came from him, you know, if she wanted something, she would sort of seed the plot and make him think he'd thought of it first so he'd feel like top dog.'

'But what about the difficult things, like when you left home or when your brother died. She wasn't able to influence him then.'

'No, you're right, she didn't succeed in everything. But ...'

'What about now though, how is she managing now that your dad's gone?'

'It's like she's a totally different person. She laugh's a lot, has started to make friends in the village. Joined the knitting circle and a book group and she's totally redecorated the house, even threw out Dad's beloved chair.'

'So what does that tell you?'

'She's free.'

'Yes, and perhaps she should have done it years ago.'

'Maybe, but there's always that stupid rule that parents hang on in unhappy marriages because of the kids. You'd never catch me getting married, it's a mug's game.'

'Don't say never Jerry. It might be because you haven't met the right one yet.'

Jerry slumped against the back of the car seat and folded his arms.

'It's not about finding the right one. I just don't trust myself not to turn into a monster like my Dad ... sins of the father and all that.'

'I could say exactly the same about my Mum. Sometimes I worry I've inherited her madness but my dad used to remind me that I shared his genetics too and it didn't always follow. Just don't let your fears hold you back.' As I heard myself speak the last line struck me, Dad was so right, but putting it into practice was another thing entirely.

'My sister did a right number on you, Jerry, but I promise you, you got away lightly. The poor bloke she's settled down with now looks totally hen pecked.'

Jerry grinned in a tight-lipped sort of way; his hands tucked high underneath his armpits. 'Yeah, I can believe that.'

'I've not seen you with anyone since then.'

'Oh, there's been a few, but no one I could really, you know, get into.'

'That's probably because you keep going for the same type. Apparently, it's something to do with your psychology, you tend to get attracted to similar personality types that match those of your formative or significant relationships when growing up.'

'Fuck Graham, where did you get all that shit from?'

'Nix, my girlfriend. She's studying psychology.'

'Bloody hell, we're all doomed then. History repeating itself and all that.'

I sat up and pointedly asked Graham 'But you can break the cycle can't you?' I thought about my mother, and the correlation between her and Blake. It all seemed to fit.

'Yes, of course, it's just a matter of being aware of the pattern I suppose.'

'Thank god for that,' I muttered under my breath and relaxed back down into my seat. A familiar tune came on the radio.

'Turn that one up,' commanded Jerry from the back seat.

Graham obliged and soon we were lost in the music as we made our way up the motorway to Liverpool docks.

We sat in the car park watching the cars board, foot passengers going last. Jerry and Graham traded observations about some of the bikes and cars they'd seen in the queue. Sometimes they bickered over certain facts, voices rising as one tried to shout the other down.

I sat quietly staring out the window, my thoughts racing, trying to swallow down the lump in my throat but my mouth was parched, my stomach feeling like it had been cinched so tight it constricted my breath. Any moment I would be leaving the safety of these two people who'd gone out of their way to help me escape. My new beginning started from this point. My chest pounded loudly in my ears, and my teeth were clenched so tight my jaw hurt. I looked at my hands, balled into little fists, the physicality of them helping me to take the first step forward. Fear and bravery are a double-edged sword.

Graham got out the car first and looked around him. He pressed a fiver into my hand.

'There, that'll keep you going for a bit.'

'And this'll keep you going and feeling mellow.' Jerry pressed a small lump of hash into my other hand.

'She can't take that. What about customs?' Graham dug his hands into his jacket pocket and scowled.

'Just stick it in your mouth up near your gums till you get on board. You'll be fine,' he looked pointedly at Graham as he said the last words.

A large motorbike swung round the corner into the car park and zoomed up to the ferry. I nearly passed out, my knees buckling slightly.

It wasn't Blake.

They walked me to the gate and gave me the biggest bear hugs, I think I'd ever had.

'Don't look back,' Jerry urged.

'Let us know you're safe. Keep Barb in the loop.'

'Sure, I will.'

I walked away from the warmth of their hugs and boarded the ferry. Being the last passenger to come on board I watched as they pulled up the walkway and loosened the ropes that tied the boat to land. It felt significant, symbolic of really cutting ties.

On deck I stood and waved as the boat moved out of the harbour and into the choppy sea. I watched Jerry and Graham's outlines get smaller and smaller, waving until my arm hurt. The goodbye only felt final though as I turned myself to face the new, whatever that was to be.

Chapter Eight

The ship ploughed on, surging up and down as a hoard of seagulls followed screeching and circling overhead. Their cries mingled with the chug of the engine and bits of tannoy announcements snatched away by the wind. Until finally all that remained was the sound of the engine, the taste of salt in the air and the seven hours that stretched ahead until we docked.

I stayed on deck letting the sea air whip around me clinging to the rail as I watched the odd dirty patch of oil float on the water; blue prisms fleeting away with the waves. This was where I was at, letting all that shiny, fickle-faced detritus go. The boat rocked and tipped as it plunged further into the Irish Channel making me feel just a little squeamish. As the wind grew fierce and biting and the overhead clouds slowed, bellies full of rain; thirst drove me below deck to get warm and perhaps buy a cup of tea.

It didn't appear to be much warmer below with the wind howling along the corridors. The air was fetid in the main congregation areas where it seemed like a mass of bodies being thrown from one side of the boat to the other. It was a strange sensation having the ground rise up before me then fall away again whilst at the same time trying to navigate my way to the café without keeling over or smashing into anyone.

Children shrieked and wailed as mothers stumbled to herd them all together. I was left with the distinct impression I was travelling on a floating zoo for all the noise and mess there was around me. I managed to find a fairly quiet area and two seats all to myself so settled down with my tea, bit off half the dope Jerry had given me and swallowed it. It seemed like a sensible idea given the circumstances and meant that I would at least get some sleep.

It was a gruesome journey, even by the ferry's standards. I felt shattered and off kilter when I got off. That odd sensation that the ground was still moving beneath my feet continued for all of half an hour afterwards. I put it down to lack of sleep, the ache behind my eyelids, the tension in my shoulders that made me feel like I was going to stay in a permanently hunched position.

It seemed to take an age to find the bus station and then get the bus out to Prosperous where Kirstie was staying. At least I hoped she was still staying. What I was to do if she had moved on was anyone's guess. I had little enough money as it was and hardly enough to get me there, let alone there and back. There was always hitching if things got dire.

The bus fare was cheaper than I'd anticipated. I asked the driver to let me know when my stop came up and headed up to the back of the bus and tucked myself away in the corner. I nodded off to sleep as the bus bounced and ambled its way along winding roads. By the time it pulled into 'Holy Corner' a place where two churches, a school and a pub were on each corner, I was the only person left on the bus.

'Miss. Miss, here's your stop.' The driver spoke softly, shook me and I awoke with a start. He must have registered the fear in my face.

'Are you alright? Are ye feeling well in yourself?' he leant in close and I could see the lines of concern etched into his face, a great furrow on his brow, the criss-cross of crows feet at his eyes, his mouth hanging open waiting for my response. Struggling, I pushed myself out of the seat and stood on unsteady legs.

'Steady now. Let's get your luggage.'

'I don't have any.'

'Oh, yes, right enough,' his smile was awkward then he shrugged his shoulders and turned. I followed him down the aisle and descended the bus. He was close behind, pulling the door to and promptly disappeared into the pub on the corner while I tried to get my bearings. It didn't take long – there were plenty of parents waiting around the school gates. It just took a couple of enquiries that set me off in the right direction. All it took was a mention of my friend's name, everyone seemed to know each other in these parts, and there I was heading down the road all with thatched cottages.

The front door was slightly ajar. It was old, its ancient blue paint peeling, showing a weathered wood grain underneath. From within came a soft voice, singing. I tapped the door and waited. I knocked again. A dog barked, more a signal than here's an intruder kind of bark.

'Who is it?' The dog appeared at the door first, it's head poking through the crack. A fluffy scruffy mongrel with a black patch on its eye and a white flash on its chest.

'Kirstie, it's me.'

'Who's me?' I heard footsteps traipse across a tiled floor then the door creak as it was heaved open.

'Oh! The Lord preserve us if it's not Frankie The Ladder herself.'

Kirstie stood before me, one arm laden with a basket of laundry. I took in the warmth of her smile that spread wide across her freckled face. Her blue eyes, framed by a mop of short blond hair, lit up. She dropped the basket and threw her arms around me. We danced and laughed on the doorstep and were joined by the scruffy dog on its hind legs.

'I wondered how long it would take you to find your way here. Come away in,' she stooped and quickly grabbed the sprawling laundry. I followed her lead until everything was back in the basket. At the doorstep Kirstie looked back at the dog. 'Droopy, c'mon, this way.'

The dog, looking like it had half a mind to wander down the path and out the gate turned and resignedly responded to Kirstie's command.

We both smiled indulgently.

'Now, have you eaten? Look at you, you look exhausted. Joe will be so delighted to see you.' She hugged me again, just to check that it was really me.

She led me into the depths of the cottage, seated me at the large wooden table and set the kettle on the range. Within minutes I had a bowl of soup before me, coddle, and a large steaming mug of sweet tea. We talked as she worked, making soda bread, cleaning the surfaces, hanging out the washing.

'Yer man, he was such a plank. You knew I didn't like him, didn't you?'

I nodded, the corners of my mouth turning down.

'I should have made you come here with me. Though knowing you, you wouldn't have come. Sometimes you just have to get right down into the bottom of the barrel before you realise that you can't fall any further.'

My head dropped, searching the floor for answers.

'I bet your mother stepped up to help didn't she?'

'I didn't tell her. Didn't see the point.'

'Don't tell me, she would've given you the 'it's your bed, now you have to lie in it lecture.'

I nodded.

'Strikes me she's about as much use as a one-legged man at an arse kicking party that one.'

I fell about laughing. 'Kirstie, you are such a bloody tonic.'

'And what about your Dad, where's he?'

'I tried getting hold of him but it's like trying to track down Big Foot. I know he cares but I'm not sure what's going on with him. Last I saw him he didn't look right.'

'In what way?'

'I don't know. It's hard to explain. He'd lost a bit of weight and looked, well, gaunt.'

Kirstie thought for a minute and sighed. 'I'd say he'll get in touch when things are better for him.'

'Yeah, sounds about right. So tell me, what have you been up to?' I searched my pockets. 'Do you mind if I …?'

She laughed. 'Here, I have one already rolled. It's for Joe when he gets home but I'm sure he won't mind.' She threw the joint across the table to me which I quickly fired up. She watched as I shook the match out and blew a couple of smoke rings into the air.

'Well, come on, spill …'

'As you know we came back for Joe's dad. He was sick for number of months after we got back. Emphysema – bloody cruel disease. He was as thin as a stick when he died, lying there gasping and gaping for breath. Joe inherited the house and then he took a job on the roads – with the Corporation. The pay's alright but the job's boring, Joe'll tell you himself but it's better than being on the brew. I took a job in the bubblegum factory down the road. I can have all the bubblegum I want,' she laughed. The job's a kip but the people are great. We're stoned most of the time, it's a great craic.

I watched as Kirstie folded and shaped the sour dough. She was quick and efficient, a smile playing on her lips. 'So, tell me everything,' she said whilst still looking at her dough.

I told her everything, spilled my heart out, cried and laughed at the table and she listened with all her heart and soul.

When I'd finished, she hugged me to her, folding me into her womanly frame. Looking into my tear-stained face she tucked a stray strand of hair behind my ear. 'Now you're to put all that behind you. You have nothing to be ashamed of ... I'd have been tempted to do more than spit in his tea I can tell you.' We both sniggered.

'I'd forgotten that!'

'I thought so. And let me remind you of how feisty you were when we first met. You were in the middle of arguing with the bar manager about the ladies' toilets not being your responsibility, remember? Then I made a comment in your defence and mentioned the ladder in your tights,' she nudged my shoulder with hers playfully, 'and you nearly bit my head off.' We both laughed. 'You were so defensive then. Took me ages to get you to trust me.'

Joe came through the front door as if on cue to our laughter. He gave a roar of a welcome but hesitated at the hug.

'Hold on, I'm filthy and stink of rubbish. Wait till I've washed and changed.'

Five minutes later he was back, changed, scrubbed and clean. The ceremonial 'home from work' joint was lit and a hot mug of tea placed before Joe on the table. Every part about Joe seemed to smile. His compact wiry frame told of the physical work he did and there was always something musical about the way he spoke.

'Sorry to hear about your dad Joe.'

'Thanks,' he said and took a slurp of his tea. 'So, what brings you here?'

'What do you think Joe. The plank, that's who. I've already told her she can stay for as long as she likes till she gets herself straight.'

'Sure,' said Joe, nodding emphatically. 'Shall we go up town and celebrate. There's a good band on. Are you up for it?' He handed the joint to me.

'Seems like a plan.'

'Great, that's settled then.'

After eating we set out, pushing the VW Beetle car down the road to get it started, plumes of black smoke belching out the back as Kirstie and I heaved and grunted to get the wheels in motion. The band was called Step Aside, it was 'deadly', everyone up on their feet dancing and clapping. The rhythm pulsing through my body. I'd never seen or heard a live band before and was utterly smitten. For the very first time I felt alive

Kirstie and Joe gave me time and space to unwind and take stock. The long lie ins in the mornings, the good wholesome food and long walks in the surrounding green countryside with its riot of birdsong and Droopy at my side eased me down gently. Their kindness restored me, enabled me to venture into a world of feeling loved and safe like I'd not experienced before. I had taken Ireland to my heart but hadn't forgotten the friends I'd left behind. I scribbled off a letter to Barb to let her know I was okay as I knew she would worry otherwise.

I was beginning to embrace the idea of making the stay more permanent. Three weeks in and I was feeling quite settled when one morning Kirstie placed a letter in front of me at breakfast. It was Barb's handwriting. I tore the letter open with some excitement. But as I read it my heart dropped.

'Frankie, it's your dad, you need to phone your Mum as soon as you get this,' I had a bad feeling, not because I had to call

Mum, more of a trepidation about the news awaiting me at the other end.

Kirstie placed a cup of sweet tea in front of me. 'Bad news?'

'Maybe? I need to call home.'

Armed with change Kirstie and I headed out to the nearest phone box.

Mum was tight lipped, her sentences clipped and short with lots of awkward pauses. 'I've been trying to get hold of you. ... and I have to find out from one of your associates that you've skipped off on holiday without even telling me. Where are you? You've always been selfish and irresponsible...'

I felt my hackles rise – if she were a mother worth her salts, I would have gone to her, told her what had happened, received support and help. My fingers wound the telephone coils tighter and tighter.

'So why did you want me to call you? It's not just to tell me off for taking a holiday surely.'

She snorted down the phone. 'I'd rather not break the news in this way but needs must. It's your father. He's very ill. It's terminal and doesn't have long left. He's asked to see you.'

My knees buckled. My head surged with a wall of questions, but I was unable to speak.

'I'll expect you to make your way back immediately.' She gave no other details, not the illness or where he was, just cut me short 'I have to go now,' and put the phone down.

I slumped on the phone kiosk floor listening to the dial tone, unable to move. Images of Dad the last time I saw him, how his cheekbones stood out and his face looked gaunt, swam in my head. I could hardly take it in. Dying. My hand was still clutching the phone when Kirstie pried it out of my grip.

I stood up. 'I need to get home.' My heart was pounding, I felt giddy and lightheaded. I tried to get out of the phone box, but my limbs weren't responding. I didn't even make it out of the door. Next I knew I was sitting on my haunches, bawling. 'Dad. It's my dad, he's dying.'

That night we jump-started the car and headed out to the ferry. The journey was unusually quiet, no high energy talks, impromptu singing or wild laughter, just the sound of the engine and its occasional mis-fire.

We arrived at the ferry with little time to spare. Kirstie handed me sandwiches and Joe tucked money into my pocket. We hugged each other with heavy hearts and made promises to stay in touch, this to me was what a family should be and from there on in I cleaved them to my heart.

I arrived at Mum's around three o'clock the next day'. Her opening words were, 'You're too late. He's gone.' Yet despite that she ushered me in. 'I need your help. Come with me.' I followed her upstairs. On the landing were several bags of black bin liners. 'You can help me take these to the charity shop.' She indicated with her chin, the look on her face was one of disdain. An open black bin bag gave me a fleeting look of the contents, men's clothes. Dad's clothes. I reached down and tipped up the bag. All the contents were Dad's things.

'He's barely died and here you are eradicating every shred of him.' My voice came shrill and broken.

'You don't get to judge me here. This is my house. You weren't here to help. I couldn't even get hold of you, didn't know where you were. I was the one that had to house him, deal with him right up until the end. And all the while you were off galivanting, pleasing yourself, doing God knows what. Don't tell me that you cared.'

'I didn't know!' I screeched, my voice at the very top of its register. 'He's my Dad. Of course, I care,' tears coursed down my cheeks as I struggled to keep a check on my breathing, my head ambushed with guilt, shock and then anger. I turned on my mother, 'I've only been gone a few weeks and obviously you've been party to this for months.'

Ignoring me she loaded the car with the bags and drove off to the charity shop. I sat in the kitchen shakily drinking tea. My thoughts lifted and fell on all the malicious words and deeds she'd had aimed at Dad – they boiled up through my belly until overload came and I threw the cup against the kitchen wall, spraying tea everywhere. If Dad had stayed with her during his last days, had she tortured him with her words? Why hadn't he told me earlier? This stupid broken family!

I was angry with myself for not seeing it coming, not being there. But worse was the guilt, it lay like some monolithic hurdle in the middle of my chest as though I was somehow responsible for it all. Dad, dead. One small light in my life gone out.

When Mum got back, she was perfunctory and explained what was to happen next. Registering the death, organising the funeral arrangements, the church, the funeral notice in the paper. It provided another opportunity for her to moan about the fact that Dad had made no provision for his family. What did she expect, he had nothing.

During the whole diatribe she showed no ounce of emotion, not a tear was shed. After the outpouring she handed me my coat. 'I'll see you at the funeral,' and that was it, I was back to square one. Homeless, no money, no job.

I turned to Barb and Tonk.

Chapter Nine

Late January 1980

I met Barb after work and we walked back to the flat, me pouring my heart out on the way. She produced a tissue each time the tears spilled, urging me to keep talking and walking. I felt lighter by the time I reached the flat. The line of empty milk bottles was still there. The sight of them gave me a warm feeling, like a landmark leading you home.

Tonk and Jerry were already at the flat sharing a bong and watching children's TV. Tonk, his eyeliner smudged, was sitting with a plastic bag on his head, bleaching his hair blond. He looked like a character from The Rocky Horror Show. Jerry was bent over an LP cover carefully sticking cigarette papers together. When I appeared they both stood up and all four of us spontaneously stood in the middle of the room and hugged. Tonk was the first to speak.

'Sorry about your…' Jerry cut him off and slung an arm around my shoulder.

'Yeah man, bummer.'

'Frankie, you don't have to face this alone. We are all here for you – and were all coming to the funeral, right!' Barb shot the boys one of her, 'I mean it stares' and they both nodded their heads in agreement.

'The next big question is, has anyone heard anything about Blake?' A silence followed.

'No. He hasn't been seen around here, but there's no doubt he'll have picked up the news.'

I felt my heart pound. My voice quailed as I tried to speak, the mere thought of Blake made my hands tremor. My eyes were brimming with tears. Barb pulled a hankie out of her pocket and handed it to me. 'Frankie you're not to worry. We won't leave you alone for one minute.'

'I don't care about me, I'm frightened what he'll do to you,' I wailed.

'I'm ready for the fucker,' said Jerry squaring back his shoulders. 'Yeah, we'll squash him like a fly,' countered Tonk, looking quite ridiculous with the plastic bag on his head.

I didn't tell them that I wasn't convinced but inside my whole body was quaking. Blake nursed his grudges, fed them with his drunken unreasonableness allowing them to grow out of all proportion. God knows what stage he had got to with my betrayal. Whatever it was, he wasn't going to give up easily. He would want to punish me that's for sure. No doubt he'd relegated me to the same rank as his mother, an *effing* C.

On the day of the funeral our household awoke early and prepared. Barb produced an iron 'from next door' she said in hushed tones and kept busy pressing shirts. Tonk borrowed the communal 'court suit' from The Madhouse. It was a little short on the leg and too wide on the shoulders for him but kind of looked okay with his bleach blond spiked hair. He went easy on the eyeliner, 'out of respect.'

We took the bus to the crematorium and sat in silence on the back seat, me staring at the bunch of lilies I'd bought for Dad, and Barb keeping a motherly eye over the whole procedure. We arrived a little early and wandered around the gravestones. A mist had come down from the hills and settled like sheets of white voile over the cemetery making it feel quite gothic and ethereal. Dad would've liked that. All it needed was a solitary bell tolling and the scene would have been complete.

The hearse made its way slowly up the drive, wheels crunching on the gravel. Dad. His coffin unadorned, no flowers, nothing that showed he was loved or meant something. Mum in her car, not far behind. She parked in the car park and was joined by a couple of friends. We all wended our way up to the crematorium.

As we waited by the crematorium door for the service to begin someone tapped me on the shoulder. 'It's Frankie, isn't it?' She introduced herself as Dad's sister Sophie. She had his eyes, and there was something about the way she bit her lip, off to the left side with her eye tooth, it was an expression he had too.

We passed a few words about how sad it was.

'All that worry she put him through, small wonder he …' Sophie stopped herself, we could both feel Mum's slitted eyes were burning through us. 'Call me whenever you want, it'd be nice to get to know my niece.' She handed me her number, gave me a brief hug, and moved on.

I passed it to Barb for safe keeping, Sophie's words ringing in my ears, causing me to ponder; can you die from worrying? Does it cause cancer?

As is custom, I sat in the front pew next to Mum. She shot me a look and stuck her handbag between us. 'Why did you have to bring them?' she indicated with her head in the direction of Barb, Tonk and Jerry who were sitting in a huddle on a pew across the other side of the room.

Picking up the order of service and examining it closely I hissed. 'Don't start. Not today.'

People began to make their way in, I could hear the shuffle of their footsteps, the occasional cough, whispered greetings, bodies settling in seats. I kept my head facing forward but when the vicar asked everyone to rise, I stole a look behind. The venue was packed to the gunnels. All these people had come to pay their respects and yet I knew hardly any of them. I was both pleased and hurt. Dad had had a life of which I knew nothing about.

I don't recall much about the service, just that it was short, and that the vicar had a stilted view of who Dad was. No mention of his military service, what he did for a living, just something banal like he got up late. That'll be mum, martyring herself again.

No reception had been arranged. It felt wrong watching all these people who had taken the time to turn up to Dad's funeral drift away. I would have liked to talk to them, get to know how they knew him, listen to the stories they had about him. Anything to keep his memory alive.

Sophie hugged me before leaving. 'Please call.' Her voice was broken and thick with tears.

'I will,' I whispered back.

Outside the air was cold and crisp. I found Barb hanging round the back of the crematorium. 'Here,' she said, handing me a large joint. 'Get your laughing gear around that!'

I lit up and sucked the smoke into my lungs. 'Thanks, much appreciated.'

'Think nothing of it. What are friends for? You okay?'

'He's gone…'

She put her arm around me as I cried softly. 'Let it all out Franke, just let it go.'

'It's not fair though,' I sobbed. 'I'm left with more questions. All those people … I knew nothing about his life. It feels like I did something wrong.'

'You didn't do anything wrong. Families are complex – but yours takes the biscuit.'

Jerry and Tonk bowled round the corner.

'We've just been watching the smoke rising from the chimney…' Barb gave Jerry a swift kick.

'At least it rose upwards.'

I gave him a steely 'not impressed stare,' to which he looked suitably rebuked, his face falling like that of a naughty child as he shifted from one foot to the other. Then we all started to spontaneously chuckle. Jerry made to punch me on the arm but thought better of it.

I wagged my finger chastising, 'Jerrington!'

I am sure he could tell by my wan smile that I was just messing.

'You're so sick at times,' said Barb, the mirth was still etched into the corners of her eyes. We giggled. It was more of a release than real laughter. Something that welded us all together.

We stood smoking, watching people come and go from the far end of the car park. A couple of strangers stopped to pay their respects, tell me what a good man Dad was. I wanted to ask them how they knew him, but it began to rain. I watched Mum as she hurried away, her body leaning into the wind, her scarf tied beneath her chin. She got into her car like she had just shoved her shopping in the boot and drove out of the car park.

'Well, at least you've given me something to do on my day off,' said Jerry jovially. 'I was going to go and pay the lecky ...'

Barb made to give him a swift slap him across the back of the neck, but he was too fast and dodged.

'But I was thinking we should just spend it on paying respects for your dad.'

'Yeah,' chimed Tonk. 'Sounds like a brilliant idea.'

'We can't go to just any pub. It has to be one Blake and anyone associated with Blake don't go to.' I needed to be cautious, this would be the time that Blake would strike, when I was at my most vulnerable.

We all trooped down to the nearest little known pub, Tonk popped in first to do a reckie. We ordered several rounds and raised our glasses to Dad, to unemployment, to not paying the lecky and anything else that came to mind.

At home that evening we settled down in front of the telly. When the film had finished Barb suddenly sat up and snapped her fingers. 'I knew there was something I'd forgotten. I've got you a job if you want it.'

My heart sank. 'I'd love to stay but ... '

'You're worried about Blake?'

'Yeah, it's too much of a risk hanging around.' I shifted in my seat.

'But where are you going to go? And you haven't got any money. You'll need to get something together. The job's not permanent and its good money.'

'Let me see. ...' I pulled a face and clasped my chin setting myself in the thinker position. Despite my joking about, I didn't feel I had any choice. 'Yeah, okay, what is it?'

'You'll be promoting Embassy cigarettes with the Embassy Bingo campaign. It goes on for a month too.'

'What?'

'Promotions. You get given a blazer, a boater and you stand about at the train station waiting for the punters to get off and hand out coupons. Easy. The pay's really good and you get 200 free ciggies. And, I'll be with you at all times and the Police Station's just across the road.'

'200 each?'

'Yeah'

'Will it make us look stupid in the outfits?'

'Course.'

'When do we start?

'In four days', time or when we get the coupons.'

'Well, it's a damned sight better than the last interview you got me. What was it, receptionist?'

Barb started to chuckle. 'That was your own fault, nothing to do with me.' I giggled.

'What's this?' said Tonk, sitting up and rubbing his eyes.

'Her interview disasters,' said Barb. 'Quite entertaining.'

'Mortified I was. Sitting in front of the panel of interviewers talking up a storm and not realising I'd tucked my skirt into my tights. How they held themselves together when I left, I don't know.'

'But the best bit was you leaving by the fire-exit and setting off the fire alarm.'

'I know. I emptied the whole building. Can't think why I didn't get the job.'

The two of us were snorting with laughter.

Tonk looked on bemused. 'And when did you realise your situation?'

'Not until I'd walked all the way down the street, and I got to those window fronts that you can see your reflection in. I glanced in the window thinking hey I must be looking good because I seemed to be getting a lot of attention. And then I saw it.'

Tonk shook his head

'Remember your first job working up the Kingsditch Estate?' Barb was on a roll. 'I can't recall the name of the firm now, but

Bean worked there too. Said they fired you because you were a crap typist.'

'I wasn't even a typist. I didn't even do typing at school, well, not enough to last a term.'

'So why did you take the job?'

'I thought it was a receptionist job with a bit of typing. I figured I'd learn as I went along.'

Barb punched me softly on the arm. 'Idiot.'

I chuckled. 'Then the next job I took on was a receptionist job for a posh architect. They wanted a dolly bird really. It was like a graveyard in there, no one called, no one phoned. And I wasn't supposed to read anything either. Just sit there like a chump.'

'Wasn't that the one where ... '

'Yes,' Our eyes locked, Barb started to keel over holding onto her sides trying not to laugh out loud. 'I dislocated my jaw copying the yoga lion pose from one of their posh magazines. Bloody phone went after I'd opened my mouth so wide it locked and I couldn't shut it.'

'Stop. Stop. I'm going to have an accident.'

'You try saying hello with your mouth locked open.' Barb crossed her legs and jigged in her seat, laughter tears rolling down her face.

'You two, you're just hopeless,' Tonk shook his head, smiling.

'God, you guys are a tonic. You've really cheered me up.'

'Yup, that's the plan.' He winked and squeezed my shoulder.

The doorbell went; one short ring, one long one. Someone from the Madhouse we assumed.

Jerry went down to answer it. It was quiet at first, then we heard shouts and crashing. Tonk ran out of the door and down the stairs.

'Stay here,' Barb stood up and peeped through a crack in the door.

'It's him, isn't it?' I could hear muffled shouting and crashing going on downstairs. Unconsciously my hands went to my throat. They trembled there, like the fluttering of a fragile bird whose beating wings sought the light.

'Barb, let me go try and sort it.' The thought of Blake hurting anyone, especially Barb, Tonk or Jerry made me want to simultaneously curl up in a ball and shut down but also run to protect them, hit out, scream.

'No,' she said firmly.

'But he'll kill them. I can't have that on my conscience. Please.'

'Sshhh, I can't hear what's happening.'

All had gone quiet. We stood leaning into the doorway, listening. Barb opened it wider. There was a faint sound of shouting in the street, various voices raised in struggle. After a while the front door slammed, and two pairs of boots thundered up the stairs.

Jerry burst into the room first, with a triumphant look on his face. He had a bloodied nose and a pink bloom where the flesh under his left eye had started to swell.

'You should see the other guy,' he joked, wiping his nose with the back of his hand. Tonk came in hot on his heels but with less bravado. 'Bastard, what a prize bastard,' he gasped, holding his side where he'd taken a kicking to his ribs.

'What happened? Where is he now?'

'He tried to force his way in. Made to punch me as soon as I opened the door but missed and connected with the wall.' Jerry moved, re-enacting the scenario, ducking and diving.

'By the time I got down the stairs they were brawling in the street,' said Tonk. 'So, I rang the Madhouse's bell. They all piled out. He got a well-deserved doing. Funniest thing though, Bean's mum was there. She came out swinging her handbag when Blake threw a punch at him'

'Yeah, she was yelling 'You leave off my boy' and laying into him with the bag. Ever seen an old biddy with headscarf on and bag in action? Fucking funny it was.'

'Has he gone?' The fear still clenched in my jaw.

'Yeah, well gone. Got slung in the back of Parsley's van. He'll not be back anytime tonight, not for a long while.'

'Serves the shit right! I'll go get some ice, TCP, and plasters. Jerry, just sit tight.' Barb bustled out of the room full of matronly purpose.

Tears began to prickle, as if the fear I'd been holding had risen inside me and was launching itself from my eyes. I hugged Jerry and whispered, 'Thank you,' while Tonk bent over still winded and blew on his knuckles.

When Barb returned, armed with her 'bruised and bashed treatment' as she called it, she sat down in a way that signified the coming of a stern talk. Dabbing Jerry's face with cotton wool soaked in TCP she spoke. 'Right. You know we can't ignore it. What are we going to do about Blake? He's not just going to give up and go away so we need to have a plan. One that keeps all of us safe.' There followed a collective sigh, relief that it had finally been aired.

'You're right Barb,' I said. 'But I just can't think for now. Can it wait till morning?'

'Yeah, let's leave it til the morning,' said Tonk. 'We've had enough excitement for one day.'

Over breakfast Jerry appeared sporting a pair of black eyes, his nose all swollen. I took one look at him and felt incredibly guilty, could hardly look him in the eye.

'I've had worse I can assure you,' he said with bravado.

I wasn't convinced. I was still too over-wrought and raw from yesterday's events. Dad going round and round in my head and Blake lurking in the background. I burst into tears, sobbing uncontrollably until Tonk barrelled through and scooped me into his arms.

'There there,' he soothed. 'I've got you. It's all going to work out my babber.'

This made me cry harder as his words reminded me of Nanny. She always had that uncanny knack of making everything feel alright. Safe and sorted. I cried on Tonk's shoulder until there was nothing more left to give. His shoulder wet with tears.

Then he made me a cup of hot, sweet, tea and said, 'Frankie, I know you have a lot going on but hear this. You are going to be safe with us for the meantime. The Madhouse will be looking out for you as will we. I'm working on an idea but need to get us some funds together to put it into place. Does that sound okay with you?'

I nodded.

'It's going to be okay, I promise.'

Several days later Barb woke me early in the morning. She could hardly contain her excitement.

'The coupons have arrived!' a smile slid across her face. It was her hatching a plan smile. Looking into the front room I could see why. At the back wall was a stack of boxes, eighteen of them, all of them containing coupons.

'Really? You're never going to get rid of them all at the station.'

'We can always burn them. There'll be enough to keep us going for a week easily,' she grinned. 'Here, look, here's our outfits too.' She held them up to the window to show them up against the light.

'Oh God, they're hideous! Looks like were going punting.' They were red and white striped with padded shoulders

'I warned you, didn't I? Come on, it'll be a laugh and it's easy money,' she bumped my shoulder with hers and gave me one of her beguiling smiles. 'Come on Frankie.'

I rolled my eyes and smiled wanly. 'Oh, alright,' then caught myself and froze. 'What about Blake?'

Barb stood up and squared her shoulders. 'Just let the bastard try it. We'll be in a public place, they have their own security guards at the train station too and the police station is just up the road. Okay?'

I nodded my head in agreement, but my chest felt tight. Fear lurked behind every thought, every move I made.

We had just finished eating breakfast when Tonk rolled home having been out all night; half bottle of wine still tucked into his jacket pocket. 'Morning campers.' He bounced in, sat next to me on the sofa and looked at the stack of boxes, his brow furrowing. 'What the hell is all this?'

'Ah, let me explain,' said Barb as she chucked a carton of cigarettes in my direction. As I broke the packet open a voucher fell out. I held it up. 'Did you get one of these too?'.

'Yes. Let's see what number you got.' She reached over and taking the voucher, scrutinised it closely. 'You've got a different number from me.'

'What's this about?' Tonk leaned forward and removing the bottle from his pocket, took an ungainly swig.

Barb pointed to the boxes and began to explain our new job.

'Do you think there's anything in it?' queried Tonk.

Barb shrugged. 'Dunno, maybe.'

'Then let's have a look,' and before we knew it Tonk was up on his feet ripping open one of the boxes. He tipped out the coupons and began putting them into organised piles – each had a specific number. Barb and I looked on thinking he'd gone a little crazy.

After an hour with various piles of coupons splayed out on the floor a pattern started to emerge. Some piles were higher than others, 'the regular numbers,' as Tonk put it. Others held fewer numbers and then there were the odd lone coupons. 'These,' said Tonk rubbing his hands together, 'these are where the gold is. All we have to do is find the corresponding voucher.'

We opened at least six boxes and sorted out the coupons. The rare ones we kept for ourselves and the regular ones we put in piles to take to the station and distribute.

I tried not to think too much about what had happened earlier in the week. Tried not to give myself time to consider the loss of Dad or the fear of Blake or anything else. Instead, I directed my attention to the Embassy Bingo coupons and the prospect of hitting the jackpot with my friends.

Chapter Ten

Mid April 1980

Tonk cashed the prize, £1,000. It felt like a fortune despite the four-way split. Barb and I waited for Tonk to come back from the bank with our ill-gotten gains while Jerry wound us up saying he reckoned Tonk would do a runner and we'd never see him or the cash again.

'Look out for the postcard from Monte Carlo,' he jibed.

Tonk appeared with a bottle of fizz, snacks, and abundance of rizla papers that he had every intention of putting to good use. He popped the champagne cork and spilled the fume into each of our mugs. We clinked and said cheers loudly. Anyone would have thought we had won the pools, the way we were behaving. The air had a buzz about it. Barb wore a tiara she'd picked up from the second-hand shop and I wore a pair of long white gloves that didn't quite go with my grubby t-shirt; the image worked provided I remained seated. We sat to the table as Tonk counted out the money, looking every bit a broker, except with eyeliner and a Johnny Rotten hairdo.

I'd already decided what I would do with my cut. It was time to move on. I had been living in fear for too long, looking over my shoulder expecting the spectre of Blake to appear at any moment, and I knew I couldn't continue like that or risk having another re-run of what happened the day of Dad's funeral.

Travel was on the cards. Where, I hadn't decided. Anywhere away from Cheltenham would have done. The decision was made for me when Tonk came home the following night looking lost and shell shocked. The company was changing hands and having to let some staff go, last in first out. When I told him of my plans he rallied and said he fancied going on a trip too.

'Why not, I've got nothing to lose have I? Jerry can have my room. It'll do us all some good.' He grabbed my hands and practically jumped up and down on the spot. 'Let's go have ourselves an adventure Frankie. Come on, what do you say?'

I'd never travelled before, not proper travelled, packed clothes, and suntan lotion type of travel. Ireland being my furthest foray, but that was running away travel and before that, Weston Super Mare with the family when I was a kid and even then, that was only a two-day holiday. A bucket and spade job on the sand with a tide that never came in. I was so disappointed that I never got to see where the mermaids lived, and Danny made a show of himself by refusing to get off his donkey ride. He squealed his lungs out as Dad prised his fingers off the pommel.

This was the real thing though, we were going abroad where no one spoke English and the sun shone all day. Just the thought of it split my face with a wide grin. Away from Cheltenham and its impending lukewarm summer, away from Blake, and Mum - perfect. We were moving out of harms reach and into another existence.

We set off that very morning, rucksacks packed, a set of backgammon, a tent, sleeping bags, one Walkman, two pairs of headphones and eyeliner. We picked up our passports from the Post Office at the end of the road. There was a bounce in our stride. For the first time in a long time, I felt alive.

Barb cried and hugged us both. Jerry wore a sad smile as he stood waving, one arm round Barb watching us climb into Graham's car.

The trees that lined the other side of the street were in full bloom heavy with pink and white cherry blossom. The wind gusted and a cloud of blossom released itself in one huge drift as Graham started up the car. The petals swirling around and dancing, as the wind carried them down the street ahead of us. It gave me a rush of hope. It felt like freedom as I watched the blossoms softly detach from the trees and launch into the air - life was taking a different turn and it was my choice.

Tonk and I leaned out of the window waving, promising to send postcards as Graham, beeping the horn, drove us off to a decent hitching spot.

We got off to a slow start. The A40 was busy; car's were rushing past in quick succession. It appeared that no one was interested or had the time to stop and pick up hitch-hikers. After an hour I began to wonder whether Tonk's appearance might have had something to do with us not getting a lift. Spiked hair and black eyeliner wasn't everyone's cup of tea, but then decided I didn't want to be picked up by someone who didn't approve. I knew something would come along, but just when?

We decided to walk further up the road, closer to the layby where the rusty burger van was parked. The smell of bacon hit us from 200 yards away and despite having a fairly decent breakfast we both felt peckish. Above us, the sky drained its colour, all its hues of blue, yellow and pink disappeared and in their stead streaks of grey spread across the sky like a nasty growing stain. Tonk looked up and pulled a face.

'Looks like we're going to get pelted on.' Then he rubbed his hands together with vigour and grinned. 'But that's all part and part of the adventure isn't it Frankie.' He looked at me pointedly and stuck his thumb out in a manner that oozed triumph. A car hooted as it whizzed by. We both waved and watched it disappear into the distance. 'Ha. It's a start!' his eye's gleamed his delight and I couldn't help but smile back, Tonk was never one to play on disappointment.

First it began to spit, then when drops of rain as fat as tears fell, we sprinted to the burger van and took refuge beneath its awning. Too late, we were wet through, our hair plastered to our heads and Tonk's eyeliner had smudged. We felt obliged to buy a burger and a coffee and stood eating while the vendor struck up a conversation.

'Where are you headed?'

'Somewhere where it doesn't rain,' joked Tonk, looking out at the rain from the shelter of the cover. 'Dover, so's we can get across the Channel and then heading down south, Spain maybe.'

'Hmmnn, good luck.' He paused and appraised us. 'You'll probably be alright because there's two of you.'

'What's that supposed to mean?' Tonk's eyebrows furrowed, his jaw set.

'Well,' the vendor leaned on the counter and scratched his chin. 'the word among the truckers is that there's nutter on the loose. People have been going missing, mostly young women. There was one from round here disappeared some weeks back and then there was that one in Cheltenham. Pittville so I was told.'

I remember that now come to think of it. Don't you Frankie? All that fuss in the Echo and on the news.' I shrugged and continued stuffing my burger. I wasn't one for keeping up with the news. Tonk and the vendor chatted for a while covering things like routes, hitching etiquette, cadging lifts with truckers across the channel, football and even punk. Tonk was delighted - someone willing to listen to him waxing lyrically about his alternative music tastes. Oh Yes, he was in his sweet spot.

An articulated lorry pulled into the layby and juddered to a stop as it changed down through its many gears. He turned out to be one of the burger van's regulars. The driver, a small stocky man climbed down from his cab and hailed the burger man warmly. By the time he pulled away from the layby Tonk and I were installed at the front of the cab looking out from our lofty view excited and fairly pleased with ourselves. Tonk sat in the middle and seemed to be in his element, striking up an animated conversation with the trucker. He took us as far as Swindon and by the time he dropped us off we were not only the best of friends but he'd arranged for another lift for us through his CB radio. Miraculously this got us all the way to Newhaven, a slight deviation to Dover but all the same the adventure had begun.

By the end of the day, we had crossed the Channel at Newhaven and made it to Dieppe. Tonk, still a little green from the crossing, lay on the grass at the side of the road taking in the sunshine, Walkman headphones clamped to his ears. His pale complexion looking slightly flushed but his beatific smile said it all.

Quite by accident we found a camp site not too far from the centre of Dieppe. Arriving relatively late, we were allocated a quiet spot on the edge of the site – Despite our reservations the tent was surprisingly easy to pitch, and nothing like my recollection of a weekend camping with grandad and using a tent that had probably serviced him in the 1950's or possibly earlier. Fortunately for us the site had a shop from which we bought some wine, bread and cheese. It seemed fitting for the occasion. Laughing we pointed to the fare we wanted, our attempts at French were pathetic and it was the only time I'd ever regretted not buckling down to my French lessons at school. Voici le garcon wasn't going to get me anywhere. Oui? Never had we enjoyed food so much, rich and wholesome with the taste of the open road on our tongues and wine in our bellies. We slept soundly that night and were woken the next day by the sound of other campers rising and preparing to greet the morning.

We ate a hearty breakfast and quaffed tea in the sunshine before setting out, edging our way down to the south of France. We rode in cabs, cars and trucks managing to communicate despite the language. Smiles, jesticulations and facial expressions smoothed the way. Kindness followed us throughout our journey that day. Families shared their picnics; truckers bought us sandwiches and coffee. One old gentleman went thirty miles out of his way to drop us at a good spot to pick up a lift. Most of our rides spoke no English and yet somehow, we communicated with laughter, wild gesticulations, and the sheer joy of moving forward on the road which only added the magic to the journey.

We slept in a hedgerow that night beneath a starry sky, watched the sun sink below the horizon and listened to cattle moving in the fields beyond. The next morning was something of a cold, rude awakening. Dew had gathered on our sleeping bags, each of us shivering awake within. Tonk was the first to stir and got the little gas stove going and within half an hour a hot brew of tea was warming us up.

Tonk. My funny spontaneous, quirky friend, the one who made crazy decisions based on a whim. I recall us sitting at the side of the road tossing a coin trying to decide which direction we went next, east, south, west – I couldn't tell which way was which until he showed me how to read my shadow, using a stick to demonstrate.

'Didn't they show you this stuff in the Girl Guides?'

'Nah, I didn't last there long enough. Got kicked out.'

'What? Thrown out of Girl Guides! What did you do?'

'Our patrol, Primrose patrol, decided we wanted to play murder in the dark. We asked the leader to turn the lights out to play the game. When she turned them out Primrose Patrol buggered off out the window and spent our subs down the chippy.'

'You were a renegade at ten then.'

'Yeah, something like that.'

'Frankie,' Tonk hesitated, the sun in his eyes making them disappear in a squint. 'Do you mind if I ask you something personal?'

'No, fire away.' I sat cross-legged opposite him wrestling with the breeze to make a hand-rolled cigarette.

'Well. There're two things I want to ask really. It's something about the way you are, tough on the outside but tender on the inside.

'Go on ...'

'Were you ever fostered?'

His question threw me, like one of those dreams you get where you're exposed and even though you're aware of it, there's nothing you can do.

I kept my breath even, 'And the second point?'

'If you were fostered, did you know someone called Nanny? Does that mean anything to you?'

The mere mention of her knocked the wind out me. Instantly, I was up on my knees, my hands to my face covering my mouth. 'You were at Nanny's too? You knew Marlon?'

Marlon was one of the children also in Nanny's care. A skinny kid with a red nose and fingers who loved to wear his duffle coat, toggle fastened at the neck, pretending he was Batman saving us from all the baddies. We looked out for each other; he was always there when I'd scraped my knee or cried in the night. 'Don't worry Frankie, we've got each other,' he'd whisper, and I had this abiding sense that he was right.

'He was my best friend.' Tonk's voice was quiet. Reflective.

It took me a moment to let the information sink in. My last clear memory of Marlon was the flat of his hand, pressed against the window as I was leaving Nanny's. Mum hurrying me up the path and into the car, no time for goodbyes. The thought of him; my younger self all fractured, held together with fruit salads and inadequate words. Something snagged, like a leaf trying to travel upstream but caught on a rock so it couldn't get past. My heart felt heavy, and the sensation travelled all the way up to the back of my throat. I rubbed the threatening tears away from my eyes.

'I'd often wondered about him. Where is he now, is he okay?'

Tonk looked at the floor and shook his head. 'He didn't make it,' he said softly then sighed, his breath ragged. 'We ended up in a home together up Shurdington Way. The foster with Nanny was only a temporary thing. He'd gone back and forth from home to Nanny's until everything fell apart.'

'How do you mean?' I hardly dared to look at Tonk but when I did I noticed his eye's glisten and blink. His words sounded muffled and thready. 'He took an overdose …' Tonk paused, took in a long breath and then continued like he had reconstructed himself. 'He talked of you a lot. Always meant to find you and help you look for your lost brother.' Tonk looked up, catching my eye and smiled briefly. 'When we first met there was something about you that reminded me of Marlon even back then. Or maybe it was because you felt familiar, you know, through Marlon.'

I reached out and touched Tonk on the shoulder, 'Why didn't you say anything?'

'Dunno. Had to be sure I 'spose, and anyway I didn't want everyone else knowing my private business. What happened to

Marlon … it hit me hard and I didn't want to come across all needy.'

I understood that so well. We sat in the golden sunshine talking, we shared a lot about what had transpired during those strange and turbulent times. It was a sharing that bonded us, more than family, more than friendship, more than lovers – something that comes from deeply knowing and trusting someone. Perhaps it was in that moment Tonk became or took the place of the brother I'd lost. The one that I'd wondered what he would have done when it all went wrong for me. It was Tonk who stepped up when Blake kicked off, he was the one to instigate travelling, just like I'd imagined Danny would have done. Then I fully understood why Tonk was so important to me. We were one and the same. He knew me as I did him, through the secrets that made us who we were.

As luck would have it Tonk kept winning the coin toss, he always chose heads, which miraculously for him, kept turning up. So, we ended up in a Biarritz camp site for a week. Our neighbours were Dutch, we swapped travel stories, beer, and smokes and ultimately food. We played Petanque and taught each other different games of cards. There was always something to raise a smile. It was a pleasant site until torrential rain prompted us all to move on. We parted company with them at the train station promising to look in on each other if ever we were in Holland or London.

Tonk flipped another coin. Another heads led us to jumping the midnight train across the border to Cadiz, Spain, sleeping in carriage luggage racks to the rhythmic sound of train moving across the track's joints and squats. Clickety-clack, clickety-clack, clickety-clack.

I woke to the sound of brakes on wheels, the carriages jostling to a slow. A platform came into sight. People started moving in the carriage, voices, a foreign tongue, strange and intriguing. I listened hard but couldn't understand the sounds, fast, guttural, fluid, and singsong. And there, outside my carriage window, the view. Never had I seen such a spectacular sight. It took my breath away. I didn't even want to blink in case it disappeared. The sun rising. Huge, glowing gold and pink. A half-circle so big it filled the sky and our carriage with its colour melting and diffusing far and wide.

'Amazing, isn't it?' Tonk propped himself up on his elbow on the luggage rack opposite.

I nodded. Tonk jumped down from his lofty perch and grabbed his things.

'Come on, this is it. We're here.'

I followed his lead as we pushed through the throngs of people moving about on the platform. We made our way out of the station and onto the main street. All the fruit trees were in bloom, their petals lifting into the bright morning sky and falling like blessings. Happy tears I thought as I stood for a moment and watched them. A few petals caught in our hair and stuck to our faces too.

We changed our money at a bank then took a local bus to our next stop. The bus was long and seemed to concertina in the middle. Its route took us through the vibrant centre of town. I thought it colourful, the roads and pavements full of people, cars, and mopeds. It was only 8am and already there was a heat in the air. As we rode the bus to the outskirts and beyond the landscape changed. It became parched and scorched. We passed rows of blossoming olive trees and witnessed clouds of red dust lift along the pot-holed road. An hour and a half later and after a good deal of bouncing and shaking, we arrived in a place called Rota, situated in the southern tip of Spain.

As we disembarked, Tonk became animated. He knew the place, had been there before some years previously, his arms flailed as he pointed out landmarks. Eyes bright, mouth working overtime, beads of sweat on his forehead while the spikes of his hairstyle listed to the right. He was keen to find his friend Antonio, see if he was still around.

'Maybe he'll be able to find us work. I'm sure he'll buy us a beer at least.' His eyes twinkled, 'He owns a bar on the main strip. Paul's Bar, I think that's what he called it. You'll like him.' His beaming grin built up the hope, even his gait had changed, he positively bounced, like Tigger.

'Don't we need to find somewhere to stay and dump our stuff?'

'Nah, let's find Antonio first, he'll tell us where the best place to stop is.'

I followed him five hundred yards or more up the street. Then he stopped outside a bar. The sign above it read Paul's Bar with an emblem of a horse with wings.

'This is it. He's still here!'

'Yeah, but it's closed and I'm not sitting outside in this heat waiting for him to rock up. I'm hungry and thirsty. So, let's go get ourselves something to eat and make some decisions on full stomachs.'

The early lunch replenished us. We tramped to the other side of town to a busy beach, spread our sleeping bags out on the sand, rolled our trousers up and paddled in the sea to cool ourselves down. We slept under the heat of the midday sun until the late afternoon blissfully ignoring all the half-clad holiday makers.

We stopped at a bar then made our way back up the road to Paul's Bar. When we finally got there Antonio practically jumped over the bar to greet Tonk. There was much hugging and a lot of smiles. Antonio must have been in his mid to late thirties. Short, dark, slim with a gap between his teeth that you couldn't help but notice.

He took us to another bar close by, ordered us food and beer. Soon, plate after plate arrived; tapas, small portions of anchovies in olive oil, fried calamares, potatoes in garlic, platters of ham. I'd never eaten the like before and ate each portion tentatively. I chewed each dish with care, letting the taste find its place on my tongue before passing judgement. Tonk watching my facial expressions closely, a half-smile riding up his face and settling in the corners of his eyes.

'Good isn't it?'

'Mmnnn, really good,' I muttered, mouth full and still stuffing in more. I ate and drank as Antonio and Tonk chatted.

'So my friend, why you here in Rota?'

'I missed you,' said Tonk grabbing Antonio's cheeks, laughing. 'I missed Spain, the madness of Rota, the senoritas.'

Antonio shook his head and wagged his finger at Tonk but his smile encouraged him further. They talked some more, Tonk throwing the few Spanish words he knew into the conversation – I wasn't sure if it was to impress me or Antonio or perhaps the words flowed because of the beer. Finally, Antonio asked, 'You got somewhere to stay?'

'Not yet. But we'll find something and we're looking for work too so …'

'I help you. You stay at my campo y la guapa, she work in my bar. Si?'

Tonk took a long draft of his beer. 'Frankie, you fancy working in the bar?'

I shrugged, 'Why not? How hard can bar work be? Besides, if I don't, we'll run out of money pretty quick.' I nodded yes to Antonio. He held out his hand to shake mine, 'Bueno. Bueno.' His face lit up, eyes dancing behind his glasses with an enormous smile that showed the gap in his tooth.

'Come,' Antonio grabbed my hand and led me back to his bar. His loose intimacy made me feel uncomfortable, self-conscious at my own discomfort, but he didn't seem to notice. He bade me sit at the counter and after a brief conversation, introduced me to one of the staff. 'This Pauline.'

She stood behind the bar, washing glasses, tea towel in hand. A petite short brown-haired girl with a suntan to match. Her eyes shone, blue as the Spanish sky that day and she flashed me a smile.

'So what are you doing here?' Her broad Dublin accent totally threw me. It was the last thing I'd expected, finding an English speaker here at the southern tip of Spain. Her accent reminded me of Kirstie, even cocked her head to one side like my old friend too. I instantly warmed to her.

'I'm to take you two to my place so you two can wash up. Antonio's going to take you out to celebrate then you'll stay at mine tonight and move out to the campo tomorrow. Is that okay?'

The shower was perfect – there's nothing better than being able to wash off travel dirt.

Pauline kindly offered to wash our dirty laundry and gave me the low down on the bar work. 'Just stick with me and you'll be alright. This is a military town and things can get a bit wild at times.'

Tonk laughed. 'She's okay with that, she's seen enough of it at home.'

Antonio picked us up in his car at 9.30pm which Tonk later explained was a normal time to be going out for most Spanish people. We drove for what seemed like an hour along windy roads into the hills and finally pulled up at a bar. There were no flashing lights and no loud music to advertise its wares, just a scattering of patrons amiably gathered. Its frontage had a long pergola covered in vines with tiny bunches of grapes beginning to form. In the courtyard, where tables and chairs were placed, shrubs of fragrant Spanish jasmine rambled over walls. Here and there stood old, gnarled fruit trees looking like something out of a Van Gogh painting. Above, a deep, wide, indigo sky abundant with glittering stars cloaked us in intimacy.

The owner came out to greet us, shook Tonk and Antonio's hands and kissed me on both cheeks. He brought tapas, glasses of sherry, copas of wine. The drink and food flowed, and the conversation ranged far and wide – not that I could really follow everything that was said.

Then the owner disappeared inside only to return with a Spanish guitar. His fingers began to pluck at the strings, gradually picking up speed. As he played his facial expressions conveyed his passion, creasing and stretching as he fought to dominate the notes. I found it mesmerizing - erotic even. Percussive notes rose and fell and then he started to sing, his face lifted to the sky as though offering his voice to the void beyond.

The sound transported me, it was from the heart, full and rending, tearing notes from heaven itself, leaving us all spell bound. Then Antonio stood up and worked his feet, striking the floor with his heels, clapping in syncopated time.

'Anda, baila! Baila.' The onlookers cried. Antonio didn't appear to hear them, lost in his zapateos, eyes closed, back arched, shoulders back, at one with the music. Pride, defiance, freedom, machismo displayed in his every move. Some of the patrons came out and joined in with the clapping, encouraging the guitarist. Ole, Ole they called and on he played.

When we got back to Pauline's that night, my head full to bursting with what I had witnessed – one of Spain's most famous flamenco guitarists, playing to us on our second night in Spain. I slept well - with dreams of dancing and music, my feet firmly rooted in foreign soil.

Chapter Eleven

May 1980

It was bar work with a difference, a far cry from working in a pub in the Cotswolds with its healthy mix of clientele, darts, footie on TV, dominos in the corner and lively conversations. The vibe in Paul's bar couldn't have been more different; maybe it was the testosterone. Young men, military men, let loose with too much time, alcohol, money and machismo to contend with. The bar reeked of sex, drink, homesick sentimentalism, beer, body odour and cheap aftershave. Some of the patrons were still boys, wet behind the ears, not old enough to drink in their own country and quite evidently not quite cut from their mother's apron strings.

The bar comprised of a long room, low lights, no windows, a juke box in the corner and fuse-ball table. No chairs for lounging, just stools around a bar worked by six girls, me included. We stood on show like treats for the punters to choose from. It felt seedy and strange, they devoured me with their eyes when I walked in, like I was some form of prey. The girls too, looked me up and down, adjusted their stance, turned their backs to me when I took my place – I was competition, and I didn't understand why. Not one of them welcomed me, or even bothered to say hello. It was okay though, I could handle it and would give as good as I got. I stuck my chin out and ignored them. Their loss, not mine.

Antonio greeted me warmly, placed me at the top end of the bar, gave me a cigarette, said 'drink as many coppas as possible.' I thought he was being generous, naivete prevented me from fully understanding what he meant. The bar wasn't very busy at first, just a few guys gathering dust, trying to make conversation with the girls – none of whom spoke English, not in any meaningful way or so it seemed.

I was glad to see Tonk barrel in and seat himself opposite me at the bar, all smiles like he always sat there. Antonio gave him a beer on the house. All the girls looked on, getting the measure of the situation.

'You okay?'

'I feel like I'm on display somehow. And this lot,' I indicated with my chin, 'aren't exactly putting out the red carpet to welcome me.'

'Don't worry, this isn't forever, you'll be alright. I'm here right beside you too.' He winked and took a slug of his beer. I felt reassured knowing that. I knew I could rely on him. We'd made a pact to look after each other, sealing it with a bump of fists and proclaiming the word 'crucial.' It was a word we applied to everything we considered amazing.

The bar began to fill up. All military, mostly marines from the American base. They sat on the stools, placed their cigarettes on the bar and looked as though they had taken residence for the night. The girls plied their trade, coaxed, cajoled and encouraged them to drink more, buy them drink at an elevated price. Love you, no bullshit, now buy me a drink. Not being a big drinker, I declined offers and quite happily chatted away.

Halfway through the night another girl joined the bar. Evidently not Spanish; slim, strawberry blond and an aura about her that instinctively told you not to mess. Her walk was confident, bold even, it had that *I can and will punch you out if I must* attitude about it. We eyed each other from the opposite ends of the bar. Friend or enemy I wondered. After a while she moved up closer, cleaning the bar and serving a few customers. I observed as discreetly as possible, feeling rather emboldened with Tonk sitting nearby. I sensed he was keeping an eye on me, a flicker of a smile across his lips. He later told me he could tell by my body language I was alert, unsure.

Next I knew this blond woman stood next to me and smiled. It was a dazzling smile that quite disarmed me.

'Hi, I'm Goodie, its short for Gudrun. You're obviously a new here, aren't you?' She had an accent I couldn't make out. It wasn't Spanish but something akin to Dutch.

'Frankie,' I held out my hand

'I can do better than that girl,' she swung round and poured us both a small glass of liquor, quarante tres and coke. 'Here,' she pushed the glass into my hand. I went to protest 'but I ...'

'I know, I've watched you. You don't really drink eh? Well, you'd better get used to it girl because this is the only way you're going to make any money. Didn't anyone explain how it works?'

I shook my head feeling rather stupid.

'Here, stick with me. I'll help you and show you the tricks. We can work it together.' Raising her glass she tipped it swiftly down the back of her throat. 'Skal.' I followed suit. 'Skal.'

She knew her trade, working the bar, hustling for drinks, teasing the punters, playing with them – just enough and no more. Each time a drink was bought for her the youth on the till handed her a chip that she dropped into a glass that was kept on a shelf near the optics. After an hour the chips began to mount up. I watched her closely then clumsily tried to emulate. It felt awkward and distasteful. My hands shook as I poured the drinks, my mouth dried up when it came to talking, I was at a loss to know what to say, aware that nearly every utterance was aimed at getting a punter to buy me a drink which I didn't really want in the first place.

'How come you're not totally drunk by now?' I slurred, my head spinning as the alcohol raced through my veins. Grinning she slyly showed me how to dilute the drink.

'Aaahh,' I nodded, still unsure I would be able to do the job with such aplomb or whether I'd be sober enough to make it through till the 2am closing time.

Tonk stayed at the side of the bar, keeping what an eye out, talking to the fellow punters. With the alcohol in me things didn't seem so bad as I initially thought. About half-way through the evening Tonk summoned me over. He'd been holding court with a group of guys playing some bar game and getting quite rowdy. I overheard bits of the conversation, words Tonk liked to throw around like imperialism, capitalism and punk rock. It generated a lively debate, his audience appearing both intrigued and amused. There was one who stood out and countered him point for point. I could tell by the way they argued and laughed there was a mutual admiration.

'Frankie, c'mere. Come and meet my new American friend. Willy this is Frankie, Frankie, this is Willy.'

We both nodded at each other and said, 'Hi.'

'He's kindly offered us a place in his flat. What do you think to that?' He was slurring his words and his eyes didn't look true.

'Great. What's the catch?' Sceptical I humoured him.

'Nothing much, just keeping it clean.'

'What! That's it?'

'Yep. That's about the size of it.'

'And who exactly is doing all the cleaning?' I raised an eyebrow looking pointedly at Tonk; he was averse to cleaning at the flat back home.

He smiled a crooked smile and leaned on the bar wagging his finger at me in an I-know-what-you're-up-to kind of way. 'Both of us, I promise.' He licked his finger and in exaggerated fashion crossed his throat. His smirk showed that he knew he'd won me over. Tonk then looked to Willy who got up off his stool, picked up his pack of cigarettes and drained his glass. He looked like he was of Italian descent, dark, well built, not exactly tall, but taller than Tonk and he had the kindest of faces, with the longest pair of eyelashes I'd ever seen on a guy. His hair, just like the other men sitting around the bar, was extremely short, cropped close to the scalp, the kind of haircut associated with Skinheads and the extreme right at home. But here it was a military requisite, especially if you were a US Marine. His t-shirt gave him away, bright yellow with the insignia of the Corps written in red, Semper Fidelis.

'You wanna see where it is?' He had a soft drawl. 'Come on. It won't take long.' He smiled and turned, headed out. Tonk held five fingers up at Antonio who was sitting across the other side of the bar and the three of us left. We walked some twenty yards then Willy paused and fished his keys out of his pocket. The flat or 'apartment' as he referred to it, was literally a stone's throw away. He opened the door and led us up a flight of stairs to a large flat with cool white marble floors, a sitting room replete with comfy sofa and chair, a kitchen, three bedrooms and a balcony overlooking the road with an oblique view of the bar.

'That's my room, that's Gary's – he's on base now but should be back sometime tomorrow and that's your room if you want it.' He pointed to an empty room.

'Perfect,' said Tonk. 'When can we move in?'

'As soon as you want. It's no biggy to me.'

For a moment both Tonk and I held our breaths and could barely look each other in the eye. Then, as if all our energy had rapidly coursed its way through out bodies, we burst spontaneously into leaping up and down, dancing and whooping.

Willy stood back and watched us, his brown eyes glistened full of smile, 'Dang, you Brits sure get excited over little things, don't you?'

'We'll be over tomorrow morning at 10am mate,' said Tonk vigorously shaking Willy's hand.'

'Thanks Willy. I promise we'll keep the place spotless.'

We all trooped back to the bar and drank to our new acquaintances. Willy's mates joined in too, any excuse to raise a glass or three.

The next day we tidied up at the campo and packed our things. It was a twenty-minute walk to the flat. Willy was waiting on the balcony looking out for us. It took us all of five minutes to get unpacked and settled. We sat on the balcony in garden chairs smoking cigarettes and drinking coke. Then I caught something move out of the corner of my eye. Whatever it was, it was swift. I blinked and looked again. The creature emerged from the corner, had big round brown eyes and a pair of long ears. A large black rabbit hopped towards us. I laughed and cooed, dropping my hands to call it towards me.

Willy registered the look on my face, 'Meet Canajo, our resident pet rabbit.' He picked it up and stroked it affectionately. 'He's quite tame.'

'Doesn't he live in a cage?' I asked, giving him a tickle behind the ears.

'Nah, I just let him do his thing. He likes to run up and down the stairs. It's his way of working out I guess.'

'Where does he sleep?'

'Anywhere he likes, but mostly in the yard out back. That's where he tends to do his business too.'

'You mean he's house-trained?'

'Not exactly, but it's not a problem really.'

'Oh!' I gave the rabbit a tickle between the ears.

'Fancy a game of backgammon?' said Tonk changing the subject. He crossed the room, to root around in his rucksack and brought out a small magnetic board. Willy was intrigued having never played it, so we set about teaching him. We spent a good number of hours playing until the door slammed at the bottom of the stairs. A figure appeared in the front room doorway.

'Guys, this is Gary. Gary this is Tonk and Frankie, they're Brits and they're going to be our new roommates.'

'Hi,' we chorused.

Gary, another marine with an exceedingly short haircut, nodded and marched quickly to his room and shut the door.

'Is he upset that we're here?' I looked to Willy.

'Don't mind him, he's just finished a shift and needs some shut eye. He's cool.'

The week drifted in and passed like the whisps of cloud travelling across the ever-blue Andalusian skies. Tonk and I spent lazy days on the balcony playing backgammon and smoking what was left of the hash we had smuggled from home. Some days we sauntered down to the beach and swam in the sea. In the evenings I'd work at the bar.

Getting the balance between knowing how much to drink and when to stop proved challenging; the first couple of nights, Tonk and Willy virtually carried me home leaving me to sleep off my hangover the next morning. Working with Goodie built my confidence, we even had a laugh too. By the end of the week, I was less reserved about asking for drinks and was able to gauge my own tolerance better, but I wasn't a fan of the job. The best bit was lining up outside Antonio's office door at the end of the night and exchanging the chips for cash. It didn't amount to much but was enough to buy food and cigarettes and just a little besides.

From the vantage point of the balcony, we watched a microcosm of Spanish life. The Blue Star nightclub that came alive from 10pm onwards and pulsed into the early hours. Sometimes fights took place and the military MPs would show up, patrol cars' blue lights flashing, the pugilists cuffed and struggling, were forced into the vehicle and whisked away.

In the daytime we'd watch whole families whizz past, precariously balanced on a moped, its two-stroke engine straining at the gears. Or the Roma, sometimes referred to as Gitanos, who sat in small groups on the kerb playing guitar and spontaneously breaking into song, syncopated clapping and footwork or all three. Most of the time they exchanged drug deals with nefarious characters looping in and moving off again.

When our hash ran out, Tonk decided to approach them to see what happened. As it turned out acquiring more was rather straightforward.

Willy and Gary came home unexpectedly early one afternoon and found us smoking. Tonk, didn't miss a beat. 'Here,' he said, extending a hand with the joint in it. Willy put it to his lips and took a long draw. He raised his eyebrows in approval and passed it on to Gary who did the same. It seemed funny how a joint changed the dynamics within the flat. That afternoon we were more relaxed, laughing, talking. Sharing information about where we each came from, music, food, Spanish life, military life.

I learned how Gary and Willy were both from New York and were sergeants. When I admitted I didn't know what a sergeant was they looked at me aghast and took pains in explaining the differences in rank and then subjected me to a pseudo test, barking at me when I gave the wrong answer, which was most of the time. In my defence I was stoned with a tendency to laugh. As the afternoon wore on it was evident, we had more in common than originally thought, particularly when laughter and some ribbing flowed.

Monday afternoon, precisely a week since our arrival, Tonk and I decided to go down to the beach and laze about. We'd bought beach mats and took towels from the flat. As we walked, I noticed Tonk wince, it was quick and almost imperceptible but drew attention to the fact that his body leant ever so slightly to the left as though he was guarding himself.

'You okay?'

He passed it off with a wave of his hand. 'Yeah, fine. It feels like I've got stitch in my side. Been there for a couple of days. Don't worry, it'll be fine.'

We lay on the beach bathed in sunshine, watching the sea surge and retreat as seagulls reeled overhead. Roxy Music playing on the Walkman. It felt like all my dreams had come true, sun, sand, sea, and a liberating sense of freedom - not a care in the world. I lay there with a huge smile on my face.

Tonk sat up. That wince again. This time the crease stayed between his brows. He looked down at his left side to just below where his ribcage finished. It was markedly swollen, and a small weeping hole had appeared.

'Frankie?' Tonk looked at me, his seemed unable to register what was happening. 'Frankie, I don't feel good.'

I looked to where he'd clamped his hand to his side, peeled back his fingers and fought hard not to recoil. It didn't look good. I got to my feet, grabbed the towels, rolled up the mats and moved us off the beach. Tonk, already naturally pale, looked decidedly ashen.

At the flat all was siesta quiet. Tonk went to lie down in our room, shutters pulled tight shut. He was running a temperature, his face flushed, beads of sweat appearing on his forehead. I grabbed paracetamol from the bathroom cabinet and looked for something to bathe the wound. He swallowed the paracetamol down in greedy gulps then lay down, his movement deliberate and slow.

'Just leave me, I'll be alright. It's nothing, probably a bit of indigestion.' He tried to usher me out of the room. I stood firm.

'No, that looked infected. It needs bathing or it'll get worse.' I'd made a concoction of warm water and lemon juice to dab the affected area with. It was all I could find. The wound was swollen and pink where the skin had broken, already oozing puss. Despite being as gentle as I could Tonk still flinched. I left him to sleep and went and read on the balcony. Perplexed, I wondered where he got the injury? It wouldn't have just appeared out of the blue. Then I remembered that day Blake came to the flat after dad's funeral. Jerry and Tonk going downstairs to sort it and the big fight that followed. Tonk coming back up the stairs, the winded hero? Jerry later said Tonk had taken 'a good kicking.' I could picture it now, him sitting in the chair in the corner of the room, tilted over, body hunched protectively the same side, the same area.

He didn't come with me to work that night. When I returned, he was still hot, despite the cool of the evening. The swelling on his side had become more pronounced and the wound was now gaping.

'Tomorrow we're getting you to a doctor, okay?'

He grimaced and nodded. The candle I'd lit threw a soft golden light, guttering when the breeze broke through. The light enhanced his features, his face fevered and thrawn, hair plastered to his head, eyes glazed and wild. The look made me shiver to the bone, like someone had walked over my grave. I fetched a cold flannel and placed it on his brow, it seemed to help but he complained of feeling cold and shuddered.

Come morning he was no better. I woke Willy up at 6am, asked if we could get him on base to see a doctor but it was no good, we were third nationals. We had no right of access and no insurance. Their medical system didn't work like our NHS, it wasn't free at source. Later in the day Tonk rallied a bit, sat up and drank some tea. His face was a puffy pink with small dull eyes staring out. He moved with care, too much care.

In the afternoon I coaxed him to go to the hospital. They poked and prodded, looked perplexed but we couldn't understand what they were trying to say. The hospital looked dirty and unkempt, blood stains still evident on the bed Tonk was lying on. Across the way a woman was trying to administer an injection to her husband and in another bed a patient was violently throwing up.

Tonk sat up and did up his shirt. 'I can't stay here, Frankie. Not with this.' He got down off the bed and I followed him, pleading and protesting. He would not be swayed.

That evening I asked everyone at the bar if they could help in any way. One of the navy guys came back with antibiotics. 'Here try these. I'm no medic but I guess he has some form of fever. These might be of help.' Two more days and still no change. I watched over him as he dozed. When he woke, I tried to tempt him with food, but he pushed it away. Just the mere effort took all this strength. I couldn't bear seeing him fade before me, he needed proper attention.

'Tonk,' I said softly, 'You awake?' He mumbled and rolled over onto his back.

'Tonk, I've decided, I need to get you home. Get you some proper help. If we pool our money, I think I could get you a flight back. Please say yes.'

He shook his head, and squeezed his eyes shut.

'Listen, I'm fine here. I've got work and a place to stay. I can hang on here till you get back and then we can go on to Greece to pick grapes. What do you say? Come on, you know it makes sense.'

He put his hand to his head, threading his fingers through his damp hair.

'Okay,' his whisper barely audible, 'Fine.'

'Crucial. I'll sort it in the morning.'

Willy accompanied me to the travel agents for support. Given I'd never been on a plane before, let alone bought a ticket. I wasn't entirely sure what to do. Fortunately, I'd taken Tonk's passport with me so securing a round trip ticket with all the correct details for him didn't present a problem. What was a problem was buying just the one ticket meant spending every single penny we had.

My emotions were in a jumble, but I had to hide how I was feeling; Tonk had to go home. There was no other practical way, and I knew that if he picked up so much of a hint of me hesitating, he would have point blank refused to leave.

I didn't want Tonk to leave. I didn't want to be left alone with people I barely knew. Granted they spoke my language, but it wasn't the same language, not really. I was afraid of what was to become of Tonk but also afraid of what was to become of me. It felt like the umbilical cord was being severed. Tonk had been a lifeline for what seemed like an age and here he was sick and about to go miles away from me. And when he got there, I'd have little chance of finding out what was to happen to him unless and until he wrote or got someone to write to me. The thought of being stranded with no real means of getting home petrified me.

His flight was scheduled to leave from Jerez airport early the next morning. Willy took him on the back of his motorbike. That night I laid out all the things Tonk would need. Passport, paracetamol – for what little good they did, items of Tonks belongings. It all happened so fast, I moved automatically, going through the motions but not really registering or connecting with what was happening.

Early mornings can be cold in Spain, the sun's heat having not warmed the ground yet. Tonk shivered as I got him out of his sleeping bag and helped him dress. I wiped his face and hands with a flannel and suddenly my mind was catapulted back to being a young kid. I was in the bathroom wiping Danny's face with a flannel. His eyes were screwed shut and his mouth clamped in a thin line as his little hands tried to push mine away from his face. 'Keep still Danny! This won't take a minute.'

A sharp intake of breath prevented the sob trying to emerge at the back of my throat. Cigarette? I fished around for the packet only to find them rather crushed under my pillow. Suitably distracted, the urge to cry passed. Willy knocked softly on the door.

'Ready?'

He picked up Tonk's rucksack and hefted it onto his shoulder. I followed them both to where the motorbike was parked on the road. They put their helmets on, me helping Tonk with his helmet strap. 'Now mind you hold tight, especially on the bends. And let me know what's happening when you get back. Straight to the hospital now.'

He was grimacing pink as I babbled, holding his head in such a manner as if to say he was allowing me to fix the helmet strap under protest.

Sensing this I changed the subject, 'The helmet won't do much for your hairdo, you'll need to fix it when you get to the other end or Johnny Rotten will have something to say.'

Then Tonk climbed up behind Willy. I lifted the rucksack onto his back, tears beginning to spill. He looked at me through his china blue eyes, 'Am I going to die Frankie?'

His question jolted me, not just because of the question but my visceral response. Inside a tiny voice was saying *Yes*, but my mouth pushed out the words 'Don't be daft, course not.' We hugged awkwardly.

'Love you Tonk, travel safe. Say *hi* to Barb and Jerry. See you on the return ticket in about a month, okay?'

'Love you too.' He put on a brave smile and patted Willy on the back. 'Let's go.'

I watched as they travelled down the road, Tonk's handheld up in a short wave. He didn't look behind. He didn't have the energy; his focus was on getting home.

Chapter Twelve

June 1980

The afternoon Tonk left, I went across the road to the romas' corner. I was feeling low and wanted to blot it all out. Hashish appealed more than drink. The roma seemed bemused with my bad attempt at Spanish, or was it my miming? There was a lot of laughter all round and sentences spoken I couldn't fathom. Either way, I managed to get the message across, and an exchange took place.

The dealer, a slim swarthy individual with a shock of black hair that fell across his eyes shouted, 'Adios Frankie Engleeesh,' as I made my way back to the flat. They all waved as I sat on the balcony, lined up a tall glass of iced coke and rolled a smoke. It was a small kindness that went a long way to brightening what had started out as a difficult day.

Gary, awake after his nightshift, joined me on the balcony. He looked at me closely. He could probably tell I'd been crying because my eyes were red and swollen.

'You okay?'

I nodded and blew my nose. 'I will be. Thanks.' I handed him the joint.

'Are you trying to lead me astray Miller? You know I love to party but the corps piss test us.'

'Nice. What would happen if you got caught?'

'I'd probably get demoted.'

'Is that a big deal?'

'Hell yeah, I'd drop a pay grade for starters. Say, how 'bout you show me how to play that Backgammon game.'

I got the game out and began to put him through his paces. He picked it up quickly, goading me as he got bolder. I realised I had him down all wrong when we first met, I thought him shy and a little awkward but here was this funny man who had the cheek to tell me he was going to 'whoop my ass.'

'It's arse.' I countered, 'if you're going to speak the Queen's English at least speak it properly.' He was getting a little bit too big for his boots.

'Get back in the hoosegow you damned colonial,' he cried as he took out another of my counters. We traded friendly insults, both laughing at how bold we were becoming. We smoked more hash and spent a sunny afternoon on the balcony playing game after game of backgammon.

At the rumble of the motorbike I looked over the balcony to see Willy pulling up. He appeared in the landing a couple of minutes later.

'Que passa?' Willy stood in the frame of the balcony door as he removed his jacket. I looked up and smiled, 'Did he get off okay?'

'Yeah, but it was a close-run thing. He's really sick, isn't he? We had a stop a couple of times. He was struggling to stay on the bike.'

I nodded, 'I've never known him be so ill. He's usually fit as a flea. Can't thank you enough for taking him to the airport.'

He shook his head. 'No biggy. You two been together long?'

'Together? No, we're not together. We're just good friends. He's like a brother to me. We shared a flat back home, then we … We decided the leave and travel.'

I didn't want to voice what had happened. I didn't want to be reminded or defined by it. I wanted to start again, and this was as good a place to start as any. Feelings? I needed to keep them stuffed way down inside, I couldn't afford to face them because if I did, they just might overwhelm me, and I had to keep it together.

My stomach tightened, my eyes prickled like small stabbing pins so I stood and looked over the balcony breathing deep. Across the road the romas waved, and I waved back.

Willy joined me. After the wave he looked surprised, might as well have walked on water by the look on his face. 'Are you getting acquainted with them?'

'Yeah, sort of. That one there seated in the middle's my dealer.' As I said it, I noticed I'd lifted my chin in a pleased-with-myself kind of way. Gary started laughing, 'Damn girl, we thought you'd smuggled it over.'

'Oh, we did, but when that ran out. Tonk found another source right on our doorstep. He's brilliant at ...' My voice trailed off. Just saying his name reminded me of how bereft I felt, the lump in the back of my throat making its presence felt again.

Willy handed me a glass of coke, there was a kindness in his smile. 'You fancy a ride on the bike? Looks like you could do with it.'

'I'd love that, thanks.'

We took off for a spin to Puerto Santa Maria. It felt good being out in the fresh air, the sun on our backs, fleeing past rows of olive trees, whitewashed cottages bright in the sun, mountains rising high on the one side and glimpses of the Mediterranean on the other.

The bodega we found was rustic with a spit and sawdust floor and friendly locals holding up the bar smoking negra cigarillos and watching a TV positioned on a high shelf above the till. They seemed to know Willy, looking up and nodding discreetly. He took charge and ordered tapas with a couple of beers.

We sat quietly in the courtyard, people-watching. Being around Willy was easy, he didn't expect conversation and seemed happy not to fill in the long pauses, yet had a ready smile, and an uncanny knack of assessing a situation. He didn't fawn and paw at me like some of the patrons of Paul's bar, just took me for who I was. I appreciated that. The bar experience put me on my guard, made me feel off-balance, even more so with Tonk gone. Being around Willy was a welcome respite.

I leaned back, looking up through the awning to where the gaps in the straw let in shards of sunlight. I watched motes of dust rise and fall quietly contemplating things. Willy handed me a cigarette.

'It'll get easier you know.'

I grimaced, 'Hope so.'

'The month will pass in no time. You may as well make the best it; you'll be okay, I promise.'

I stiffened at the word promise. Such a loaded word, filled with expectation and hope, like the Christmas present you'd dreamed of waiting for you under the tree only to find it was nothing like what you'd expected. Still, I didn't want to seem ungrateful, Willy was trying to be supportive, and he didn't need to be.

'Yeah, you're right, but it's still hard. I've never been this far from home before.'

'What about your folks? Couldn't they come get you or send over some money to get you home?'

The thought of having a family like something from the Waltons made me sneer.

'What? Did I say something funny?'

'Kind of. You don't know my family.' I stared down into my glass trying to shut down the conversation. After a lull Willy asked, 'What do your folks do?'

'Tell me about your folks first.'

'My Mom, she's a typical Italian American Mom, fusses over you, wants to feed you up, nags like hell when your home. And what she says goes, she rules the roost,' he makes to salute as if to emphasise the point. My mom has a heart of gold, she even sends me a parcel of pistachios every month.'

'Pistachios?'

'My favourite kind of nuts.'

'Never heard of them!'

'She'd love you; have you chowing down bowls of pasta in no time to fatten you up. As for my pops, he's a technician, works for a telephone company. Had the same job all his life. He's kind of old fashioned but he's caring and a good dad. I've two brothers, one older one younger, and a sister. Melissa got married last year. You want to see a picture of my nephew?' he reached for his wallet. 'There, that's Lucas,' a bonny baby with big brown eyes stared back from the picture. Then he flipped to the next, 'Michael, my oldest brother he was in the Marines too. Did a stint in Vietnam, came back an alcoholic. It's put my mom through hell. Oh and here's a picture of my folks. I really miss them.'

We both leaned in to look. Willy bore a striking resemblance to his mum, barring the moustache that Willy had been trying to grow.

'You look like a close family,' I felt a pang of envy, what I would give to be part of something like that.

'Yeah, we're real tight.'

'So why did you join up then?'

'I couldn't think of anything I wanted to do at the time and I didn't want to end up working in the local factory. Half the neighbourhood works there. I wanted something different and knew I wanted to travel. Being in the military it's a given, and you get training.'

'Do you like military life?' Willy pulled a face.

'Nah, not really. I've got two more years to go and then I'm outta here. I get fed up with its BS. So, what about your folks?'

'My mum's a secretary and Dad,' I paused to swallow, talking of him in past tense was still difficult, 'Dad was a mechanic.'

'Your dad's passed?' concern drew Willy's brows together.

I lit the cigarette and took a deep draw. 'Yeah. A while back now. Actually its four months and I'm still raw.'

Shock registered on Willy's face, his eyes got wider as if the lens changed and he looked at me in a different light. He shook his head. 'Dang.'

'Fucking cancer! I think worry brought it about. If it weren't for that I'm sure ... '

'I'm sorry.' He leaned forward and touched my hand. 'How did your mom take it?'

'You don't want to know.'

'Try me.'

I hesitated for a second but then something changed inside and as the words formed and found their release I found myself talking more and more.

'When I was a kid she was very ill in here,' I pointed to my head with my forefinger. 'My brother died and it sent her over the edge. She got sectioned – kept in hospital under the Mental Health Act and I went into care for a while. My brother was always her favourite. I thought it would change after he died but it seemed like she blamed me or would have preferred it to be me instead. So, I left home at 16. It was tough for a while then I ended up sharing a flat with Tonk and two other folk, Barb and Jerry. They were, no, *are* like family to me.'

'So why did you leave?'

'Yeah, why did I leave?' I pulled on my cigarette and carefully knocked the edges of ash off into the ashtray.

'I got involved with this guy who liked to use me as a punch bag and …' I felt my stomach lurch just thinking about the other way's he abused me, a flash of how I'd drifted away up into the corners of the ceiling that night. I caught my breath and pushed the thought back down. 'He was a nasty piece of work who could more than handle himself and I had to get away. That's where Tonk came in,' I could feel tears prickling my eyelids and began to feel uncomfortable.

Too much was coming up for me to keep the lid on. And I still couldn't bear the idea of Tonk not being around, but it wasn't just that, I had an uneasy sense of something awful heading my way and I couldn't quite shake it. 'Can we change the subject? Maybe go home now?' Grabbing my jacket and helmet I stood, signalling an end to the conversation. From the corner of my eye I could see that Willy looked perplexed, then he shrugged, picked up his keys and said, 'Sure, let's get out of here.'

A couple of days later the flat was quiet, both Willy and Gary were away working on base. I was lying in after a late night at work, made even later by going on to the Blue Star nightclub with Goodie. We got pretty wasted and danced under the glare of the disco lights. Goodie, was on form that night, strutting her stuff, showing off her 'wild Icelandic side' climbing on tables and dancing, knocking back tequillas like they were going out of fashion, and encouraging me to do the same. She had no inhibitions, all her actions were large, bordering on the outrageous. She happily demonstrated this on the way home by suddenly dropping and squatting behind a bush, teetering on her high heels laughing as rivulets of pee trickled across the path.

Despite all her wildness and bravado she was extraordinarily kind. She didn't need to team up with me in the bar or look out for me. When I asked her why she just laughed and in her booming voice said 'Girl, you looked like a fish out of water that needed loosening up a little.' When she left me at my door that night, she said she would drop by sometime, show me around Rota, she hugged me before zig-zagging her way down the street.

It was 10am when the buzzer went, one long loud buzz followed by three short ones. It sounded pretty insistent to me. Half-dressed, I opened the shutters and stuck my head out the window, half expecting to see Goodie. Below was a dark-haired Spanish girl. She looked up smiling.

'Hi Frankie? You let me in? I friend of Willy's.'

'Just a sec.' I threw on some clothes and pressed the intercom.

She came up and followed me into the kitchen where I put a saucepan on the stove to make tea. We went through into the living room and sat. There she explained in her quiet, hesitant voice, that Willy had sent her, told her that I could do with a friend.

'My name is Angela or Angie. I married, my husband he working in the base. He friend of Willy's.'

'Is your husband Spanish too?'

She laughed, 'No, he Marine, like Willy.' She lit a cigarette and picked at her red nails. 'My husband is in the jail now – on the base. He fighting with another Marine. It so fucked up.' She pulled a disapproving face and shook her head.

The buzzer went again, two short raps. I opened the balcony door and looked over. Goodie, flicking her hair back, hip stuck out striking a pose. 'Girl, are you just going to leave me standing here all day?'

I beamed back, Angie pressed the buzzer to let her in.

I introduced Goodie to Angela, they kissed each other on both cheeks, a Spanish custom that intrigued me. A far cry from how we greeted each other at home but one that said so much. I liked its openness, the kisses at the beginning and end of meeting, like a capital letter and full stop in sentences. You knew where you were, everything out on display.

We relocated to the balcony and stood there talking and looking out onto the world beyond. The romas were across the street in their usual location. They looked up and waved. Laughing I waved back.

'You know them?' said Angie, eyes wide.

I beamed like I'd been given the biggest ice cream ever. 'Yep, the one standing up is my dealer.'

'You like to party?' she said with a cheeky grin.

'If you mean smoke, yep, sure do.' Then I produced some rizla and all the other rolling essentials. We sat around for a bit chatting, smoking, and laughing, sometimes Angie and Goodie broke into Spanish. It sounded like a blur of vowels and consonants to me. They tried teaching me specific words too, greetings and swear words, the ones they deemed important. After a while Goodie suggested we all go down to the Puerto to hang out there. It seemed like a good plan; the heat was still rising; it would be cooler there. We left, all three of us balanced on the back of Goodie's moped like we'd done it a million times before. This soon became a regular occupation, meeting up, partying, going to the Puerto on the moped to hang out. Sometimes we'd see some of the romas there that gathered in the street opposite the flat. I always made a point of saying hello.

That night in Paul's bar Antonio made a point of introducing me to one of his friends, the Police Commissioner. The Commissioner was dressed in civilian clothes and, maybe, because I was a little worse for wear, he looked pretty much like most of the Spanish men of his age. Not too tall, slim, dark hair, dark eyes, and a beard. After he'd left, Antonio impressed upon me the importance of being nice to this man because it was down to him whether I could or couldn't work or even stay in the country – apparently, I should have had a permit.

The following night I'd arrived at the bar just a little late, stoned but ready to work. When Goodie arrived, the fun started, chips racking up, and lots of coppas being downed. Later into the evening, a dark-haired, bearded, slim Spaniard came into the bar.

He stood directly in front of me, watching me closely. It was at about this time Goodie started to feel unwell and left early so I didn't have my side-kick to rely on. The bar was dimly lit so I couldn't really make out the Spaniard's features. I could sense him clocking everything I did, I thought of the Police Commissioner and Antonio's caution to be on my toes when he was about and the power that he had. Being stoned and it being dark I couldn't quite remember what he looked like. Was this him? Then this stranger said something in Spanish I didn't understand. Was it that he would be back for me later? He beckoned me to come closer, I leaned forward and he stuck what I thought was a piece of liquorice in my mouth and left.

The taste was nothing like liquorice, it was bitter, devoid of sweetness. I screwed my face up, wanting to spit. Then realised, I knew what this acrid taste was - hashish. Why was the Police Commissioner giving me this? Was this a set up? Was he going to come back later and have me arrested and thrown into prison then frog marched out of the country?

Paranoia and being stoned is not to be under-estimated. I left the bar in a total flap; I didn't even stop to collect my chips. At home I sat for a full hour half expecting the police to be at my door dragging me away for all kinds of misdemeanours.

When Willy arrived home, I tearfully told him what I thought had happened. Calmly he told me to sit tight while he went next door to the bar to find out what was going on. Half an hour later he returned and delighted in telling me that it wasn't Police Commissioner. I'd mistaken him for one of the romas from across the road who happened to live at the Puerto.

Antonio, especially, thought it hysterical. 'How could you mistake a Police Commissioner for a roma?' He later asked me, I couldn't really say, not without sounding offensive, so just shrugged and smiled. To me Spanish guys from that region all looked very similar, dark with black hair, bandolero moustaches, short and slim like whips with the same kind of shoes, like cowboy boots only not in boot form. Neither Willy or Antonio was buying it.

I felt a little dumb but mostly relieved. After that, the roma was referred to as the Police Commissioner and I was ribbed relentlessly.

Willy had some annual leave due. We spent a couple of days cruising around the area on the bike. For the final day we drove up to Pamploma to see the Running of the Bulls. It was a long drive, we were so stiff when we finally got off the bike, I thought I'd never straighten again. Having never really heard of the event we'd come to see I wasn't entirely sure what to expect. First, we heard the pounding of hooves on the cobbled street, then we rounded a corner to a herd of bulls charging wild and loose. It was made more intense because the streets were narrow, and the houses were all terraced. Even though we were watching from a safe distance it was frightening. Some of the youths taunted the bulls to get them to chase them, narrowly missing being gored or trampled as they dived into doorways, through windows or over walls. The bulls were massive, powerful creatures. I could feel their laboured breaths, almost touch their mouths all frothed with rage and energy, their withers covered in sweat. These beasts were so wound up they crashed about, charging at anything and everything. Until then I hadn't really understood the expression raging bull, but it became all apparent when we witnessed this.

We left late in the afternoon and drove back in the semi dark, the wind and cold wrapped round us. By the time we arrived home all the barbers were shut. Willy had to have a haircut before going back to work the next day or suffer the consequences. There were no scissors in the house. I called at Angie's but she wasn't in. Goodie had the night off and was away somewhere too. I trudged back to the flat empty-handed knowing that Willy was desperate. The only cutting implement available was a pair of nail clippers. I sat him down, put a towel round his neck and made the best of it. To call it a car crash of a haircut is an understatement. Uneven, chunks of hair missing, some bits longer than others and the odd bald patch here and there. I watched Willy leave in the morning, his face set like a chastised schoolboy who'd been told he wasn't getting out to play.

Only Gary came home that night. When I asked him what had happened, he replied; 'Willy got confined to barracks for a month.'

'For a haircut! You are having a laugh, aren't you?'

'No Maam, this aint civvy street. One whole month.' To say I was disappointed was an understatement. I left and went to work. When I got home that night Gary had company, she was just leaving as I came in. He didn't make any introductions and I didn't bother to ask. From what I could make out it didn't appear to be a loving connection. No loving gazes or tangled fingers, just a perfunctory cigarette and a curt goodbye at the door. After it slammed shut, I heard Gary's feet coming back up the stairs, taking them two at a time. He tripped over Willy's rabbit wandering about the hallway and cursed. I stood listening from my bedroom doorway, smiled, and turned off my light.

Some afternoons I hung around the flat to play backgammon and get stoned with Gary. There was something about him that intrigued me or maybe there was more to it than that, more than I wanted to admit. He had charisma, in a self-contained and self-assured sort of way. I liked that about him, in a way he reminded me of Dad. Perhaps it was his detachment, he appeared aloof, quietly observing; whatever it was I found it very alluring.

Somewhere midst all that, the liking him changed to finding him attractive. I realised the extent of the change when I needed one of the shutters in my room fixed. He was standing halfway up the ladder plying a screwdriver. My job was to keep the ladder secure. As it was the height of summer, he wasn't wearing a t-shirt. All I could see was the length of his body from the thighs up. I found myself thinking about his smooth tanned skin, the muscles on his arms, the beginning of his happy trail at the top of his shorts and my lips just inches away.

I couldn't stop thinking about him, imagining what I'd do to him if only I had the nerve. When he spoke, I'd find myself blushing, my voice becoming reedy high. It was embarrassing.

The more I became aware of it the worse I got. Then there was the sneakiness, I'd check him out when he wasn't looking. I mean really check him out. I was becoming a perv. Do you get female pervs? What was happening to me I was twenty not twelve for God's sake? Pure lust, the likes of which I'd never experienced before floored me, but how to act on it? How does anyone act on these things? I felt cack-handed and gawky around him; what was happening to me? I'd never been like this before.

Sunday night, the only night Pauls Bar was closed, Gary and I were lying on the rug in the living room playing backgammon when he suggested a game of cards. 'Sure,' I said as I watched him produce a pack and deftly shuffle.

'Ever played fifty-two card pick up?' he arched his eyebrow, mischief in his half smile.

'No,' I said, expecting him to teach me something new.

He fired the whole pack at me, laughing as he did so.

'You bugger!' Feigning annoyance, I made to slap him. His hand caught my wrist and pulled me close. I felt his breath on my face, sensed the heat of his lips, smelt his fresh shave. I closed my eyes as he kissed me. His hands reaching up to cup my chin. I could feel his fingers settle on the small scar I had to the left. I almost gave myself up to him but there it was, that reminder, surfacing when I really didn't want it to. I pulled back quickly, heart racing fighting for air.

'What is it? Are you okay?' Gary sat up, a puzzled look on his face.

I felt the heat rush to my face. 'I need to ... to get a glass of water that's all.' In the kitchen I splashed my face and filled a glass of water, gulping it down before returning back to the living room. Slowly I eased myself down on the rug, we smoked a number and kissed softly until I initiated things to go further.

That night he was tender and loving, the intensity of the lovemaking explosive. His lips covered every inch of me in ways I'd never imagined. It left me wondering what the hell I'd been doing prior to that, I felt things I'd never felt before. And once that appetite was whetted, I knew there was no going back.

In the morning, things changed. Gary had cooled; he dressed and left for work. No mention of what had transpired. Confused and ashamed I wondered did I do something wrong? I couldn't understand why he didn't feel the same way as me given the intimacy and intensity of what had transpired the night before.

Too embarrassed to confront him and yet too besotted to want to rock the boat, I struggled to know how or what to think.

I talked to Goodie, she just shrugged, 'He's a Marine, girl. It's just sex to him. Don't expect anything else.' I didn't understand, how could he shut down his feelings? I felt used and rather stupid. I'd got myself into something I didn't understand from the outset, what did I expect?

One Friday, late afternoon, almost two weeks after the card episode, Gary came by with a spring in his step. Already on the balcony enjoying a smoke he disarmed me appearing with the backgammon board.

'Are you up for a thrashing then?' He put the set on the table and dropped into the chair settling himself like a concert pianist, hands hovering over the board as he set it up. Without looking up he handed me the joint

'In your dreams sunshine.' I took a long drag and blew the smoke out slowly as I gave him a steely eyed look.

'First, a game of darts. Here, take this.' I handed him back smoke. 'I warn you. Only take me on if you think you're big enough.' I arched an eyebrow and sashayed off into the hall where the dartboard was situated.

'Throwing down the gauntlet, are we? Then bring it on.'

We gathered our darts and flipped a coin. I won.

Standing on the oche I could feel the heat of his body. He stood directly behind me, his breath on my neck, barracking or bumping me every time I attempted to throw.

'C'mon Miller, what's keeping you?' he jibed, laughing, and bumped me once more.

I swivelled round to find his face close to mine and before I knew it, I was in his arms, kissing him deeply. Our hands peeling off the few clothes we were wearing. I woke early the next morning in his bed and this time I was the one to rise and leave first. He followed me into the kitchen and stood close as I made us coffee. When I'd finished, he pulled me into his embrace.

With my hands still curled around his neck I looked him in the face, I felt exposed, shy even, but forced myself to speak. 'You know I hardly know anything about you and I'm not in the habit of kissing strangers.'

His smile was indulgent. 'Well shoot, what do you want to know?'

I wanted to say everything but my inside my head I skidded to a stop and threw out something random. 'I don't know. Tell me how come you and Willy ended up sharing a flat together.'

'That's easy. We're both from New York, both Italian, well, I'm half Italian, half American Indian on my mother's side. We're catholic and we're both sergeants in the Marine Corps. And, we were both in the same platoon together in Okinawa. Although Willy is more an admin man, he works in the office whereas I'm a bona fide Grunt. I get extra kudos for being a sharpshooter.'

'So how come you got the flat given you are doing different things. Your platoon must be quite big no?'

'Willy's popular, everyone knows him. He knows all the legal stuff, gets your leave sorted and shit. He got the apartment and was looking for a roommate and I was wanting to live out. It's better to not live and work on base, you need to get away from it. Don't get me wrong, I love the corps, but it can be quite intense. I just happened to hear about it and moved in that day. Now my turn to ask questions. How come you're hitching around Europe and what's the deal with Tonk?'

'Tonk? He's just a good mate. I shared a flat with him, Barb and Jerry.' I chuckled, 'Jerry lived in the bathroom.'

'But you two are tight. Really tight.'

'And what's wrong with that? We've been through a lot together. He's like a brother to me.' I paused on the brink of telling him about Blake but thought better of it. There was still a rawness around the subject for me, leaving me vulnerable and feeling stupid for getting in so deep.

'That ain't natural, not where I'm from. Damn, you Brits are weird. Ain't your parents worried about you some?'

I sighed and shook my head and stuck out my chin. 'Chance would be a fine thing. My dad died a few months ago and my mum … I don't get on with her. It's complicated.'

'That's rough. I'm sorry about your dad. He must have been young.'

'Yeah, in his forties. Cancer. It took him less than three weeks after he was diagnosed but the signs were there when I think about it.' Gary lifted my chin to his face with his thumb and forefinger and kissed me tenderly. In his arms I felt safe and held, like nothing else mattered and nothing could touch me. I could have stayed there for eternity. I believe that was the moment he stole my heart. We stood like that for some time until the doorbell rang, a delivery for Willy.

Chapter Thirteen

Early August 1980

Tonk returned as promised, later that morning. As I stood on the balcony I felt giddy watching him climb out of the taxi, my buddy back again. A taste of home, someone I knew to the core and could rely on. I waved wildly. So did the romas.

As I turned to go downstairs and it struck me that his arrival meant change. Soon we'd be heading out again, hitching across Europe to the vineyards of Greece. I tried to push aside the vague sense of disappointment and my feelings around Gary that were evidently growing and taking hold.

I ran downstairs and greeted him on the street with a huge hug. I knew that he still wasn't right the moment I was up close. He'd lost weight, and tilted slightly to the right as he walked. His face had that ravaged look about it that Dad had had the last time I saw him. My heart sank. As I held him tight with my face buried in his shoulder I prayed silently that my fears were wrong. I couldn't look him in the eye, he'd know. I needed a moment more to steel myself.

He paid the taxi as I picked up his rucksack and hefted it onto my shoulder. We made our way upstairs talking about the flight, who sent their love, how everyone was doing back home. It was light and breezy. I set the saucepan on the stove ready for a proper cup of tea and Tonk produced a large packet of Tetleys, a double packet of Custard Creams, and a jar of Marmite care of Barb. Jerry had sent a large bar of Cadbury's fruit and nut 'for the munchies' and had also sent a stained beer mat with a smile and the word Frankie written on it. It made me grin. 'How is the ole bugger doing? Still up to his usual nonsense?'

'Yeah, but not for long. Silly sod got caught shop lifting in Cav House. Slippers.'

'Slippers?'

Tonk was grinning. 'I know. You know what he said when I asked him why?'

I shook my head. 'Tell me …'

Tonk began to giggle. 'He said …' laughter escaped from his mouth. He tried to compose himself but more giggles erupted. 'He said … coz I just fancied them.'

I could just imagine him saying it. Sitting in the chair in next to the sound system in the front room, legs splayed, pointy cowboy boots facing in opposite directions and probably a joint tucked into the top pocket of his jean jacket. 'Idiot.'

'That's our Jerry for you.'

'Will he do time for slippers?' We both giggled again.

'Nah, doubt it. Probably a fine and a community thing like sweeping the streets or loading bags in Sainsburys.'

'Hope so.'

We stayed inside out of the reach of the sun and heat, keeping to the pleasantries and not what I really wanted to come straight out with. Finally, I asked him what it was that made him so poorly.

He shrugged, nonplussed. 'It seems to have cleared up, look,' lifting his t-shirt he showed me his scar. It still looked pink and swollen but the wound had knitted.

'But what did the doctors say?'

That twitch appeared, the one where a side of his mouth lifted into a swift half smile. 'I went to the hospital,' he began, 'they checked me out. Even kept me in overnight but couldn't find anything. Said it's probably down to indigestion and gave me antibiotics.'

'And did they make you feel any better?' I was dubious, his twitch going ten to the dozen.

'Yeah, sort of.'

'What's that supposed to mean?'

'Well, I was told it would take a while to recoup. I suspect it still needs a bit of time that's all.'

'And Barb, what did she make of it?'

He dropped his head and covered his face with his hands. 'To be honest she didn't want me to come back either.'

I handed him a joint. 'Either? Who else agreed with her?'

'Well, Jerry said something along those lines too.'

'You're a bloody idiot you know that?'

He looked up, eyes grinning through his eyeliner weary eyelashes.

'Jeeze, you know you're not in a fit state to be travelling like that?'

'Yeah, but I reconed I'd just hang out here until I felt better. It's not a bad spot. So, what about you. What's been happening?'

I told him about work and teaming up with Goodie and how much we'd earned, adding that I still thought the job was cack. He'd noticed that the romas and I were on waving terms, and laughed till he coughed when I regaled the time I'd first scored hash from them. My mistaking the Police Commissioner with the roma had him in kinks, but that might have been the facial expressions I added into the story.

'So, how's it going here then?' He looked around the flat as though expecting Gary or Willy to appear.

I shifted in my seat and crossed my legs.

'Frankie?' he leaned forward like I was about to tell him a big secret. He could read me like an open book. 'Tell me. Come on …'

I didn't quite know where to start or how to explain it as I wasn't quite sure what 'it' was. I nibbled at a ragged nail before starting.

'Well, Willy's been grounded on base for the past month, should be home any day now – I'll tell you more about that story later, but it all came about because of a haircut or lack of one. And Gary, well, I'm not entirely sure what's going on there.' I blushed, giving the game away.

'No,' Tonk sat back in his chair, 'Frankie, please tell me you haven't.' He levelled his gaze at me.

Enjoying his shock I looked him in the eye, emboldened. 'Fraid so.'

'Really? What were you thinking? It's like shitting in your own nest.'

'I know, I know. Don't say anymore or I'll have to stick my fingers in my ears and *blah blah* you out. It was lust on my part. Honestly I've never...'

'Stop, just don't go there. That's too much, I don't need to know the intricate details of your sex life. So, are you two an item now?'

'No. I'm not sure what we are. I don't think we are anything really.'

'Oh, awkward.'

'Yeah, it is a bit confusing.' I focused on a ragged nail on my index finger.

'Just don't let it get out of hand like Blake. I can't be rescuing you again in a hurry. Which reminds me, want to hear the latest on that tosser?'

'I'm not sure. Is it good or bad?'

'Depends on your perspective, but I think you'll like it.'

'Go on then.'

'He's up on a murder charge. On remand in Gloucester at the moment awaiting trial.'

'Murder! Really?'

'Fuck yes, and I'm only glad you got away from that psycho. It could have been you!'

'Yeah, it could have been,' I shuddered.

'Don't you want to know all the gory details?'

'No. I don't want to give him a moment of my time.' My heartbeat quickened. 'Anyway, here's to us and all the crucial times we have ahead of us.' We chinked our mugs of tea, sloshing it as we did so.

'Yeah, here's to that fucker's ill health and long-term imprisonment.' And then Tonk changed the subject. He brought me up to speed with other events back home, the Madhouse being raided, again. Bean leaving for India and being chased by rogue elephants when he got there; the thought of Bean reminded me of that time when I had gone to see mum and how she had been so awful. Bean, bless him, came to the rescue and scooped me up like Cinderella, biker style, and we did get to the party afterall. As an afterthought he mentioned that Jerry was doing up his Triumph for the umpteenth time.

'When is he not doing up his bike?' I laughed. Tonk nodded in agreement. 'This must be the third time at least.'

I made sandwiches for lunch and watched as Tonk nibbled at his. He left half of it saying he didn't feel hungry and needed to rest. He'd had an early start after all. Come the evening when he got up, he didn't look all that refreshed. He didn't seem to sit in his usual way either, it was more hunched and considered. I dismissed it thinking he was probably still a little tender where the wound had been.

We sat out on the balcony in the cool of the evening, the scent of jasmine growing in the window box next door caught on the air. Tonk's usual liveliness failed to appear. I put it down to him being tired from the journey but something niggled. He came with me to the bar and sat on his usual stool chatting to Antonio but come eleven o'clock I could see him flagging. I took him back to the flat, got him settled and went back to the bar. Even Antonio commented, 'Is Tonk still sick? You sure?'

Willy returned three days later with a better haircut than last I saw him, all the bald patches had grown in. After an evening with Tonk he also commented that he didn't look quite up to par. But every time I asked Tonk he played it down, said it was nothing, that he was recuperating, that it just needed a little time.

We were at the height of the Spanish summer the heat relentless and fierce. Tonk's health declined rapidly. His listing walk became more pronounced, from barely noticeable to something you could tell from one hundred yards away. His ascent up the stairs got slower as the days progress until he started making excuses not to go out. Night times I sensed he was awake and uncomfortable with all the tossing and turning. Sometimes he cried out in his sleep. Ten days on, he lay listless on the sofa, brow beaded with sweat, eyes glazed with pain. Finally, he owned up to 'not feeling right' and after my insistence, allowed me to check his wound, I could see it had swollen and started to fester. Most of my earnings went on bandages and ointments that I changed twice a day. Then the wound began to smell bad too. I was hopelessly out of my depth; it felt like trying to sweep back the oncoming tide. Sometimes I found myself crying quietly in the toilet, coming out with my brave face on, putting on a smile that hid the panic. Someone, anyone, fucking help me. I think he's dying, and I don't know what to do.

He spent most of his time sleeping or when awake, complaining about the heat. I filled the freezer with ice, even fetched some from the bar. I'd wrap flannels in the stuff and place them on his face, neck, hands and feet, watching them alternate pink to white, white to pink. The veins on his forehead standing out, like they couldn't pump enough heat around him.

Willy bought a fan cooler to try and ease things, but it made little difference. Two weeks on and it got to the stage where I could barely tempt him to eat. I had to resort to spoon feeding and washing him. This was the deal breaker.

He was so vulnerable then. As though all the fight had gone out of him, leaving only fear behind his eyes. His fingers clung to me like those of a small child and sometimes when he said my name, I could hear another voice within his, one that said Frankie in a certain way. It was petulant, loving, small, funny, needy.

Memories of Danny would surface, played out in short vignettes. Sitting to the table, laughing, head back, mouth full, eyes squeezed shut; in the garden, digging for worms, ruddy face and snotty nose wiped clean with a grubby coat sleeve. Bath time, bawling, tears gathered on long eyelashes and action man drowning at the bottom of the tub with my barbie doll. Sitting on the stairs listening, a pair of chubby toes lined up next to mine. A whispered, 'night night' Frankie, through the darkness.

I had no real time to stop and think. Too busy 'doing' just to keep that tide from coming in. This time we didn't have the funds to buy an airline ticket, not even a single. The best I could rustle up was a ticket on the Magic Bus to London. It meant a twenty-four-hour journey but there was no other choice. The ticket used up all the money we had. Acquaintances at the bar said I was mad to cover the ticket again, tried to convince me to leave him to it, but how could I? This was Tonk, they didn't understand that

that's what you do for a friend, a real friend and besides we'd made a pact to look out for one another.

I was back to square one. Going through the motions of trying to persuade him to go home. I tried from every angle, pleading, cajoling, getting angry but he was adamant he was going to get better and just needed a little more time. I didn't feel he had the time to waste, I knew in my bones that something more sinister was at play. My dreams were full of foreboding; I'd wake in tears, hyperventilating. Dad and Tonk fusing into one.

Grief and worry can do strange things to a person. Rationally, I knew it was all down to that, but it still didn't stop how I reacted. It even took me by surprise. Tonk's situation was dire. Finally, I stopped dithering and bought the ticket, presenting it to him like a fait accompli.

It was an ugly scene on a blistering hot day with a dry heat that would have cured the marrow of your bones given half the chance. Tonk lay on the sofa, covered in a white sheet, eye's half-closed, listening to the BBC World Service. It would have been laughable had the circumstances been different, he despised anything that smacked of what he defined as Empire, but now, the radio babble gave him something other than himself to focus on.

When I told him about the ticket he raised himself up on his elbow, his face cracked into a frown and swore 'I'm not fucking leaving you.'

Something inside me imploded. All reason and kindness shunted sideways making way for all the angst I'd been wrestling with.

'It's not all down to you!' I screamed, 'Stop behaving like an idiot, it's pathetic. You're not doing me any favours; I don't need you to martyr yourself on my behalf. You must go back home where you can get the right medical care and attention. I'm not a fucking nurse.'

Tears streamed down my face as I made a sharp exit to the bathroom and slammed the door. It was the worst row we'd ever had. I hated myself for what I'd said. I heard my mother's voice in those words and detested myself some more.

Why could he not see that it was an act of love? Why was he so desperate to stay when his health, possibly his life, depended on leaving? That wounded look on his face killed me, as good as taking a knife to the heart. But I had to get him home.

Then it dawned on me ... what if he...? But we've always loved each other – like brother and sister. I'd never considered it to be anything else but what if ...? No secrets, we'd always agreed to that. I stepped out of the bathroom with a different sense of purpose.

Willy refused to take Tonk to the bus station, 'He'll not make it. Look at him,' he whispered, peering at him through the balcony's glass door. Tonk lay on the sofa like a sinking ship, pink faced, semi-conscious labouring with the heat. We'd hardly exchanged a word since the row and when I looked at him it was as if he'd shrunk, given in to what was making him ill. We all could tell he wouldn't have the strength to stay upright on the back of the bike. In desperation I broke my promise to Tonk. He had begged me not to mention his illness to Antonio – he didn't want charity. This had gone way beyond charity, he needed help.

I went to the bar early before anyone else arrived that night. Antonio was visibly shocked when I told him, he pushed himself off the bar and stood upright throwing back his shoulders. 'Why you not come to me earlier? Why you not think I not help my friend?'

'Antonio,' I said, levelling my gaze at him. 'Tonk is a very proud man. He finds it hard to ask for help from anyone. He thought he would get better but this, this has got bigger than he can deal with.'

'I come for him tomorrow and take him to the airport myself. If he sick, I pay for flight tomorrow and we go there together but I not take you.'

'Why ever not?'

'I talk to my friend, man to man,' he thumped his chest. 'I give him money to get him home from airport. He won't want it if you are there to see. You understand?'

'I think so.'

'Bueno, it's a deal. He fly home then.' he slapped the flat of his hand down on the bar, 'entonces, estamos listos?'

Saying goodbye was hard, but in a different way to before. I didn't have the same fear for myself as I had then. This time I felt a little more secure. A place to stay, a job, albeit crappy and some friends around me. As I waved Tonk off I felt a huge wave of relief, he'd rallied just before getting into the Antonio's car – a quick view of the old vibrant Tonk on show, giving advice, making jokes, trying to be brave.

He hesitated before climbing into the car and looked at me in earnest. 'Don't go falling in love with a Marine, he'll only break your heart. Go for someone in the Navy – it's a much better pay scale. Better still, don't get tied down at all. Live your life, Frankie.' His face had flushed in patches as he climbed into the car and waved from the front seat until the car was out of sight.

I almost envied him going home but pulled myself up short, he was returning out of necessity.

His words had jolted me though. He said them in a way that sounded final, like an ending was coming. *Live your life, Frankie.* Then I thought about what he'd said about not falling for a Marine. How could he be so calculating? Love is love. You can't just fall in love to order and anyway, who was he to say that one was better than the other?

Bits of our conversations came back to me, threading in and out in my mind's eye. I could see us back there, sitting on the balcony, the backgammon spread out before us. This was where most of his nuggets of advice were given. The last time we'd talked about matters of love or my utter car crash of a relationship with Blake he put it like this:

'You're just too gullible, you get all stuck on the wrong things. It's like you've no sense of self-worth and can't see what's really before you. You need a guy to love you for who you are and not try and adapt yourself round him like some weird chameleon. Believe in yourself, Frankie.'

His words made me balk and question myself. Was I that malleable, was it that obvious? I sucked my teeth, wondering, then shrugged as if to physically shirk it off. Like they say, many a true word ...

I slept that afternoon right through to the next, waking just an hour before needing to go to work. There were no more dreams, just sadness. I knew then that there were no sights, no sounds that could make the word *goodbye* anything other than what it was.

Chapter Fourteen

October 1980

    I knew the post was slow, but as the days turned into weeks I was desperate for news of Tonk. Barb sent a postcard from drizzly Cheltenham Spa, it didn't contain much news, just a few comments from Barb and the Madhouse; Jerry had signed his name. I told myself that no news about Tonk was good news.
    I wasn't sure how to read the situation with myself and Gary: all I knew was that the energy crackled like powerlines when we were in the room together. My head went on scramble when he was about; I became awkward and self-conscious, my heart pumped faster and my stomach flipped. I was addicted, I hung around the flat like some lovesick puppy waiting for him to appear and when he did, I'd act like I was indifferent. I lost sight of why I was playing this game and yet somehow, I couldn't stop myself. Was this love or lust? What did I want to achieve? I wanted him, heart, body, and soul. I ached for him, but realistically I knew deep down we were too young to settle. I knew he still wanted to play the field, feed the sexual animal within him. I knew a military life was stifling for people like me, somewhere along the line I'd grow bored and mess up somehow. And there was still the spectre of my mum's mental health. What if I had inherited it and it hadn't shown it's colours yet?
    And if I told him how I felt how would he react? What if he laughed in my face? I didn't think I could cope with rejection. It

was too hard to contemplate and so I stayed silent, trapped by my own fear and imaginings.

Some nights we'd end up together. He always came to my bed made up of two sleeping bags spread over a mat on the floor. Our lovemaking was intense and tender and after, we'd wrap arms and legs around each other until one of us rose in the morning.

In time there was a softening of heart. Early one morning Gary came home from work and knelt beside me as I lay sleeping. He folded me into his arms and whispered, 'You smell good,' before getting into bed beside me. Sleepily I mouthed the words *I love you* as we kissed and it seemed like he did the same, as though we were sewing our souls together with our lips.

Willy wasn't happy. He and Gary circled round each other like caged tigers trading thinly disguised insults. I knew it was because of me but didn't know how to deal with it and so chose to ignore the growing animosity.

Occasionally when Gary was away working on base Willy and I would take off on the bike, go down to Puerto de Santa Maria, go people-watching, act crazy, mingle with the locals. My relationship with Willy was completely different from the one I had with Gary. I could talk to Willy easily, we'd cover all manner of things openly - as if we were on each other's wave-length. He got me and I got him, and I loved him for that - but I couldn't discuss what was or wasn't going on with Gary. Maybe it was shame, maybe it was loyalty to a friendship, to a lover. I suppose I wanted to keep both of them. I didn't want to have to choose. Between the two of them they made me whole.

There were times when I wished things had been different, that I'd not fallen for Gary, but I couldn't help how my heart felt. If I could have fused Gary and Willy into one I could have made the perfect boyfriend. As it was, Willy didn't like Gary and made no bones of showing it. He'd corner him in front of me at every opportunity trying to make a point. Trying to open my eyes.

'Didn't I see you on base taking Sandy to the movies?' or 'Wasn't that Melissa you were with at La Playa bar?' He'd throw curve balls at me too. 'Have you ever noticed that Gary never takes you anywhere?' Or 'What you two do together only ever takes place in the apartment.' He explained that Gary was a cheater, that he couldn't help himself. He's a hunter and loves the hunt. On the base he had kudos because he'd been a sharpshooter with an elite battalion, all the guys looked up to him and all the girls wanted him to take them to bed, he even admitted that's why he chose him to share the apartment with. 'You deserve better than this, Frankie, way better. If you were mine, I'd marry you in a heartbeat.'

I was too loyal for my own good and made my ears deaf to his words and my eyes firmly shut, I resolutely refused to see what was going on beneath my very nose. I was drunk on the titbits Gary fed me, no promises, just a tantalising hint of what my imagination thought was to come. I understood Willy's reasoning. He was my friend and was looking out for me. He wanted me to see things for what they were – I couldn't dive that deep, I swam with water-wings of hope on the surface. Sometimes he fed me morsels of hope too.

One night, at the Blue Star nightclub, Gary came to my rescue. I was drunk and got up in the face of a guy who called me a cheap whore because I refused to dance with him. Gary deftly manoeuvred me outside for some fresh air, I sobbed as I gulped it down, teetering in my heels. He lifted me into his arms and carried me back to the flat, with me bitterly voicing how I thought they were all a bunch of shits, everyone except him and Willy. In the morning he brought me tea and a paracetamol and out of the blue said, 'What would you say to us getting a proper bed?' But I was too hung over to fully process it and said nothing.

It didn't register until later that day. And when it did, hope rode high then. I felt ebullient, like he'd made a wild declaration of his love. I spent the whole day with a smile on my face and a spring in my step, it was as though someone had turned the light on in my heart. In my head I'd rehearsed a thousand times what I was going to say to him, how I would bring the conversation back to his proposition, going on to decide on the criteria for a good bed.

He didn't come home that night - a nightshift on base. That night I slept dreaming that I had my arms around him in our new bed. The following morning, he came home looking sheepish. His voice gave him away first, all hesitant and considered. It seemed he couldn't look at me directly, his movements quick and clunky. He sat me down out on the balcony, made us a coffee and rolled a joint which he lit it with excessive attention, lifting his head and blowing smoke up high before he spoke.

'You'll have heard that the Marine Corps Ball is coming up soon.' I nodded, watching him closely, trying to read his body language. 'You know, I wanted to invite you …' And there it was, the pause before the 'but,' I leaned back on my chair and exhaled. 'So, what's the but?'

He handed me the joint then hooded his eyes with his hand. 'I'm really sorry Frankie, I kind of invited someone else and I can't get out of it.'

I ditched the joint in the ashtray, rose out of my chair and threw back a caustic remark as I left. 'Kind of? You either did or you didn't.' As I crossed the threshold of the balcony door I hissed 'Do what you want, we're both free agents.'

There I was again, denying how I really felt. Pushing it back down and pretending everything was okay, but it wasn't. My head was boiling I was so angry and devastated. I wanted to hit out, kick something. Not a good idea with flipflops on. I could feel it welling up in my chest, that urge to shout, really shout, call him all the names under the sun or to use his terminology. *Goddam mother fucker, no good sonofabitch,* so he didn't mistake how I felt. But it doesn't have the same effect when issued with an English accent, it just sounds like I'm at a function serving sandwiches with their crusts off. Anyway what was the point?

I wanted to push him away so he'd feel bad and grovel his way back. But what if that plan backfired? No, I wasn't going to give him that. Disdain was a subtler sword and a better way of showing my disappointment.

Bile gathered in the back of my throat. Why would he do that? I tortured myself with all the reasons why and kept coming back to what Willy had said 'he's a hunter and likes the hunt.' What was I to him then, roadkill? I wanted to curl up and cry until my body dried into a husk. Who was this other woman? What did she have that I didn't? How long had it been going on for? Was it something serious? Why hadn't I seen it? How could this bastard do this to me? Wanker!

Willy was right – he never did take me out, not properly out. I had a flurry of thoughts all coming at once. Any normal person would have told him to fuck off, but I still hesitated even in the midst of my anger. It was as though I was sitting there just waiting for more, pushing myself to the very edge of destruction. And then all the negative self-talk would follow. Why was I not good enough? Did I deserve this? Had I brought it upon myself?

I stayed away from the flat all day, and went to Goodie's. We picked up Angie and sped off to the marina to drink beer. Physically I was present but there was a huge disconnect. I'd retreated into my thoughts, my fingers played with the rim of the bottle as I drifted off, trying to wrestle some semblance of understanding, niggling at it from different angles.

'Why you not happy, tia?' Angie clicked her fingers. 'Hello in there.'

A flicker of a smile crossed my lips, but my quivering chin said otherwise. 'It's Gary,' I hung my head and sobbed, telling them what he'd done. Angie stood up, her chin set to feisty, 'I go on the base now and tell him what an asshole he is. That is so fucked up.'

'Forget him.' said Goodie resolutely, raising her hand to summon the waiter and order shots.

'How can I when I'm in love with him?' I wailed into Angie's shoulder as she hugged me.

Goodie wasn't taking any prisoners. 'You think you're in love with him? Do you really know what love is? You want a man to treat you like this? You let him get away with this and it will end up a whole lot worse. You have to love yourself first.'

'She right.' Angie downed a shot and encouraged me to do the same.

Goodie jerked hers back and slammed her empty glass on the table. 'Now girl you get a hold of yourself. He's not worth it. If he don't appreciate you for the beautiful mujere that you are then tell that hijo de puta to go. Dignity and pride. Viva las mujereres.' She stood up and threw another shot down the back of her throat and Angie and I followed.

Perhaps it was the drink, or maybe it was the company or even a mix of the two. Somehow the words that had always stopped short at the edge of my mouth found a way to break free. Words I found difficult to articulate let alone hear it said in my own voice. 'I make bad decisions when it comes to men.'

'Don't we all,' Goodie blew her cigarette smoke out of the side of her mouth with some force. 'I'll never really trust them completely after what I went through.' She signalled to the barman to bring three more beers and shots.

Angie and I turned to look at her. The expression on her face was dead pan, her eyelids heavy, as though weighed down by the thought of it. 'I was only seventeen when it happened. My first date. I was so excited and yet so naïve.'

Angie leaned in. 'Que pasaste tia?'

Goodie flashed, 'What do you think?'

The barman placed three shots on the table before us. Goodie lifted hers and threw it back, slamming her glass down when finished.

It took Angie a moment to process what Goodie was trying to convey.

'No! No me digas.' Angie's hand shot up to her mouth. I caught her horrified expression and looked from her to Goodie.

'What? I'm missing something here. What happened Goodie?'

She held my gaze, her eyes narrowed, steel cold. 'The arsehole raped me.'

I don't recall whether it was me or Angie that responded first. My mouth fell open. I remember wanting to give Goodie a hug but could tell she had more to say. It was in the way she sat forward, gripping the bottle like she was ready to pour more than just beer. So a hug wouldn't have been appropriate. Away off in the far corner of the bar the fruit machine was pumping out a jackpot to flashing lights and a patron jumping up and down excitedly. It was midst all of this commotion Goodie spoke, her voice barely audible above the din.

'I was a virgin too.'

'Por Dios, no.' Angie was out of her chair, her arm around Goodie's back

'He claimed that I was being seductive and that I provoked him. That I was asking for it. He was brutal with it too. I was covered in bruises.' Goodie's eyes were cold and clear, like she had distanced herself, putting the hurt to one side and the anger to the other, her words merely citing what had probably been said a thousand times.

'Are you telling me he got away with it?'

'More or less. He only got six months. It totally messed me up for a long time. Still does.'

'I'm so sorry,' Angie hugged Goodie close.

'Why do they always have to resort to violence? Why do they always get away with it?' I felt the anger welling up, my throat constricting, heat flushing into my face. Before I even realised tears were coursing down my face and then I began to sob, real shoulder shaking sobs.

Goodie hugged me. 'It's okay,' she soothed, 'I'm dealing with it.'

I shook my head, wiping my tears. 'It's just so unfair. Why?' I reached forward and took a long swig of my beer then lit another cigarette, fingers fumbling with the matches. 'Bastards – all of them.' Wiping my eyes, I drew myself up in my seat. 'I didn't tell you how I came to be here did I?'

'No,' said Angie. 'I thought you were just hitching with Tonk. Having some wild adventure.'

'I had to leave. I had to get away from the man I was living with. He was violent ... and it was getting worse. Tonk helped me, to keep me safe.'

'Yeah, come to think of it you never really talked about your previous boyfriend. Is that how you got that scar on your chin?'

Goodie reached out and traced a finger over the scar.

'Yes.' I nodded. 'His ring caught me side on and knocked me clean off my feet. All because I'd moved something of his and he couldn't be bothered to look for it. Bloody stupid really.'

'Did he do that to you a lot?'

'Not at first.' I dropped my head, it was a compulsive reaction, something I couldn't help, I was well versed at hiding my emotions. It's what kept me safe.

'Why didn't you tell anyone?'

I felt heat flush at the back of my neck and cheeks. I closed my eyes. 'It's difficult to explain. He'd make me feel like it was all my fault, like I had to apologise to him. Sounds bloody mad. And then I felt embarrassed, like I was making too much of a fuss. I'd try and convince myself I could handle it and I didn't want to involve other people.'

I sat for a moment, sifting through the many reasons why I didn't tell anyone and becoming fully aware of my own discomfort, the tension in my shoulders, my gritted teeth, the knot in my belly. Finally, I lifted my head and looked at them.

'I did tell people eventually,' my eyes searched Angie and Goodie's faces for a reaction. 'What stopped me was fear. I was too frightened. I'd got into a place where I didn't dare speak up. If he didn't have me, he would go for the people dearest to me. Friends tried to help but he threatened to smash their places up. He said he would beat them so their own mother's wouldn't recognise them - and I had no doubt he would have done so too.

My one saving grace was my friend Kirstie, she lives in Ireland now, just a little north of Dublin. I worked with her in a bar too.' The thought of her brought a small smile to my lips. What I would have given to have seen her cheerful face at that moment. An image flashed before me of her and Joe standing in the kitchen drunkenly singing Spancel Hill at the tops of their lungs.

'You remind me of her Goodie. She was strong and smart like you. I never actually told her what was happening at the time, but she later told me she suspected as much, said she'd seen someone close to her go through it so she knew the signs.

When she left for Ireland she gave me her new address and told me to keep it safe. I hid it from Blake so it was the one place I could go that he didn't know about.' The thought of being so bold made me chuckle. 'Weeb was and still is a very good friend. When I first ran away from Blake it was her that I ran to. And I knew that Blake wouldn't have any way of finding me there.'

'Does she know where you are now?'

'Yes, she should do. I wrote her a couple of weeks back,' A smile spread across my face, in my mind's eye I could hear her voice giving me a gentle slagging and laughing raucously. 'But she's terrible at writing back.'

Angie piped up, 'So why you leave Ireland if you happy there?'

'My Dad was dying. I needed to get home to see him.'

Her eyes widened 'He dead now?'

I puckered my lips in response.

Angie shook her head and muttered, 'That is fucked up.'

'I'm so sorry Frankie,' Goodie reached out and clasped my hand.

'Me too, he died just before I got back. Then, to make things worse, Blake got to hear about my return. He turned up where I was staying and caused a big fight. Tonk got hurt in the process. He got kicked just here.' I indicated the spot on my own body.

'That is too much, tia, too much.'

'I'm glad you made it here. At least you are safe.'

'Yes, I'm safe living with Gary and Willy. They'd make mince of him.'

'Mince?'

'Ground meat,' I explained. 'But I still get scared. I don't like being around drunk men. They're too unstable, unpredictable, especially the angry ones.'

'Aaah, so that's why you got all paranoid the other day in the bar.'

'Oh, yes, I remember now, the day when the fleet came in and those two guys started fighting?' Goodie said. 'I saw you didn't turn your back on them once. And when the fight started you grabbed a bottle didn't you.'

I shifted and looked down at my feet, ashamed. 'I was scared.'

'Tia, tell me, do you think you'll be in danger if you go back home?'

'I'm not sure. Last I heard Blake was in prison awaiting sentence. Someone got killed.'

'Killed? He sound nasty. I hope he go to prison, and they throw away the llaves. Vamos, let's drink to that.'

'llaves?'

'Keys,' said Goodie.

Chapter Fifteen

I crawled into the flat early that evening, navigating the stairs on my knees. I'd lost a shoe somewhere along the way and had managed to acquire a number of bruises up my leg. I spent the rest of the evening crying and clinging on to the toilet. Willy was on hand to help, fielding coffees, water and paracetamol, telling Antonio I was unwell and unfit to work, putting me to bed, making sure I lay on my side. Goodie called by the next morning and gave Willy a blow by blow account of my drunken activities while I slept.

I surfaced later that afternoon with a pounding headache. After my shower Willy called softly, 'Coffee's waiting for you here if you want it – and toast too.' I stepped onto the balcony still drying my hair, then wrapped it in the towel and slumped into a chair. Willy observed me with knowing eyes and a wry smirk.

'God, I feel rough.'

'Hate to say it but you look it too.'

'Couldn't help myself. I got a bit of bad news.'

'So it appears.'

'Willy,' I paused, struggling to find the right words, 'I'm so sorry for yesterday. I ... '

'Didn't I tell you? But you wouldn't listen, would you?'

Just hearing him say that stuck in my craw. It made me want to slap him for being right but it also made me want to slap myself too. I could feel his eyes on me. I bent forward like a hinge

'Yes, you were right, but can we not do this right now.' I put my head in my hands, pressing my temples.

'Okay,' he patted me gently on the back. 'I think you've been through the mill enough.'

I nodded in agreement, still facing the floor.

'I do have something I want you to tell me about at some point later though... this guy you were with, are you worried he might come looking for you here?'

'Willy, not now. Some other time okay.'

'You know I'd take you to the ball but I'm already taking someone.'

I shook my head, 'No. It's okay Willy. It's fine, don't worry about it. But thanks.' Normally I would have been excited for him. A date. Under any other circumstances I would have quizzed him about this mysterious woman, was she American or Spanish, were there romantic intentions? I was happy for him but was too wrapped up in myself. I didn't think I could handle seeing Gary with someone else, seeing him being all solicitous – having fun, out together in public with this woman lapping up all his attentions. The skinful of alcohol hadn't eradicated that thought. I was left feeling spiteful and jealous. Wishing all kinds of bad things on him and his ball-date. It was an emotion I'd never really experienced before, and its power threw me.

I wanted to do something drastic, something that would make Gary notice me, react, show me how he really felt. Or perhaps I just needed to see it for what it really was for myself, so I could stop hoping that the worm would turn and realise that there weren't always happy ever after endings.

I pursed my lips thinking, maybe it was time I went home.

At work that evening I could barely raise a smile. My chirpy chatter exchanged for grumpy one-word responses. Everything seemed sullied, as though the colour had been rinsed out of everything and my world had been turned into sepia.

Then Matt, one of the marines, the sweetest of guys, asked if anyone was taking me to the ball. He'd been something of a regular, popping in a couple of nights a week and spending time talking to me. He wasn't showy, didn't drink too much, didn't smoke either. A steady guy, unusual for a marine as most of the regular grunts were rather unpredictable, rowdy and not always the brightest cards in the deck – but my impressions were forged from the other side of a bar so really what did I know. When I said 'no' his face lit up as though he'd just found the winning lottery ticket.

Stealing himself, he gulped at his beer. 'Would you do me the honour of accompanying me?'

Put that way how could I refuse? I knew he had a crush on me and for that my heart went out to him; but was it kind or fair to accept? Seeing me waver he used his persuasive charm.

'It's the Marine Corps celebration of the year, you'll love it, and all the other guys will be as jealous as hell when they see me with you. The charm worked, boosting up my sagging self-esteem and so I said yes on the proviso that he understood that this was not going to lead to anything afterwards.

I had a week to find a suitable dress, I searched the local shops but there was nothing suitable within my price range. Rather than finding it fun it was beginning to become more of a burden. I wanted to look good, not just for Matt but for myself too. I wanted to look drop dead gorgeous, or enough for Gary to regret his decision. As the day drew nearer the urgency became more pressing. Goodie took pity on me and turned up at the flat the day before the ball. At the sound of the buzzer I leaned my head over the balcony to see her standing there, hands on hips, looking up.

'Come on, get dressed. We're going shopping. Anda tia. I'll wait for you here.'

I dragged a comb through my hair, washed my face, threw on some clothes and ran down the stairs. We took the bus to Cadiz and scoured the dress shops, Goodie encouraging me to try on outrageous items and joining in too. We filled the changing rooms with dress after dress, prancing about the shop floor, posing before staff and customers. We put on quite a show. Acting like money was no object. We decided on a purple dress, one that was modest, no plunging neckline, but hugged my figure and shimmered in the light. Goodie scraped my hair from the side of my face and held it up.

'It looks better like that, sophisticated. He's going to feel sick when he sees you on the arm of another guy, what was his name?'

'Matt.'

'I know the guy. You'll be safe with him. Just make sure you have fun.'

Mention of the Ball was like a no-go zone, we each skirted around it like it was a huge crap in the middle of the room and any talk of it meant they'd be duty bound to clear the crap up. It was awkward, I was dying to quiz Willy about what he knew about Gary's date but I knew he was enjoying watching Gary squirm and was probably hoping that it spelled the end for us. I still didn't have a clear idea of what the Ball was all about or what to expect. A glitter ball in the middle of the room? Live band? Neither Goodie or Angie had ever been to one so they couldn't enlighten me. Matt just said, 'You'll love it,' which left me none the wiser.

This mystery woman of Gary's burned me, like a hot coal melting its way through my skin. I tortured myself wondering what she looked like, what she had that I didn't. I was half hoping that she was fat and frumpy with a spotty face and uneven teeth but knew that Gary wouldn't date someone like that. Willy did a great job of mentioning I was going to the Ball with Matt within Gary's earshot. If he was put out about it he certainly didn't show it, just lifted his head from the book he was reading and said 'He's a good guy and will take good care of you.' I wanted to scream from the top of my lungs 'I don't want him to take care of me. I want you! I want you to take me, make a fuss of me, make me feel special,' but instead I retreated to the kitchen and cried into the sink as I banged some pots about.

On the evening of the ball Matt arrived early to pick me up looking sharp in his dress blues. Gary was still around the flat when he arrived. They made polite conversation on the balcony as Matt waited for me to put the finishing touches on my makeup. It felt uncomfortable seeing Gary all smartened up in his dress blues, he looked so handsome. It was even stranger knowing that he'd spent the previous night in my bed, arms entwined around me. I couldn't help but wonder what the hell I was getting into.

Matt was so attentive and kind, lighting my cigarette, helping to fix the corsage he'd brought me, complimenting me on my hair, my dress, keeping the conversation light. And all the while Gary sat there, watching me, agreeing. I couldn't look him in the eye. It hurt too much. My heart pounded so loud I could hear it in my ears and yet there I was doing the typical British thing, stiff upper lip, holding my feelings in check, making polite conversation with Matt until he looked at his watch and announced it was time to leave.

As we left, I heard Gary call after us, 'Have a good time you hear.' I paused in the doorway and looked back, our eyes met, and I'd swear I saw his soften. There was a hint of his shoulders sloping and his face turned down making his brown eyes seem wider.

Was that a moment there where things could have been salvaged or was it a look of pure regret?

'You too.'

I lingered for a moment then turned and swept down the stairs after Matt and away in the taxi.

I'd never been on a military base before. Being a third national I was told it wasn't usually allowed. When we stopped at the gate the guards peeked in the cab window, nodded to Matt and waved us through. He was all smiles, cracking with the guards through the window like the cat that had got the cream.

When the cab stopped, we stepped out onto a red carpet and walked up to the entrance where two guards stood as sentinels at the door. Above it, the American and Marine Corps flags flew which gave a regal aire to the occasion.

Inside, photographers' bulbs flashed, lights of all hues lit up the room and ladies wearing long dresses and posh hairdos escorted by Marines milled about. There were a lot of people. I didn't realise there were so many Marines on the base and felt a little overwhelmed. Matt was greeted by a couple of his colleagues and took the time to introduce me to them and their partners. Naturally the event had been timed with military precision. A call went out for us to take our seats. We sat at a long, white table. It was tastefully decorated with flowers and miniature American and Marine flags. More announcements followed, including a message from someone important stating it the Marine Corps birthday, I was rather confused. I thought we were at a ball? Matt put me straight telling me the two were one and the same. After prayers the band played, heralding the arrival of numerous personnel accompanied by lots of quick marching and finally a huge cake appeared and ceremoniously cut with a sword and handed out. After the Marine Corps birthday ceremony was over, the ball began with a bang.

Despite looking, I didn't get to see either Willy or Gary. In a sense I was glad, although curious, I didn't want to torture myself by seeing another woman on Gary's arm. At one point I went to the ladies and while sitting on the loo I picked out Gary's voice in the room next door. He sounded quite animated, I both loved him and hated him in equal measure at that moment. How could he have done this to me?

None of us at the flat mentioned the Marine Corps Ball after the event, it was as if the very mention of it might set something off and we'd fall through the cracks.

After a couple of days Gary and I reverted to where we were – he'd come to my bed at night. Perhaps I was a fool to allow it, but it was what I wanted. I couldn't help myself. This time he was more solicitous, opening up, telling me things about himself, trading intimacies. He told me about his family, how his dad had once travelled as a hobo riding the trains across America, that his mother was native American from the northeast coast and still spoke the language; that his little sister was wild and he was forever having to haul her ass out of trouble.

I glossed over my family. It seemed too much to tell him all my past, especially my mother's health. I often worried it might be something that was passed on. Although I did tell him about the family dog, Bonzo and how he had a whitened muzzle and would close doors if you asked him.

Gary even left some of his things in my room, a t-shirt, a pair of shorts, the book he was reading. Then his alarm clock appeared. It felt like a permanent fixture, like the kisses I received when he came back after a shift.

One evening he came in to see me at work, stayed all night at the bar, watching me. When we got home, he sat me down and took my hands in his.

'Frankie, I can see you hate the bar work. You don't belong here, you know that. If you need money to get you back home, I'd be happy to help you, I have some savings. All you have to do is ask.'

I was stunned. No, no, no. This is not what I want. I shook my head, unable to speak. It was almost too much. We were doing so well. My eyes focused on the jar I had stuffed with jasmine earlier in the week. All that remained were dying petals now scattered on the surface of the sideboard. The last thing I wanted to do was leave. It was him I was staying for and here he was giving me the opportunity to go home. I wasn't sure what to make of it. Was this because he wanted rid of me or was it an act of altruism? I was on the verge of telling him that I couldn't leave because I was in love with him when someone began shouting his name from beneath the balcony. He was needed back on base and our conversation was cut short.

Pushing a stray lock aside from my eyes he kissed me tenderly before leaving. 'Just think about it, okay?'

He didn't come back that night. I woke to a grey day, jasmine petals drifting into the room as I opened the shutters. Angie appeared later that morning, her black hair shining like a raven's wing as she looked up at me peering at her over the balcony. I buzzed her in and went to the kitchen to make coffee. Her heels clicked across the floor towards me then she greeted me with a kiss to each cheek.

'Que passa, tia?' she lifted her chin and pressed her lips together into a downturned smile. 'Frankie, you know I love you as a friend, si?'

'Of course, Angie.' I handed her a cup of coffee.

'Can we sit down? I have something to tell you.'

Now I was the one frowning. We sat on the sofa, and she handed me a cigarette, flicking on her lighter as soon as I put it to my mouth. As I inhaled, fingers fidgeting with the rim of the cup, brushing away non-existent ash. Angie cleared her throat and pulled on her cigarette.

'I was on the base today and I heard something you need to know,' she tossed her hair aside and took another sip of her coffee. 'It's about Gary.' She crossed her legs. 'They say he got a woman on the base pregnant.'

I dropped my cup, watched the pieces scatter as if in slow motion, coffee pooling in the middle of the floor. Instinctively I wrapped my hands around my head. 'No, Angie. No.'

I knew it to be feasible, possibly true, but I didn't want to believe it. It would sit right between us like rancid meat in a triple decker sandwich. 'Does he know?' My mind raced, picking up the pieces of our conversation earlier, him offering to pay for me to go home. *You don't belong here... Think about it!* Was this why he'd brought it up. Did he want me out of the picture, was that it?

Angie shrugged. 'If he didn't, he probably does now. Everyone on base knows.'

I was digging in sinking sand, asking question after question, making things worse by assuming the answers. 'Do you know if she's going to keep it?' I wanted to hear the word *no* and hated myself for it. This was a life we were talking about, a life that Gary had created with another woman. I looked up at Angie.

Her mouth turned down at the corners, she lifted her hands, palms up. 'I don't know. Lo siento, tia.'

I doubted it was planned. Life is complicated, like the weave of a cloth under fine white thread, stitch by stitch we tell our stories. And this is some story. How could I wish the life of that little baby away – my own had started the same way.

Angie left shortly after leaving me the rest of the morning to brood over the news and wait for Gary to come back.

At three o'clock I heard his footsteps coming up the stairs I slammed the balcony door shut then sat with my back to the door pretending to read. I must have read the same paragraph twenty times, but nothing went in. Eventually he slid the door across, leaning out through the frame.

'You alright?'

I kept my head down as if engrossed in the book responding stiffly. 'No, not really.'

'What's up?'

'You tell me.' I flashed him a look clocking his sharp intake of breath.

'Were you going to tell me? And don't try to pretend you don't know what I'm talking about because you damned well do.'

'Frankie, calm down. Let's talk about this. I was going to tell you, but I only just found out. I needed some time to get my head around it.'

'Calm down?' I threw the book down and sprang up out of my chair to face him. 'I'll calm down when I'm good and ready, and not when it suits you.'

He lowered his eyes.

'So where does that put us? Is there an us? Or was I just a convenient fuck?'

His head reared backwards; he wasn't ready for this response. My being so blunt hit a nerve. He'd never really seen me angry before, not properly angry. I think it unnerved him

'Obviously, you were fucking both of us at the same time.' Hearing the words out loud hit me like a swift punch to the gut. Betrayal. Such an ugly word. It snagged my lungs and caught my breath so it came out thready. My throat felt swollen and barbed, I knew I was going to cry, could feel the tears threatening behind my eyes. I pushed past him and locked myself in the bathroom. He followed me tapping on the door saying my name softly.

'Come on Frankie, open up. Let's talk about this. Please?'

I sat on the toilet snivelling and blotting my face with a tissue. I didn't want to be smooth talked, oiled with more lies and deceit. I just wanted to retreat and lick my wounds, with half a mind to hurt him back.

I watched his shadow hovering from the crack beneath the door. After a while he went away. This made me feel even madder and I started to cry again. He could have at least tried a little harder. I hadn't been that awful to him, had I? Even though I had told him to go away it was the last thing I wanted him to do. But the tears turned to laughter when he returned a couple of minutes later and started blowing smoke from the joint he'd quickly rolled underneath the door.

'If you don't come out, I'll smoke you out,' he said, mischief in his voice. More smoke appeared. 'Oh Frankie,' he half sang my name, blowing yet more under the door.

'Wanker,' I opened the door a crack and looked down to find him on his knees.

'It's a peace offering. Chief Gary make big pow-wow with HRH Frankie.' He held the joint out to me and made his bottom lip tremble.

As I took the joint from him, he stood up and drew me into his arms. 'I'm so sorry Frankie, really I am.'

We stood for a while as I leaked silent tears onto his t-shirt. He held me close, stroking my hair and kissing my forehead. I stood there listening to the steady beat of his heart wishing I could stay there forever.

He led me to the sofa and we sat side by side. 'I know I really fucked up. This was never meant to happen. I dated her a couple of times before you showed up. Then she went home on leave for a month. It was never anything serious, just …'

'A casual fuck.'

He grimaced, I could tell by the look on his face he found the remark tasteless like he didn't want the truth to be dressed up so starkly. Or didn't like that I was seeing and saying things exactly as they were.

To me it underlined the fact that he'd misjudged me. Perhaps it would have been more palatable if had been delivered by one of his machismo marine brothers.

'Come on Frankie, you gotta know it was an accident. I'm just twenty-one, for fuck's sake. I'm a young guy with needs,' he looked at me now as if it had been obvious all along.

I shrugged, and took a long pull on the joint, now it was me not wanting to hear the truth.

'I'm not planning to settle down now, not at this stage. Not in the military.' I sighed and looked away. That last statement stung, a recoil sting, like burning your tongue on a hot drink. It made perfect sense, but all the same I didn't like it and Gary sensed it.

'If it were you, it would be different.'

'How? You just said yourself, you're too young to be settling down.'

'I know but …'

'So what are you saying?'

'I'm not in love with her.'

I looked at him and started to cry again.

Downstairs the front door slammed, and Willy's feet were heard charging up the stairs. He came into the front room bringing with him a waft of warm air.

'Que passa?' he stood, his eyes taking in my red tear-stained face and Gary, all tensed up like wire pulled to snapping point. He had that look on his face that said it all, at last the truth's out.

'Ahh a joint, just what I needed.' He crossed the room, relieved Gary of the joint and taking a big toke said. 'You'll never believe the shit that's going down on the base …' as he disappeared into the kitchen and I heard him heft the fridge door open, 'Anyone want a coke or a beer?'

'Yeah, I'll take a beer.'

'Frankie, you want one?'

'No thanks.' My voice was flat, all the emotion stuck at the back of my throat.

Gary squeezed my knee and whispered, 'We'll pick this up later, okay?' Reluctantly I nodded. I listened to Willy rummaging around in the fridge, the hiss of his beer can as he opened it. He appeared momentarily round the kitchen door frame; a beer can arced in the air and was caught neatly by Gary. Then the doorbell went. A frantic sort of buzzing. Gary got up, his movement slow and deliberate as he went to look over the balcony. I heard a male voice and Gary answering back. He came back into the front room looking flustered.

'I'm needed on base.' He disappeared into his room briefly, grabbed some kit and stopped to kiss me on the forehead before heading out. I heard the door slam and the tyres of the taxi squeal as it took off in the base's direction.

Willy sat in the chair opposite to me and took a long slug of his beer. 'So, you know then?'

I nodded, 'Yeah, unfortunately.'

'Too bad,' he took another long slug. He looked up and opened his mouth as if to say something, but I held up my hand.

'I don't want to discuss it right now, okay.'

'Sure, if that's what you want.' He shifted in his chair, 'Hey, did I tell you that the phone box behind the Blue Star is dishing out free calls, so if you want to call home, now's your chance.'

I checked the time on my watch. If I hurried there was still time to catch Barb, we were an hour ahead and if I was lucky, she would be at work. Suddenly I had to hear her voice, tell her what was going on, get her advice. I needed to speak to someone that really knew me, that understood without me feeling like I had to save face, be something I wasn't. I needed to be reminded of who I was through our many shared experiences and who would talk to me straight. I needed to hear from and about home. Something to anchor me because at that moment in time I felt like a boat without a sail. I needed something solid away from the madness here.

I ran down the stairs to the phone box. Someone was just finishing a call, an American emerged with a big smile on his face as he held the door open for me.

'Was it a freebie?'

'Yeah, sure was. You just need to insert one coin and the rest is free for as long as you want.' He must have seen my face fall because I didn't have a coin on me. He reached into his pocket and flipped me a twenty-five-peseta coin.

'Thank you so much,' I smiled.

'Think nothing of it.'

I dialled the number and within two rings Barb picked up. There was much excited chatter to start with. It was so good to hear her, like the first cup of tea in the morning or the glorious sound of the jackpot paying out on the pay machines. But after the initial buzz the conversation's tone changed. Barb's voice lowered, taking on her serious tone, like the one she used when setting out the flat ground rules.

'Frankie, I need you to listen. What I'm about to tell you is going to be hard. It's Tonk. He's really bad and he's been asking for you.'

'Oh shit. No. How bad?'

'It's cancer.'

'Cancer?'

There was a beat while I tried to take it in.

'But he'll be okay won't he? I mean, he's too young ...'

'I don't think he's sure yet, they're still doing tests. But if you want me to be really honest I think you should get back home quick.'

Holding on at the other end of the phone I struggled to speak.

'Frankie, you still there?'

'Yes,' I said weakly.

'I can cover your fare, you can put it on my card. Have you got a pen and paper?' She read out the details and I took them down, writing on a cigarette packet with a shaky hand.

'Just get yourself back here on the next flight, if possible, okay?'

I stumbled weakly out of the phone box and made my way to the travel agents. A flight home was leaving the next morning at 10am from Malaga. I asked them to hold a seat for me while I went to get my passport details. The rest of the evening was spent frantically packing and hoping that Gary would be back in time for me to explain.

He got home at 3am, shattered from a long shift and crept into bed. Within minutes he was out cold, I tried rousing him, but he was lost in a deep sleep. His body heavy, deeply relaxed. I let him sleep, he obviously needed it. I lay there in his arms wishing for the night to last forever, savouring every moment, and dreading the first light of dawn.

I woke at 6am, could hear the birds and life stirring outside beyond the bedroom shutters.

'Gary,' I whispered. 'Gary, wake up. Please wake up.' He roused briefly. He looked so peaceful lying there, a half-smile on his face, I felt guilty knowing I was about to shatter that peace. A car stopped outside, engine still running, without needing to check knew it was my taxi. I shook him awake. '

The taxi beeped its horn. I ran to the balcony and signalled I'd be down in a minute. Kneeling on the bed I shook Gary again, he opened his sleepy eyes and propped himself up on his elbow.

'I have to go,' I whispered, my voice caught on a sob. 'I love you Gary, I really love you, but I'm needed back home. I'll write you, I promise. I've left my address ...'

He sat up straight and rubbed his face in his hands. 'Babe, what's happening?'

'I'm so sorry, I couldn't get hold of you yesterday. I need to get home. I'll be back, I promise.'

The taxi beeped its horn again.

We embraced, both kneeling up on the bed. I trembled as he squeezed me tight 'You're something special, you know that?' Leaning back, I studied his face, he was choked I could tell, particularly when he swallowed hard, suddenly looking every bit the vulnerable boy. He rubbed his eyes with his thumb and forefinger and put on an unconvincing smile. 'You'd better go, your taxi's waiting.'

As I left the warmth of his embrace, I knew this was something I'd probably regret for the rest of my days.

Willy was already up and helped me downstairs with my rucksack. He hugged me just before I got into the taxi, tears in his eyes. 'Take care Frankie and keep in touch.'

I looked up just before I got into the taxi to see Gary standing on the balcony, holding up the flat of his hand, a silent wave goodbye. I watched him from the back of the taxi until finally, he disappeared from my sight.

Chapter Sixteen

End of November 1980

The journey back was fraught. Long lines of tired passengers, screaming children, noisy tannoys and having to shuffle from one place to another. The flight didn't serve tea and I was parched from crying. All I could think about was Gary and what I had left behind. It felt as though my heart had been prized from my chest leaving a gaping wound that physically and emotionally hurt.

I composed a letter to Gary en route back home. Finding myself with time on my hands at the boarding gate, and, later on, on the train back to Cheltenham. It took numerous attempts to write. I experienced a whole gamut of emotions as I watched the familiar landscape flash past the train window. Distant hills I'd once ranged, out early with the dog, the song of the skylark rising against the dewy whispering grasses and murmuring breeze. Things I loved, that grounded me and yet they fell away to nothing given the heaviness in my heart. Getting heavier as the miles between Gary and I grew, and the miles between facing the reality of Tonk's situation shrank. But Tonk was too painful to even think about.

I had regrets, things I wished I'd said and done. Would the last outpouring before I left Gary do the trick? Would he understand, really understand? I could still see his face, the cut of his jaw, the softness in his eyes, the flex of his biceps as he held me close before I closed the door on us, shutting out the light pouring in from the shutters. All I wanted was to hold is face in my hands, feel his breath on my neck, his hands caressing me.

And yet here I was trying to write but words failed to hit their mark. It was so messed up. I realised he was trying to apologise before he went on base that day, that in his own clunky way he was trying to tell me that he loved me, or at least I think he was. And I'd gone and left with no time for us to say what we should have said and probably messed it up more. I cried continuously as I wrote, the ink disbursing on the page. I sent the letter that day, dropping it off at the post box in Cheltenham train station. I'd put more than the required stamp on the envelope to ensure that it didn't get held up.

Dear Gary,

Sorry, more than anything, I'm sorry. It was never my intention to hurt you - far from it, you're the last person I'd ever want to hurt. If truth be told I hurt myself more - that's what comes from keeping things buttoned up and not saying what you really feel isn't it?

I really meant it when I said I love you and I'll admit my timing left a lot to be desired. I should have told you how I felt long before, not waiting 'til the taxi was parked outside.

Leaving was the hardest thing I've ever done but was a necessity I couldn't avoid at the time. It had nothing to do with you or us. God know's I wanted to stay, hold on to what we were building but it just wasn't possible at the time. I hope you'll come to understand that. I do want to be with you, It's the most certain thing I've ever felt in my life and I will, I promise, be coming back if you'll have me?

For now, I'm just asking you to trust me. Tonk is very ill and I needed to go home. We are, I assure you, just good buddies and nothing more. I know that is a hard thing for you Americans to understand being of lesser evolved intelligence, but I promise you it's true. He's always been like a brother to me.

I miss you Captain Gringo. I miss you so much it hurts. I miss your terrible backgammon (you still need more of my tutoring!), I miss you trying to wind me up but most of all, I miss your arms around me at night.

Never forget, I love you. There, I've said it again – I'll say it a thousand times if it helps.

Love, love, love,
Frankie aka HRH Frankie xx
ps: Tell Willy I said hi.

My train had got in late and I went straight to the hospital from the station. Tired from the travel, all the delays, the curled British rail sandwiches and chalky tasteless tea. I was already emotional from events earlier that morning and close to tipping point.

At the hospital information desk, I was given a lecture about turning up outside of visiting hours. The officious cow on the other side of the desk turned me away telling me to come back at six. I staggered away unsure of what to do before sliding down a wall and weeping in the corridor. A porter found me and took pity - he took me to the appropriate ward.

I'd expected to see Tonk sitting up in bed looking his cheery self. I made ready with the bag of grapes I'd bought for him. When I'd bought them I had it all figured out, he would use them to fire at the other patients that kept him awake. The thought of it had made me giggle, I knew he'd appreciate the gesture. Particularly as he'd told me in great detail, of the time when he'd had his wisdom teeth out, all the snoring had driven him to the edge of reason. His eyes had taken on a wild look as he retold the incident, like he was possessed. It was deliberate exaggeration for my entertainment. I thought the grapes would make him laugh.

To my surprise he was in a ward all by himself.

When I got there the doctor was just leaving. He hurried past, eyes downcast. I sensed something was wrong before I got to Tonk but kept my smile firmly fixed. This wasn't just a nasty infection or the removal of a small offending body part, this appeared to be more sinister than that. Barb's letter said he was ill, to come home, but I never ...

Light was streaming in from the tall windows, dwarfing him in his hospital bed, giving a childlike impression. He was half sitting up, still wearing his hospital gown, propped against his pillows, barely recognizable with his hair flattened down on his scalp, no eyeliner, no hint of Johnny Rotten. That would have pissed him off no end, he always managed to keep up appearances no matter what he was up to.

His pale face made his blue eyes stand out, red rimmed against his sweeping blond eyelashes. He wiped his eyes hurriedly when he saw me.

'You alright?' I said as I reached out to grip his hand.

'Frankie?' His face seemed caught between being happy to see me and dealing with something awkward.

'Frankie, he just told me ...' His hand, clammy in mine, clutched me like a frightened child. It unsettled me.

'Told you what?' I said dumping the grapes on his side table.

His voice broke as tears welled in his eyes. He was searching for the right words, fighting to keep his breath even.

Now I was concerned, he never, ever cried, not unless it was a Bambi film. This wasn't like the Tonk I knew. The one I'd hitched with across Europe. The one I'd danced, or in his case, pogoed, in the middle of the street during a lashing thunderstorm or made wishes to shooting stars at the southern edge of Spain with. The one who threw bricks through old landlord's windows.

Watching him gasp, hearing the rasp in the back of his throat and feeling his nails dig into my hand as he squeezed ever tighter both shocked and frightened me.

'Told you what? Slow down, take your time.' I was swallowing hard, trying to match my breathing with his, inwardly praying that the words he was about to speak were not what I feared. He gathered himself and started again.

'The Doctor just told me I have three months.'

I gasped. 'Three months! No, that can't be.'

'It's terminal Frankie. I'm going to die.' He dropped his head, gulping in air.

Now both of my hands were folded round his.

'No. Tonk. It can't be true. They must be able to do something.' Inwardly I was screaming *but you're not even 24 yet.*

We're going to see The Ramones on tour. Hitch to Greece and hang out in olive groves ... Go to Delphi and consult the Oracle. He was going to be my chief bridesmade if I ever ... and the one to organize the divorce party, which he said was a given.

He looked at me slowly, searching my face for a nugget of hope, shaking his head still trying to come to terms with the news himself. I made a clumsy attempt at hugging him, which was hard to do without dislodging all the attached tubes and wires. My arms like a flailing octopus trying to find a place to hold.

'Did they say what it is?'

'It's cancer. Bowel cancer.'

'Oh, Tonk, I'm so sorry.' Words failed me, my head spinning as I told myself not to lose it, not to fall apart in front of him. I snuggled into his shoulder. It felt all frail, light and angular like my grandma felt when I hugged her goodbye. We stayed like that for a while, my tears splashing onto his pillow until his breath steadied and he pushed me away. I knew he was going to need someone strong around him. I needed to be his shoulder, like he had been mine, my rock.

'Frankie, can I ask a favour?'

'Anything, ask whatever you want.'

'Will you stay with me 'til the end? I know it's a lot to ask, but we've been through so much together.'

I squeezed his hand. 'Of course. Whatever you need. Cruicial.' I gave him a weak high five.

'Cruicial.'

He smiled weakly.

'Frankie, if you don't mind, I need to rest now. Will you come and see me tomorrow?'

'Sure. I'll see you tomorrow. Just get some rest.' I leaned over and kissed him tenderly on the forehead. 'Love you buddy,'

'You too,' he whispered and closed his eyes.

Chapter Seventeen

January 1981

Night times were the hardest. We were now two months since the terminal diagnosis. I'd lie awake going over the events of the day; wondering if there was anything I could do differently that would help? Was there anything Tonk could try that would change things? I was camped down at our old flat on the other side of town. He was staying with his Mum, which was both easy and hard for him. It brought other demands; he kept those cards close to his chest. I'd worry about him, the time he had left, what he was still physically capable of doing.

The first thing I noticed was that the distances he could walk; gradually got shorter and shorter. Then the weakness in his limbs. The day he couldn't make the stairs, as he clutched at the rail, gasping for breath. I tried to pretend I'd not seen his embarrassment.

'Remember the time Barb and I hauled you, blind drunk, up the stairs to the flat after you'd managed to projectile vomit through the letter box of that girl who'd just dumped you? Was it Louise? The one Barb and I had named Headache, for obvious reasons.'

He had dined out on the letterbox incident for weeks. It even went into local legend coming back to him one day in a highly embellished form like a scene from The Exorcist. He loved the notoriety, said it was his claim to fame.

Now his sickness came from less exalted impulses.

'It's the drugs! They numb the pain ... they numb everything,'

I could see him giving up. Letting go of little things – he stopped wearing black eyeliner, his safety-pin came out and then he just stuck to wearing his pyjamas.

'What's the point of changing? It's not like I'm going anywhere, is it?'

Our conversations revolved around the inevitable, planning his send off. In a strange way he relished it, considered it with panache. It was just bravado, him trying to make light of it to make it easier for me. Sometimes I found that lack of honesty hollow, there was so much to say and so little time. His lack of energy was hard to comprehend, he had been so full of life and energy and still should have been, at only 24. It was like he'd turned into an old man overnight. I could hardly meet his eye.

'What?' he snapped; his mouth curled into a snarl.

'Nothing.' I shrugged acting nonchalant. We both knew it was a turning point but neither of us were ready to deal with it. I disappeared into the small kitchen, thinking as I put the teabags into the pot, this is the moment where I can really see him slipping into the abyss; those small pieces of him going, day by day. My concentration lapsed and I poured hot water over my hand.

I yelped, quickly shoving it under the cold-water tap. The distraction, although sore, provided the jump-start I needed. As I stood at the tap, I realised something else was churning within me. We were angry, like elastic bands stretched to snapping point. I remembered reading something about it in the leaflet the Macmillan nurse had left.

He was too young. We were too young. It just wasn't fucking fair. Why him? I felt my chest constricting as though a scream was forming and ready to take flight.

'I gotta go.' I left suddenly, closing the door on Tonk's protestations before crashing down the first flight of stairs. On the landing I kicked and punched the wall until my boot split and my knuckles hurt. My face was wet with tears and snot. We shouldn't have been spending our waking hours thinking about death. About how it would be at the end. Or whether there was anything on the other side? It was all moving so fast. In my head echoes of my conversation with him earlier in the week bounced off my anger:

'So, do you recon they'll let me in through the pearly gates?'

'What? I thought you told me you're an atheist, Tonk!'

'Yeah, when it suits. Sometimes I catch myself, wondering, you know, like the Buddhists.'

'Eh?'

'Well, they believe in life after death.' His nosed twitched, a tic that appeared when he was nervous. 'I might come back again as an ant. Or I might just hang about and watch the side show of you lot scurrying about down here.'

'Are you getting all religious on me?'

'No. I don't know. I was just thinking about those spiritualists who contact folk on the other side ...'

'It's all a scam.'

'Is it? Maybe we should have a code, just in case. So, if I do get to communicate. I could give you the football results for the Pools.'

'I think that would freak me out. I'd worry you'd be hanging about watching.'

'Yep, I'd catch you dropping big farts on the bog!

'Stop!'

'Seriously though if we had a code word what would it be?'

'Do you need to ask?'

'Crucial?'

'Yeah, crucial.'

He wanted The Sex Pistols to play him out, just for effect. Holidays in the Sun or God Save the Queen? He oscillated between the two. Making an impression right to the end. He relished the idea of his Auntie Rita, a royalist, being highly offended with the latter. How he laughed, the full head back, face creasing. A laugh that showed off his fillings until the tears of mirth fell.

'Rita'll be so rankled, just watch her face. She'll suck in her cheeks and poke her fat face forward like a turkey, double chin wobbling in disgust. Bloody snob with her Jubilee mugs, and Tory leanings.'

In the stair landing I tried breathing deep, letting my shoulders fall, letting the anger wash over me.

Then I thought of Gary – what he was doing? I wondered whether he thought of me or had he forgotten and moved on? Two months had passed and still no word. How could I get through to him? Would he still be there if I went back? There was no telling when that would be and I didn't want to wish my time with Tonk away.

Gary was always there, occupying the in-between moments that weren't taken up with the stuff of life, inhabiting the back of my mind. Shadowing what I did in the day. Every day. I'd catch myself thinking *Gary would like this*. Or *this would make him laugh*. I'd recall our conversations; I'd even imagine new ones. The things I'd tell him about my day. Silly things like the woman down the street that walked her ferret on a lead, or the huge spider in the bathroom that I was convinced was stalking me. Or, how I was struggling with loosing Tonk. How Tonk's mother thought I could be the one to turn things around and magically make him better; that she saw more into us than we were, and I didn't know how to respond. That I'd wanted to protest 'You've got it all wrong. I'm not his girlfriend.' That it would feel like snogging my brother! That she'd pat my hand and with dewy eyes tell me they were all counting on me, oblivious to what I was trying to say. I wasn't a miracle worker. I was following through a promise – like I know Tonk would have done if our situations were reversed. It was that pleading look in her eyes: *Heal my son. Please, heal my son,* that overwhelmed me.

Tilting the landing window open I lit a cigarette and watched the afternoon traffic pass on the main road beyond. Blowing the smoke out of the window felt like a soft release until I heard a voice shout.

'Oi, you're not allowed to smoke on the landing, stupid. Come back and have a real one and make me that cuppa you promised.'

Smiling, I stuck two fingers out the window and shouted, 'I'll be up in a minute.' I still needed a bit of breathing space, a bit more time to think. My mind switched gear again and Tonk's grumpy confession popped into my head. He told me he felt burdened by friends and family coming round, wringing their hands, weeping beside him – as if the tears were meant to convey how they really felt.

'It's like they want me to absolve them, tell them it's alright, like I'm some priest or something. I hate it,' he spat. 'All I want is for everyone to treat me as normal – treat me like they used to. I'm not fucking dead yet.' He gripped the arms of the chair, holding onto his pain, holding on to his anger.

'How can anyone treat you as normal when you're wearing that ghastly smoking jacket?'

Humor, it was always my way of changing the subject. Taking the piss, deflecting by giving him the digs about that old silk house coat his mum had given him to wear.

It was another thing for me to take on board, treat him just like you always have. Never let on what's going on inside. I was breaking, not wanting to let go. Tonk, the one who'd wave his bare arse from the back window of the 29 bus during rush hour 'because he could'. He even kept a tally of the number of irate elderly ladies who had hand-bagged him. Was it twelve or thirteen?

Tonk, who claimed he was a punk because he had a safety-pin in one ear and the same hairstyle as Johnny Rotten but who hated spitting! Who was confrontational, sometimes obnoxious just for effect, but was a sweet mild-mannered wuss at heart. We all saw it when Barb's granny visited the flat, he ran down the shop to get her Battenburg Cake and even walked her to the taxi rank. She hung on to his arm even though she didn't need to, giving him her coquettish dentured smile.

Tonk, who cried in the cinema dark at Bambi and swore it was just a sniffle.

After I'd gone back up and made the tea Tonk became reflective. 'Frankie, remind me again of how we first met. Just humor me, will you?'

'Course, I'm happy to remind you how you got me into drugs and rock and roll and had me consorting with mad bikers.'

He chuckled and lay back on the sofa bed cushions, eyes closed, blanket pulled up to his chin. His freshly laundered pyjamas with the white hankie tucked into his top pocket made him look like a dandy, even more so with his spiked hair

His Mum popped her head round the door.

'That's me away now love. I've left your food on a plate in the fridge. I'll be back at six. Now remember, Pete'll be round early this afternoon. Play nice! Bye Frankie.' She nodded and disappeared. Her face looked pinched, all the worry etched into each crease and line.

I heard the front door click and the clipped sound of her heels descending the communal stairs. It was a prim and proper buttoned up kind of sound, the antithesis of Tonk who clumped and rolled as he walked, a swinging sort of swagger that looked more elegant than it sounded.

'Pete?'

'I know! They got back together just after I told Mum I was sick.'

'But he's an arse.'

'Don't remind me. He's the whole reason I left home. Only now I don't have to put up with his bullshit, and he knows it.'

'I thought you left home when you met Marlon?'

Tonk opened one eye. 'That! That wasn't of my choosing.'

'How do you mean?'

He closed his eye again and settled his head into the pillow. 'When Dad left, he'd shacked up with some woman in Gotherington. Posh house, looked like one of those chocolate box pictures with thatched roof. He went off and lived the life of riley and left us with nothing. Mum, she did her best but wasn't managing. Got caught shop-lifting and did six months. It was enough to completely fuck both of us. Now do you understand?' He turned his head to check my reaction.

I didn't flinch, just steadily held his gaze. 'Yeah, it all makes sense now.' And it did, Tonk was built on brittle foundations. I understood that, but he was loyal and deep down had a big heart.

'I never bothered to mention it because it's in the past and besides Mum's still mortified by it. Hates people knowing,' he propped himself up on his elbow. 'So I'm trusting you to keep it to yourself.' He tapped his nose with his forefinger and raised an eyebrow looking pointedly at me. I nodded in agreement. He lay back down, pulled the covers up and closed his eyes. 'So, go on then ... '

'Go on then what?' I teased.

'You know what I mean, stop being a wind-up.'

'Where do you want me to start?'

'The first day you turned up at the flat... You know we all knew you were homeless, don't you? Meagher was quite a softie for a landlord. He told us you were kipping on the sofa in one of his flats, terrified of one of the tenants boa constrictor getting loose.'

'What, so you put me through a fake interview ... '

'Something like that. He had a good heart for a capitalist landlord did Meagher. But what I want to know is how come you left home so young?'

'There's not much to tell really. I didn't really understand it then. Still don't now. My mum's not like yours.'

'So, tell me. What happened?'

I settled myself on the sofa and began rolling a spliff. 'It was all bloody bollocks! I'll admit, I felt a sense of relief, defiance even leaving home at her insistence.'

'Your mum?'

'Yes, who'd ya think? She was doing my head in. Shutting the door on her felt like... It was a piss poor relationship by anyone's standards, the nagging, the shouting, the humiliation and not to mention the emotional blackmail. But its end came about so quickly that I'd not had time to prepare on any level.'

'She put you out?'

'Hey, stop interrupting. I remember pulling the door to and an eddy of old blossom swirled at my feet, scattering as I stepped forward. That blossom was me Tonk; I was going to be as free as it was. Does that make sense?'

Tonk nodded, 'Go on ... '

'As I marched down the street, my sense of indignity played out with every step.'

'Did you have a pet lip and jut your chin out?' Tonk stuck his lip out for effect.

Smiling, I shook my head indulgently. 'But then my stride began to falter. I started thinking What am I going to do? I was angry, stupid angry. I stood on the corner, in plain sight of the house, making a thing of taking a cigarette from my back pocket and lighting it, blowing the smoke out insolently. I hoped she was watching that she'd noticed I'd stolen one of her fags just before I left. I wanted to provoke her but at the same time I wanted to show her that I didn't care. She wasn't going to get to me.'

'Right. Where was your dad when this was happening?'

'Dad.' I shrugged. 'I tried calling him. Went to the phone box. God, it was awful when I think of it. I dialled the number; the bloody thing rang for an age. When the pips went, I felt this rush of relief. But a voice I didn't recognise answered. *Who?* she said in this hoity-toity voice, the kind that sips sherry in the afternoon. Her voice threw me. *Can I speak to Mr Millar, my dad*, I said. *No, you've got the wrong number. There's no one lives here by that name,* she snorted. *Oh. Okay. Richard then?* She said *No*. Her voice sounded all smug like she was enjoying being a pain in the arse. I remember muttering, *Sorry to have bothered you,* and slamming the phone down. I was all confused and disappointed. Could feel it gathering at the back of my throat, constricting tighter and tighter. That's how it always starts when I panic. I'd nowhere to stay and just one 10p piece left. I dialled again, saying each number out loud and tracing it round with my finger in the dial.

Tonk laughed, 'Bet you had your tongue out too, just like my niece does.'

'Hey, just coz you have terminal cancer doesn't mean I can't slap you'

'I'm only messing, you know that.'

'Okay, so where was I?'

'In the phone box.'

'So, the number rang and was quickly picked up. I pushed my last coin in and all I got was ... *Oh. It's you again. What number are you wanting?* I read the number back to the voice at the other end. *Yes, that's my number, but there certainly isn't anyone of that name living here. Don't call again.* I rang off. But that was the number he'd given me ... and then it occurred to me, when had I ever used it? Never. I stood in that stinking phone box that smelt of piss and cigarettes and cried for some time. There I was, 16, homeless and all I had to show was a pathetic carrier bag with a few useless items in it. I had no way of contacting Dad, not without a work or home address. So, I went to a friend's snivelling all the way. She took me in for a couple of days. My journey started from there really.'

'But that's not the same as when you got to our flat.'

'No, it took me months 'til I got to the flat. Kipping on people's floors, I even slept rough in that park near the Sarah Siddons club for a while. I hated being cold, tired and being at everyone else's mercy.'

'You were so innocent.' Tonk chuckled, holding his stomach as he laughed. His face, caught on a shard of pain made the expression look waxy. I had to look away as he grabbed for some morphine and swallowed it down with loud gulps. I tried to carry on as though nothing had happened.

'Yeah, I still remember the day I turned up to see the flat. Standing outside the grownup terraced houses checking the address held tightly in my hand. I climbed the steps to that bottle green front door - that colour always reminds me of school and getting my head stuck in the railings.'

'I'd forgotten it was bottle green. Railings?' his voice trailed off as his eyelids drooped.

'Yeah, Sshhh, that one's for another time. Course, if I tell you I'll have to kill you. But back to the story line. I had hesitated; finger poised over the bell. God I was nervous. I straightened my coat, polished each shoe on the back of my legs then pressed the bell. Meagher met me at the door with that bloody great dog of his. Midas, wasn't that his name or was it? Remember it used to root out Jerry's smelly socks.' I looked across at Tonk. He was fast asleep.

Chapter Eighteen

March 1981

Finally, Gary wrote. I could hardly breathe when I saw the envelope, the FPO address, his scrawl across the front and all the stamps. It had taken its time to find me, travelling from Spain to the States to be processed and then back to me. I made a cup of tea and sat down at the kitchen table. Barb had gone to work early. This was my moment to savour, alone in the flat.

> *December 14th 1980*
> *Dear Frankie,*
> *It's two in the morning and I'm on base, almost at the end of my shift. All I can think about is you. I've been going over and over things in my head. I know I screwed things up with the Sandy situation, which was, I promise you, a total accident. I thought you understood that when I told you. But now, you've got me so I don't know which way my head is up. First you tell me you love me and then you run out on me. A man can only take so much.*
>
> *I'm not the kind that gets close or attached to someone easily, but you are one big exception, girl. You're something special, you know that? The house is so cold with you gone. I'd do anything to hold you close right now or wind you up and watch you try and act mad. And by the way, I think it's you that needs more tuition with the backgammon – don't think I'd let you away with that one!*

>There's none of your bad cooking for you to poison me and Willy with – remember your ratatouille? I even miss that reggae music you liked to play so much.
>By the way you left your commie watch behind so if you want it, you'll have to come and get it – If you think you're big enough. I'm not done with you yet.
>Take good care of yourself Frankie and write me soon.
>Love G.
>ps: I'm sorry to hear that Tonk is sick. I hope he gets better soon, say Hi to him from me won't you.

I kissed the letter and put it down on the table in front of me, fingers tracing his words. I'd never seen his writing before. A scruffy print pressed hard like it had been chiselled, like writing was an alien activity. I imagined the hand that had penned it, broad but surprisingly soft with clipped clean nails. The hand that had touched me tenderly. The same one that had tucked a stray strand of my hair behind my ear, cupped my face before kissing … He'd sent the letter from his FPO address, not ours the one we had shared together. Maybe he was worried my letter might get lost or that Willy might pick it up. I sensed he was jealous of my friendship with Willy.

My face ached I was smiling so much. It felt like I was smiling from the heart up. He cared, he actually cared! I read the words again and again for good measure – they fed my emotional psyche, soothed my angst, like someone had thrown out the rocks that had settled on my heart. For a minute Gary's letter removed me from the grip of despair at Tonk's illness.

Gary had told me I was something special. I could hear his voice as I read, the nuances of his up-State New York accent. But wait, he'd not reciprocated, not said outright that he loved me. What did that mean?

Yes, it was a positive letter, encouraging but it didn't swear undying love – didn't beg for me to return, just offered an excuse. Was it because he didn't think he was good enough for me – or the opposite, that he didn't care as much as I did?

Perhaps we were too young. We had a whole lifetime ahead of us. How could we know we had found 'the one' at this early point? Or was it that he was playing it cool and acting like the tough marine he thought he was – playing out a part, one that he'd interpreted from the films he watched that influenced him? Maybe his reticence was out of his sense of responsibility towards a pregnant girl – even if he didn't care for her.

I decided to hang on to the good bits despite my numerous insecurities.

That afternoon I'd promised to call in on Tonk. I stopped to pick up a hot sausage roll and a sweet-dough, full of grease, dripper, from my local cake shop - the forbidden food. There was a queue, the woman at the counter was slow. I ended up missing the bus, watching the number 34 moving up the Lower High Street. Tonk had begged me to pick the pastries up even though his mother was on a mission to get him to eat properly. She had it in her head that it would reverse Tonk's prognosis.

Tonk, realist as ever, protested loudly, 'What's the point, Ma? Let's face it, I'm on the way out. At least let me enjoy what time I have left.'

She responded every time with tears and pleading which Tonk couldn't abide. He'd relent and we would be reduced to covert food missions to which I was complicit.

It was another hour until the next bus came so I decided to hitch. Why not, I'd hitched round Europe, so covering 4 miles shouldn't be a problem. I didn't give any heed to the fact that recently young women had been going missing in Gloucestershire. Pulling my coat tightly around me I walked to the main road, head down against the wind and finding a decent hitching spot stuck my thumb out. I must have been there for ten minutes when a truck loaded with building materials pulled over. He said he was going my way, so I got in.

The cab was grubby, the passenger footwell brimming with empty cigarette packets, old sandwich wrappers and discarded paper cups. It reeked of stale cigarettes, the ashtray overflowing with buts. The driver wasn't very communicative either. On profile his cheeks were full and rounded, his forehead broad and high, brutish even. His unkempt curly hair framed his face and reached his collar. It was the kind of face you would never forget.

We were getting close to Tonk's place, the block of council flats on the main road with the words *Tories Out* spray painted in red on the wall, you couldn't miss it and it always made me smile. Tonk's handiwork perhaps? A bus stop was directly outside his flat.

'Just here will do fine.' I geared myself ready for the truck to pull up. He wasn't slowing down, his eyes still fixed ahead staring into the moving traffic, broad rough hands on the wheel; nicotine stained, fingernails edged black.

Had he heard me? I gripped the door handle. Could I jump if needs be? I raised my voice above the hum of the engine trying to sound sunny and confident as though I knew what I was doing.

'Just here, thanks.'

He tilted his head, flicking his eyes over me, predatory like. The tip of his tongue darted out to the corner of his mouth like a lizard. Yes, that's what he reminded me of, a lizard.

I sat up and leaned forward, half poised to reach for the handbrake. I needed to do something quick. Then the traffic slowed. I could jump if needs be. He saw my move and, letting out a loud sigh, indicated and pulled over. Maybe he figured I would be trouble. Maybe he figured he couldn't quite get away with it in the middle of busy traffic. Or maybe I was just being paranoid, I'd had a couple of close calls over the past weeks hitching.

I can't say I scrambled out of that truck with any decorum. Barely had it stopped when I was out, two feet on the floor and slamming the door shut; him staring forward. The guy was a creep, more than a creep, he felt dangerous, and I was glad to be out of his company. Something was definitely not right about him and I felt like something significant had just happened.

I stood at the side of the road shivering as the traffic hurried past, and put my hands in my pockets. I felt the tepid heat there of the sausage roll and it brought me back to the here and now. So I hastened to Tonk's door.

I swung in, heading straight for the kitchen singing my greetings as I went. 'Need a cuppa? I'm putting the kettle on.' I popped my head round the front room door. Tonk was lying on the sofa, all bundled up, eyes closed. Golden sunlight illuminating his face giving him an angelic sheen that I know would have annoyed him. The kettle clicked off and I went back into the kitchen, smiling.

'I've just had a weird lift,' I called, pulling down the cups from the cupboard and sorting out the tea. 'Thought I was going to have to punch the bastard, he wasn't slowing down and for a minute I thought he wasn't going to let me out.'

Tonk shouted through from the front room. 'I thought I told you not to be hitching on your own... There's a nutter on the loose out there at the moment. It's not ...'

I carried the cups through and put them down on the table, 'Safe. Yeah, I know, but I didn't want to hang about for another hour, not with these bad guys waiting for you.' I pulled out the pastries.

'Ho ho, now you're talking.' He reached out and grabbed the sausage roll, closing his eyes as he ate, the sinews of his jaw working over-time. His face had lost its ruddiness, you could have hung coats on his cheekbones.

When finished his eyes checked me up and down. 'You look perky, what's changed?'

I beamed.

'No! Has he finally written then? I hope there's a grovelling apology in there for taking so long to write. Does he want you back? If he does, he's going to have to pay for your flight coz you're not going to hitch it alone. I can't come with you this time – and knowing you, you'd end up going in the wrong direction or get picked up by some other weirdo.'

I didn't want to answer his questions – afraid of what he might say – I couldn't bear to hear the I told you so's. What I felt for Gary was all consuming and I didn't want to hear anything negative, anything that would make me see sense. I didn't want sense in the equation. I just wanted Gary.

Tonk leaned forward and peered at me with a quizzical look on his face. 'There's something you're not telling me.' I shifted uncomfortably in my seat, knowing he would disapprove of the pregnancy, tell me I was mad or worse. After all, who in their right mind would fall in love with someone with that kind of noose hanging round their neck? Gary had assured me it wasn't planned, and I took it at face value because it suited me. I had it in my head that he wasn't in love with her. He wasn't going to marry her but there was that nagging question, was he going to support her?

Tonk would see it for what it was. But would it worry him? I suspected it would niggle at him; he'd nurse it like a raw wound until it grew to enormous proportions. Didn't he have enough on his plate without me adding to it? Then again he was there for me, always had been. I didn't quite get it until that day when he told me about Marlon and how my childhood friend had put Tonk on the path of looking out for me. He understood, right from the deepest seam, like it was ingrained in our DNA, and just like Marlon all those years ago, he had my back, taking up the cudgels where Marlon left off.

'Come on, spit it out!'

I sighed, 'You're not going to like it.'

He arched an eyebrow, 'Let me be the one to decide. Come on,' he urged.

'Well,' I smoothed my jeans with my hands and picked at a bit of lint, 'I didn't quite fill you in on the whole picture. But with what I'm about to tell you I don't want you to put two and two together and come up with ten, okay?'

He nodded, steepling his fingers and placing them under his chin, his counsellor pose.

'Just before I left, I found out something ... Gary was going to tell me, but Angie got there first which rather confused things.'

'Go on,' Tonk shifted in his seat to sit up fully.

'He found out he got a girl pregnant on base,'

Tonk dropped his head in his hands.

'Go on, say something!' I looked at him sideways, but he didn't move. 'Apparently it happened sometime after I got there.'

'So, he was shagging her and seeing you at the same time. Nice. Classy Frankie.'

'Yes, but we weren't exclusive.'

'You mean **he** wasn't exclusive. I know you remember,' he lifted his head and gave me a look that filled me with his disappointment.

'Since when were you so perfect? Haven't you ever played the field? He's a marine Tonk, that's what they do.'

'I'm not buying it and who's to say that they stay faithful when they're in a long-term relationship?'

'I don't know, but it's a chance I have to take.'

He looked at me for a moment, all tension in his face and cords of his neck. Then he visibly relaxed before me, 'What the fuck!' his body melting into a slouch as he let the air out of his mouth nosily. 'I know you'll go and do what you need to do no matter what anyone tells you. I told you before, not to go falling in love with a marine. You're heading for heartbreak, there's no two ways about it. I love you Frankie and want the best for you. I'm telling you - he is not the best.'

'You're probably right,' I conceded.

'I'm always right,' he said with a smug smile.

'Wanker,' I said, nudging him with my shoulder, relieved that we'd avoided a big bust up.

'I have just one question though.'

'Yeah?'

'What is it about him that makes him stand out from the rest?'

The first thing that came to mind was the sex, its white-hot intensity, how it had moved something in me that I'd never felt or experienced before. When I was with him it was as if nothing else existed, we were our own little universe. More than that, I felt physically safe, there was nothing about him that made me feel threatened; he had a way of making me laugh with his ribbing, treating me like one of the grunts he ordered about, but it was all good natured, loving even. Before I left, we'd got to the stage where we could read each other, anticipate each other's needs. I'd rub his neck when his head hurt, or he'd cook me something when he could see I was tired and hungry.

Was it enough? I still hadn't talked to him candidly, not without being guarded. There lurked an element of insecurity within me where I didn't want or wasn't prepared to expose all my vulnerabilities. I was terrified of rejection and feeling that way had caused a gulf between us.

Tonk broke through my reveries. 'Frankie to know what real love is? You have to love yourself, know yourself and what you want and need. If you hitch yourself onto someone else's dreams, you're only fooling yourself and that way madness lies.'

That night in the still of the night I wrote to Gary:

> April 1981
> Dear Gary,
> You'd better be on your knees as you read this – being in my wonderous presence and all that. Like I've told you before, a little grovelling goes a long way and it would be a shame to waste all that training I put you through.
>
> I meant to write you earlier than this, but things have been difficult despite being pretty much the same. It's midnight here. I can't sleep, my head's turning all kinds of nonsense round and I don't seem to be able to switch it off. Tonk's getting sicker and I have that sense of the clock ticking even more than before. I'm dreading the day, just thinking about it hurts, he's been like a brother to me. And his poor mother, what a mess she's in.
>
> Tonk's impending passing makes me think of other, deeper things, (I know, you're going to tell me to stop taxing my little brain), like the meaning of life, what it's all about. I'm not the religious type but it does lead me to question - if there is a God up there why he does the things he does? Like taking Tonk so young when he hasn't had all the things we come to expect in life.
>
> I spose we can't go around expecting everything to just fall into our laps. Things happen when we least expect it …. like when I lost my dad. I was left bewildered, holding on to a load of things I'd wished I'd said and done, things I thought would be a given. This isn't the type of stuff I generally talk about, with anyone, but tonight it's pouring out of me, and you happen to be the one I'm sharing it with. I hope I don't sound weird.
>
> So, talking about the things I want from life – dare I be bold and tell you – I want you. I want to be with you. I feel it like I've never felt or known anything so surely before. I know this is a lot to take on board, afterall we haven't really known each other for that long – and you don't really know all that

much about me – and likewise me with you. I 'spose what I'm trying to tell you midst all this waffle is that I love you and hope you feel the same way too.

Tonk's dying brings losing my dad back up to the surface. Makes me realise that life's short and you need to say what's going on before it's too late. When Dad died, there was a lot going on for me at that time, too much for me to try and tell you here. It's complicated (when is life not complicated?) suffice to say that one day I'll explain all.

Sometimes I find the situation I'm in at the moment too hard to bear, especially when Tonk needs me to be the strong one. At times I think my head is going to burst. I've not cried in front of him; he said he couldn't deal with everyone's grief when he's still here, but it's been a close thing. Bet you're appalled with this stupid English stiff upper lip approach. It seems inhuman at times, doesn't it? Even I don't understand it – the conditioning goes so deep.

Enough of me moaning on. How's life on base? What have you been up to aside from dressing up as a tree and shouting at people? Ha ha, I can be cheeky from this distance. Looks like your discipling and training me has gone out the window, though I'm sure you'll have a go at instilling it again when I'm back. You can at least try and I'll respond with my usual belligerence.

I miss you so much it hurts. Can't wait to be back in your arms again. Might take me a while though coz it all depends on Tonk and then I have to get the money together for a flight.

I love you more than you can imagine. You can get up off you knees now.

Frankie xx

Ps Write me soon.

Tonk still had plans. He wanted to squeeze in as much as was physically possible before 'the lights went out' as he put it. A steady stream of visitors called by, keeping his mum, whom I now called Thelma, busy making cups of tea and fussing about whether she should be buying in Tetleys or Co-op's own brand. Some visitors brought flowers for Thelma, leaving money discreetly stashed on the sideboard before they left. It was the least they could do. Tonk was well loved and by extension, so was Thelma.

People knew that this was the time to say their goodbyes before it was too late, before he was a dribbling mess dosed up with morphine. He wanted to keep his dignity, not be seen like that – word had got round. I felt the strain, Tonk even more so. Friends calling by trying to be positive and jolly, making small talk, not knowing how to address what was really going on. Jerry was the exception. He was more real than most, had Tonk in stitches calling him a cunt for 'getting off the bus early.' Even asked if he had a credit card he could borrow to go and whoop it up round town. Typical Jerry, no holds barred. It was refreshing until the time came for Jerry to leave.

I saw him out. He strode out the door without a backward glance, in a hurry to get his denim jacket on. I called after him, but he didn't answer, footfalls clattering down the first flight of stairs. Then the sound stalled. Leaning over the banister I saw him, sobbing so hard he couldn't stand up properly.

It really hit me then that our circle of friends was about to change irrevocably.

Tonk had decided he wanted a bucket list and had us in stitches with some of his elaborate ideas. He learned to knit thanks to Barb and made some elaborate creations for friends, insisting that we wore them, it was his own private joke that we indulged. Jerry's should have been in a museum - I'd loosely called it a jumper with its overly long sleeves and short body knitted in a lurid assortment of colours. Jerry couldn't help but roll his eyes at the mere mention of it, making an over exaggeration of the suffering he had to go through to wear it.

Tonk also insisted on going ice-skating because he'd never been before. We made an afternoon of it, travelling through to Bristol on the train and having a riot in our own little carriage there and back. The ice-skating was a bit of a disaster, it was too cold and Tonk could only manage half an hour on the rink, teetering like a spindly legged foal. It was the last time we were all to be together from the flat. Each of us making a big effort to keep it light, laugh a lot, not overly fuss yet being hyper vigilant at the same time. I still have the picture of all four of us, Tonk sat in the middle, his thick eyeliner making his tired eyes pop out, and us in our jumpers hunkered around him wearing big cheesy grins.

The big one on the bucket list was seeing Bowie in concert. He was one of Tonk's musical heroes. It was a convoluted trip and took an enormous amount of planning which Tonk took charge of. He surprised all of us with how skilled he was at it, even referred to it as his lost calling.

Mad House Bob kindly offered his converted taxi for Tonk's use. It took on the essential role of getting Tonk to the venue. By the time preparations had finished it looked like a boudoir with Tonk wearing an impish smile, lying at the centre of it beneath a mound of blankets. Bob, complete with leather chauffeur hat, drove with care, avoiding all the bumps and potholes in the road that he could. Then there was all the dashing about in the wheelchair flashing special passes and getting waived through areas where others couldn't pass. Tonk smirking like he was the Pope, loving the speedy entrances and exits. However the excitement really took it out of him – he slept for two days straight afterwards.

He still looked piquey after emerging from his extended sleep, but then it became apparent, he'd caught a cold. He must have picked it up at the concert. It started with a cough, he coughed so hard his eyes rimmed red and streamed. He tried to pass it off as nothing but when the McMilllan nurse left that morning her face was etched with worry. She shut the door to the kitchen as she spoke to Thelma. The muffled sobs were unbearable.

When I arrived the following day Tonk's face reminded me of a tortoise, lined and emerging slowly from beneath the duvet. He opened his hooded eyes as if they were leaden when I caught his hand. 'It's time, isn't it?' he croaked.

'Not yet Tonk. Please not yet,' I whispered fervently.

He went from a cough to a streaming nose to a sharp rise in temperature that continued to rise. He couldn't get warm enough, complained of the cold. I rubbed his feet and his hands, fetched hot water bottles and blankets but when the shaking took hold, I knew we were on the downward slide. The McMillan nurse took over, stripped him of his blankets, leaving him lying there in his flannel PJ's, all skin and bone shivering and chattering teeth.

The ambulance came within twenty minutes, standing quietly outside the flat, engine still running. As they stretchered him out I went to grab his standby bag but one of the paramedics staid my hand and shook his head. This was it, the count down.

By the time he got to hospital, every major organ was showing signs of trying to shut down. I arrived just before the sepsis had kicked in. They had put him in a quiet room to the side of the main ward. I watched from the door as the nurses bustled about around him in their soft squeaky shoes, speaking in hushed tones, and monitoring him regularly. His mum sat beside him holding his hand. She looked like a bird, thin from worry, her mouth working but no sound coming out, just her body shaking and tears rolling, big and fat, down her cheeks.

She stepped out when she noticed I arrived, 'Just needing a ciggy, back in a sec,' the lighter and cigarette already in hand.

When she returned, I could smell the smoke off her more than I could her perfume, it was as if she was curing her grief in five-minute cigarette intervals. It made for a jarring mix, even overpowering the smell of the disinfectant and for that I was glad.

Tonk was restless, drifting in and out of consciousness, the veins on his head standing out proud. At one point he opened his bloodshot eyes and gripping my arm said, 'Live your life. Promise me,' his breath came short and fast.

'I promise,' I whispered, taking his hand.

The sepsis had all but taken hold, his body swollen, he was fighting but the infection was winning, it was just a matter of hours. The clock above his bed seemed to tick even louder than it had before.

Thelma and I sat there talking or singing to him, knowing that hearing is the last sense to go before … I was quietly singing the line 'I'm stepping through the door. And I'm floating in a most peculiar way …' when his breathing stopped completely.

The time was 3.15 am.

I never thought I would welcome that kind of silence. One gilded with relief and sadness, like a soft cloaking veil, bleak yet somehow a serene release. His passing was a profound moment, one which I knew would be forever etched in my memory.

Then his mother's keening pierced the silence, summoning the nurses' soft shoes, busying themselves switching off monitors, smoothing sheets and marking clipboards. They brought us cups of sweet tea and retreated leaving us to deal with the first waves of sorrow.

The rest of the week I walked around in a haze. Numb. Nothing seemed to register, like I was outside myself, turned inside out and washed on the wrong setting. I had difficulty motivating myself; rising out of bed, even deciding what to wear proved challenging. My usual routines were upturned. Had it not been for Barb's kindness, giving me time and space but not enough to lose myself in, I could have fallen through the gaps into the abyss.

I had to face the fact that Tonk was no longer here – no more of his banter, just an empty silence, and a dent in the cushion on the seat he'd once occupied.

All the old friends and more gathered for the funeral; the chapel so crammed that people had to stand outside. A wave of nods of approval occurred as he went out to the Sex Pistol's God Save the Queen. I made a point of looking for his Auntie Rita and sure enough, she had that disapproving look on her face he had described that day. It made me smirk despite my inner turmoil.

The vicar did a great job with the eulogy cramming in many funny stories about him, he even said at the end that he wished he had known him. If that isn't praise, I don't know what is.

Standing by his graveside was surreal, even down to the cawing crows hidden among the cedar trees. I felt disassociated from it all, one step removed. I couldn't cry, just stood there dry eyed and then felt bad because I wasn't behaving like everyone else. I'd done my grieving months earlier and now I had nothing left to give. Part of me died when he passed.

At some point I'd gone to visit Mum. I thought she might have understood how I was feeling, perhaps even emphathised? But she just dismissed it telling me off for wallowing and being self-indulgent – that I knew nothing about grief as if she had the sole monopoly on it.

It took me a good month to rally. There was so much to deal with in my head. Tonk, Dad, the spectre of Blake (I suspected that this would be the time he would pounce, when I was most vulnerable. It would have more effect for him then).

I found temporary work, my approach was virtually robotic, disconnecting mind from emotion and coming home to smoke stupid amounts of dope to numb the pain.

'Live your life,' he'd laboured to say, insistent that I promised.

The trouble was I didn't know how I wanted to live it. I hadn't really dared to dream. I thought I wanted to settle down, have a family, but now I wasn't so sure. I wanted to go back to Gary – his pull on my heart was beyond rational. It was something like being a homing pigeon, responding to the heart's compass as it battled to find its way home.

Was that my sole purpose in life? I thought of my mother and her marriage at eighteen, I wasn't that much older. I didn't want to end up like her - trapped, resentful and unfulfilled. She obviously hadn't known her own dreams. If she did, had they'd got lost between marriage, children and work. Disillusioned, she had anchored herself down with armfuls of grudges, built herself a pyre of martyrdom and ignited it with layers of long forgotten misunderstandings, arguments, hurts, slights and verbal bile. She couldn't see the potentials and possibilities because she was hell bent on blaming everyone else for what was wrong with her life. If only she had used that energy in positive ways, to live life as she was meant to live it.

I knew that my situation was different, love was involved. But what if I was too naïve and young? What if I changed my mind? I nudged these ideas around my head like food I didn't like on my plate.

I knew I had to snap out of my lethargy – it served no one. I'd remind myself; this isn't what Tonk or Dad would want for me. Spain was calling. Time was slipping past, and the flight had to be paid for.

I was starting to get impatient and impulsive. One night, dosed up on smokes and Barb's favourite drink, Tequilla, she and I hatched a cunning plan.

'It's high time I had me a proper holiday,' Barb announced. 'And what better place to go to than Spain.'

I could see right through her plan. She was dubious of my intention of going to Spain alone and wasn't keen on Gary. He didn't have a good track record; didn't write regularly, had made someone else pregnant and she had seen my hopes dashed every time the postman turned up empty handed, which was 98% of the time.

'I'm going to check out whether he passes muster myself. Besides, Tonk would approve I'm sure,' she slurred.

Chapter Nineteen

June 1981

The next morning I was up first and made coffee to alleviate our dry mouths and swollen tongues. I'd put the radio on to fill the silence.

Barb sauntered into the kitchen, switched the radio off and settled herself in her seat, and leaning forward towards me, with the mug cupped in her hands. 'So, I just want to check that you're really intent on going back?' Her blue eyes fixed me in that *this is not a good idea* way that she had.

I shifted in my seat and fidgeted with my lighter. I felt compelled to plug the silence that followed her question. What I said sounded more like compulsive babble than something measured and well-reasoned. 'I have to Barb, I love him. It's the way I feel when I'm around him. When he turns his attention on you it's like there's no one else in the world and nothing else matters. He doesn't want anything from me either - there's no shoulds, musts, have-tos - and he makes me laugh. Besides, I feel safe around him, like if Blake turned up, he could really deal with him. Know what I mean?'

She arched an eyebrow. 'Frankie,' her voice was low and serious, 'what do you know of love? Think about it. Do you know what it takes to make a healthy relationship work? How do you know that this isn't just lust? You said yourself the sex was white hot, but what else? I'm going to ask you a bunch of questions I want you to think carefully about. I ask you because I'm your friend and I love you. Okay?'

I nodded.

'Answer me this: How long have you known this man? How much do you really know about him? Can you, hand on heart, say that he would be wholly honest with you and really have your best interests at heart? Have you thought about what might happen if you get there and things don't turn out the way you planned?'

I turned my head away, jigging my knee up and down in irritated fashion – I didn't want to concede. It hurt too much. It meant I'd have to re-evaluate everything. I remained resolutely silent.

'Okay, so here's the plan. How 'bout I come with you – make sure you get there safe and sound. I'll check this guy out on my terms. You can either listen to what I have to say or not, your choice?'

Barb was never one for rose-tinted glasses, she saw things as they were. She was practical, realistic. I liked the sound of the plan.

'Better still, why don't we have a mini holiday before going to Spain. You can't just turn up looking pale and interesting. Let's start off in Portugal, have our own fun, get a tan then hitch over to Cadiz. We'll fly to Faro; Cadiz is only a couple of hours away and flights are cheaper.'

Barb already had it figured out. The plan seemed simple enough. It made perfect sense. Besides, I thought I'd never return to Cheltenham, that Gary and I would sail off into the distance, loves young dream. The Faro stop would be mine and Barb's last hurrah together.

Faro was a tiny but busy airport bathed in sunshine and smelling of salty sea air and aviation kerosene. We took a taxi to the Old Town, and it didn't disappoint with its cobbled streets and little alleyways. Some of the buildings were dilapidated which rather added to the area's charm. The driver stopped to proudly show us the huge cranes nests above the main gate with these huge birds staunchly sitting there like they were guardians of the entrance. Then he set us down in the main square just by the cathedral.

All around the orange trees were in blossom, their delicate white petals caught in the breeze and bathed in golden sunshine. Barb and I basked in their beauty as we set about exploring the area in search of a suitable *pension* – what they called a hotel there.

Our small suitcases rattling along the cobbled streets sounding like trains going somewhere in a hurry. My shoes pinched, vanity high heels and cobbles don't make for a great mix, and several times almost upturned me. Our arms soon grew tired of dragging our suitcases and bags loaded with Duty Free, but the charm of the place kept us going.

We wandered from pension to pension. Ideally, we wanted something with a balcony or at best a nice view. There were so many to choose from but not everything met our criteria. I felt like I was caught up in a middle of a Goldilocks story, only our version being just a lot of beds being too hard or too soft, the 'just right' one hadn't quite appeared. In the end exhaustion drove us to deciding. We flipped a coin, Barb liked one and I liked another – they both had their merits. As a compromise we decided we would book one, stay there a couple of nights and book the other for the remaining nights.

It felt liberating having the choice and added to the sense of adventure. After dumping the suitcases and having a wee freshen up, we pottered round the town in our flipflops and summer gear, getting our bearings. We had fun figuring out what looked like the most interesting bars and eateries and more importantly, where to take the bus to the beach – all very civilised.

As the saying goes, mad dogs and Englishmen, or in our case, Englishwomen, go out in the noon day sun. On our fifth day we were rather overzealous with the sunbathing and fried our tender white skins to what felt like a crisp. It was a miracle neither of us got sunstroke.

'We look like radiation victims,' winced Barb as I dabbed on the generous amounts of Aloe Vera to parts that looked like they were still cooking. I glanced at myself in the mirror and clocked my bright red face, knowing full well it would peel and knowing my luck, just about the time we were setting off for Spain.

By the evening we were feeling rather sorry for ourselves. Especially because something had upset our stomachs and it was a race to see who got to the bathroom first.

'I don't think we should drink the water,' said Barb, as she appeared from the bathroom for the third time in twenty minutes. 'We'll have to take some loperamide because we can't go on like this.' She produced a packet of diarrhoea tablets and threw them on her bed.

I was rather in awe that she even thought about bringing something for an occasion such as this. It hadn't even occurred to me. She must have been a Girl Guide or a descendant of Florence Nightingale.

'Have we got any bottled water to take them with?'

Barb shook her head forlornly, 'No, but we've still got some voddie,' she held the bottle aloft, smiling.

'Aha, well, isn't that a coincidence,' I grabbed the bottle and unscrewed the top. 'This'll just have to do.'

We stayed in our room playing cards between forays to the toilet. There didn't seem to be any point in going out to eat. Besides, we couldn't be sure our stomachs wouldn't ambush us.

Late the next morning we stepped out to find tea and a late breakfast. The cathedral bell was striking noon and making the cranes squawk in loud rattling bugle calls. 'A penance for all the party revellers,' Barb shouted, hands covering her ears.

We took our time to find the right place to eat, still sore from the sun burn and rather washed out from our bodies' purges the night before. The bar was quieter than usual and had a shaded courtyard. We ate omelette and toast and sat with our pots of tea and English papers retrieved from the paper shop next to our pension.

'Bloody Thatcher,' Barb sat up and shook her paper. 'She makes my blood boil.'

'She did more than that for Tonk,' we caught each other's eye.

'God, he hated her with a vengeance didn't he!'

'Yeah,' I said wistfully, 'do you remember that march we went on? The one where he tore up his bed sheet and painted Out Maggie Out, only he'd spelt it owt.'

Barb started to laugh, 'Yeah. And when I pointed it out to him, he got all indignant and claimed it was in solidarity for his northern brothers-in-arms.'

We both creased up laughing. I raised my cup, 'To Tonk.'

'To Tonk,' said Barb then took a sip. 'You know what? He'd have a fit if he could see us now toasting him with tea.'

'Better than nothing at all,' I quipped. 'I miss that silly bastard.'

'Yeah, me too.'

Having had a siesta and taken paracetamol for our sunburn, we set out early that evening. Our quest was for a kiosk, to exchange money, but we quickly found they were all shut until Monday. This left us with next to nothing to see us through the weekend and we were already starving.

'Come on, let's see if there's a chippy, or an Irish bar,' said Barb as she stopped and applied some lipstick with a flourish. She didn't usually wear lipstick and immediately I was alert. I tried to motivate myself, although it was hard when your skin feels like it's going to split at any moment, however, once we'd started to move my hunger pangs took over.

Our stomachs moved us on from place to place in search of food. Some were just too cheap and nasty to consider, others too noisy. The last thing I fancied was to eat in a busy, smoky bar against the background of football revellers watching a game. Then we happened to pass a restaurant, the smells coming out of its doors were exquisite. Our stomachs lurched and seemingly deposited themselves on the doorstep as we walked past.

Then Barb quickly about turned. 'Follow me,' she hissed, 'I have a cunning plan.'

She threw back her shoulders and positively sashayed into the restaurant with me playing keepy-uppy behind. This was a new side of Barb I'd never seen before. As we were seated, Barb asked the waitress if she could speak to the manager. I looked askance at her, trying to signify without words, 'What the fuck?'

She gave me a sideways-glance and when the waitress was out of earshot whispered, 'Don't worry.'

I watched the waitress talk to a man seated with a large party of people. They were loudly celebrating something and by the bottles on the table had imbibed a fair amount. He rose and came across to us, greeting us warmly in broken English.

I caught the glee in Barb's eye. She crossed her legs and licked her lips, as though tasting the food we were hopefully about to savour, then launched into a speech.

'Good evening, we are representatives of Phalaxy Tours, a new but up-and-coming tour company and we would love to consider your restaurant as part of our exclusive tour package.'

The manager got the jist of the speech and positively lit up at the prospect. 'You English tour company? You be my guest, try my food. Come.' He bid us follow him to the table with the large party of people and sat us both at the top next to him. He remained standing and addressed the party, lifted a glass and, looking pointedly at Barb and me.

'Bem vindo, Phalaxy Tours!'

We smiled politely and lifted our glasses. The rest of the table stood and with glasses charged loudly repeated 'Bem vindo, Phalaxy Tours.' I didn't dare look Barb in the eye for fear of falling apart, a giggle lodged itself behind my lips just waiting for an excuse to erupt.

'What is your name?'

Barb was quick with her response; her eyes had that sparkle about them.

'This is Enis and I'm Clit.'

I almost spat my drink out, my eyebrows shooting up as I stifled a cough. Barb's face had flushed with delight even more so when the party echoed our new names raising their glasses to us again. I clamped my teeth firmly shut and put on my tightest smile then mouthed to Barb as we sat back down 'I'm going to kill you!'

She flashed me her ha-ha-deal-with-it smile, loving every second of mischief she created. It was a joy to behold and who was I to be a party pooper?

We dined like queens that evening, polvo a lagareiro and bacalhau (the latter Barb deposited in her serviette – it was too salty) and a never-ending amount of beer. Our host was so generous and hospitable but as the evening wore on his questions about Phalaxy Tours were becoming difficult to answer – largely because the drink was making us less able to remember what we had said earlier, so we kept contradicting ourselves. Barb had developed a bout of the hiccups and sat there, tight as a tick with a smile smeared across her lips. I managed to convince her she needed to visit the ladies.

'What are we going to do if they present us with a bill?'

'Oh, I hadn't really thought of that. I've been too busy having fun. It's great, isn't it?'

'It won't be if we end up getting slung in jail for stuffing our faces and not paying.'

'Well, what do you suggest we do then? Come clean and tell them out there?'

I didn't like the prospect of that either, who could tell how it would go. I looked up at a large moth fluttering round the light in the ladies loo. Then at the window above the sink. I figured it was large enough for us to climb out of and with some shoving and heaving we climbed through it and out to the back yard the other side. I was the last to climb out the window, Barb pulling me through from the other side trying to stifle her drunken giggles. As I inched through, I lost one of my shoes in the sink. There was no danger I could climb back in to get it. So, I left it there, a smelly stiletto reminder of a modern-day Cinderella that had dined at the manager's table. From there we slipped, or in my case, hobbled, down the side passage alongside the restaurant and legged it barefoot home, laughing so hard in places, we could hardly run.

Sunday, we lazed around the locals' bar near to our pension. It seemed friendly enough and we were mostly left to our own devices. The owner didn't seem to mind the fact that we made a couple of beers go a long way. At some point we struck up a conversation with one of the locals, Jose, a middle-aged man who turned out to be a travelling salesman, or that's what it loosely translated into.

When we told him we were going to Cadiz the next day he could hardly contain his excitement. 'You come with me. I go to Cadiz tomorrow.'

It was a gift we just couldn't refuse. Somehow, midst his poor English and our total lack of Portuguese, we arranged for him to pick us at 9.30am from outside our pension. Door-to-door service, the gods were surely smiling down on us.

That night I could hardly sleep for excitement. This time tomorrow, I said to myself, this time tomorrow I'll be in his arms. I took a long and leisurely shower, shaved my legs, moisturised, and tried to deal with the peeling skin on my nose and shoulders. At least I looked less like a lobster than I had a couple of days previous. When sleep finally found me I dreamt of how the reunion would be; me running into Gary's arms, being lifted up and whirled round, our lips meeting, our bodies melting into one. His first heartfelt words 'Frankie, I've so missed you ...'

'That must have been some dream you were having last night.' Barb looked at me, bleary-eyed over the rim of her coffee. 'All that sighing and fidgeting, Oh Gary, oh Gary. Yes. Yes. Yes.' She mimicked a climax, throwing her head back and tilting her chair so it teetered on two legs.

Laughing, I threw my bread roll at her. 'Stop! Was it that bad?'

She tightened her lips into a forced smile and raised her eyebrows. 'I don't want to be anywhere near you two tonight if that's what it's going to be like thank you,' then she took a bite out of my bread roll as if to impress her point.

Jose was prompt. He sat outside the pension in his white van, wearing shades and smoking a cigarette. When we popped our heads out the entrance, he beeped the horn and waved with so much enthusiasm it made the van squeak and rock. The van had seen better days, there was a dent in the passenger door, rust round the wheel arches and the windows were covered in a thin film of orange dust, not that we cared, it was a free lift. 'Beggars can't be choosers,' muttered Barb as we skipped out the door towards the van.

Jose bundled our cases into the back. Barb and I tried to help but he was insistent – probably trying to show off his machismo. It felt a little awkward watching him puff and pant trying to lift the suitcases, his face red from exertion. We had to look away and certainly not catch each other's eye for fear of laughing. When finally, he'd shoved them in place, I followed in alongside and made a makeshift cushion with my coat towards the front. I noted Jose's work items – a small, battered leather briefcase with frayed stitching, a pair of black slip-on shoes that looked as though they had walked the Gobi Desert and back, and stacks of what I thought were journals loosely covered with newspaper. I paid little attention to them. My head was elsewhere, we were on the road to Spain and that's all I could focus on. Barb got the comfy seat in the front.

We set off to the funky tune of *On the Road Again* by Canned Heat and all of us boogied about in our seats testing the van's suspension. It all seemed perfect, the sun was shining, the sounds were apt for the moment and the mood among us was high.

Jose's English was limited, but he made up for it with lively gesticulations and when they didn't work, reverted to shouting. Everything went perfectly for the first hour or so. The conversation between us stopped and started, until we ended up looking out the window, watching as the landscape changed from rows of flat vineyards to the ground lifting and undulating, growing steeper as the mountains loomed larger. Then we hit a pothole at some speed, a suitcase toppled, a journal stack spilled, sending glossy covered magazines sliding over the back of the van. They lay there like fluttering birds as the breeze from the open window breathed life into them. I clambered towards the back to gather them up.

Initially I saw a pretty woman's upside-down face smiling up at me, then something made me balk. I blinked as though my brain had registered it wrong and looked again. Closer this time. No, I didn't get it wrong. The body belonging to the face was completely naked. Not a stitch on, everything splayed and out there for all to see. I clambered back to the front, could see Jose watching me in the rear-view mirror.

Then I leant forward and spoke softly in Barb's ear. 'Don't want to alarm you but we're travelling to Spain in a porno wagon.'

'What?'

'The goods he's selling. They're all porno mags.'

'Porn?' Barb blurted out loud simultaneously twisting her head round to look.

As soon as she'd said it the driver turned and looked at us with glad eyes.

'Si, si, porn.' His full smile revealed his blackened teeth. 'You like?' His head nodding like one of those irritating nodding dogs you find on the dashboard of some cars.

Barb bristled and gave him one of her killer stares until he visibly shrank in his seat. 'Me,' she pointed to her chest, 'no like porn. You,' she stabbed her finger in his direction, 'very bad.' The menace in her look and voice was unmistakeable, even for someone who didn't speak English. Then she turned to me, speaking through the side of her mouth, 'If he tries any stupid nonsense, I'll punch him and we'll leg it. Are we clear?'

'Totally.' I wondered how exactly I would leg it while sitting in the back of the van. Not that it mattered, I knew Barb could handle herself and that was enough to give me the naïve confidence I needed.

Jose looked from Barb to the road to his religious tokens hanging from the rear-view mirror and back to the road again, as though seeking advice from higher quarters and trying to figure out what was going to happen next. He seemed jittery, like a naughty schoolboy who'd been caught out and expecting a thwack to the earlobe at any minute. My eyes fixed on his long tapering fingers gripping the steering wheel and for a moment my mind was elsewhere.

A jolt in the road brought me back to his nicotine stained fingers with a constant cigarette clipped between his middle and forefinger. His religious medallions, Mary and Jesus, a silver cross that glittered and chinked with the movement of the car. I decided he was not the type to be a threat to us. Besides, he was so slight we could have blown him away like the wolf in the three little pigs. All the same, people can be strange, and I wasn't going to let my guard down.

We drove for another half hour. The animated mood that accompanied us at the beginning of the journey had changed into something more sombre. Jose remained tense as he drove, eyes squinting into the sun, finally he turned down the radio and slowed the car down. This is it, I thought, bracing myself for something unpleasant. But Jose, swallowed hard and merely said in a cracked voice, 'I sorry, I very sorry. I not bad man. I work for to care my family. Three childrens. Understand?'

'Don't expect me to absolve you – it's still bad, its exploitation, objectifying women. Baaaaaad.' Barb wagged her finger at him then sat back in her seat, folded her arms, and fixed her glare straight ahead taking in the arid earth and its dust rising beyond the grimy windscreen. Jose glanced sideways, gripped the steering wheel, and sped up.

Dusty warm air circulated around the van the pages of the loose magazines continued to flap and flurry. From the corner of my eye I caught a flicker of porno images, tits and bums, women languishing on their backs with come hither looks. It struck me how utterly mad the whole situation was and suddenly I found myself rolling about laughing until the tears leaked from my eyes and spread all over my face.

Barb craned her neck, looking askance at me, her frown had drawn her eyebrows down, this made me laugh harder. Jose clocked me in the mirror and began joining in, a titter at first building until he was laughing so hard, he was thumping the steering wheel and accidently beeping the horn. Finally, Barb let go, her shoulders shuddering until her whole body was wracked with mirth and she ended up hanging out the window, open mouth, screaming and flailing her arms.

The outburst broke the ice and when we finally calmed down, I edged closer to the front, keeping my eyes on the miles of tarmac ahead but this time with a smile on my face. No one spoke, all that could be heard was the sound of the tyres gripping the road and the rush of air as it passed the van. Each of us, in our own way, lost in willing us on to the end of the journey.

The sun had climbed to its highest point. The sky was the kind of blue a child would paint, all one colour and scudded with the occasional whisp of fast-moving cloud. It was a blistering heat, making the middle-distance shimmer and shift, like an exotic mirage. I half expected to see a herd of camels and Lawrence of Arabia cresting the hill. The wonder of it was diluted as within the van, despite the open window, it was hot and stifling.

We had crossed the border and were travelling along the main highway. Our destination was but half an hour away and still I hadn't seen anything that looked familiar. On the barren golden hillsides stood large billboards of Spanish bulls and the silhouette of a caped man in black advertising a famous sherry. If I shut my eyes, I was convinced I could get a hint of fermented grapes, or rich raisin slightly crushed and left out in the midday sun; the smell you'd find in the bodegas when all but the hard-core drinkers would be honouring siesta hour.

The thought of it made my heart quicken; behind the flat in Spain there was a bodega. Its smell reminded me of warm evenings, bringing the sun-dried washing in from the yard, music drifting out from the open kitchen door. I was getting closer to where I'd left my heart, to where my life was going to begin.

We pulled into a petrol station and Jose got out to refuel. He came back with cold cans of coke and sweet buns for each of us. 'Please, I sorry,' he pointed to the back of the van. 'Here, Magdalena for you. Eat. We friend for sure now?'

It was a welcome and sincere offering which I readily accepted. I tipped the coke down the back of my throat and licked my fingers when I'd finished with the bun. I hadn't realised how hungry and thirsty I was. Barb took a little while longer to accept Jose's offering but by the time she had finished eating the Magdalena she had come round. Her face had softened, her lips sporting an almost beatific upward curve. She wiped her mouth with the back of her hand and turned to Jose giving him a wide smile and a thumbs up.

'You're alright Jose even if you are a bit of a wanker. But you obviously have your reasons.'

Jose dropped us off in the centre of Rota. As he pulled away from the curb, he brandished one of his mags out the window at us, grinning wildly, 'You want souvenir?'

Laughing, we waved him and his van full of porno mags off and watched as it disappeared down the main drag. I wondered where he was going with those magazines in this strictly Catholic country. How did he justify what he did with his faith? Surely, if he got caught with them, he would be in big trouble. And what of his wife, what did she make of her husband's goods, selling filth to feed his family? Perhaps it was a matter of making do with what you had. Who was I to judge? There was a kindness in his heart, and he had delivered us safely to Rota after all.

I marched us to the flat, Barb pausing every now and then to marvel at the exotic flowers hanging in doorways, draped in window boxes, all brightly coloured and glorious. We walked up the street past row upon row of gaudy, noisy, smoke-filled bars, each in competition with each other.

'Jeez,' said Barb, 'Looks like the worst of the world's detritus has been coughed up here.' She pulled a face as she side-stepped a hefty pool of vomit. 'And you want to come back here to live?'

As we got closer to the flat, I saw the familiar gathering of roma seated on the corner. I paused outside the gate as a voice called out 'Ola, Engleeesh.' I looked back across the road to see a small crowd of smiling faces.

'You back for good?' the Commissioner stood, every part of him looking like he was about to break into a flamenco dance.

I shrugged, 'Tal vez, no se.'

'Come see me when you want,' he patted his jean pocket. 'Si?'

'Si, for sure,' I shouted back.

'Who the hell's that?' hissed Barb. 'He looks like a gypsy.'

'That's because he is.'

'How come you know him?' Her gaze followed in his direction, she was practically drooling, her fingers lingering on the gate.

'Put your tongue away! He was my dealer.'

'Really? Smokes and gorgeous.'

'Yeah. Great guy and sells some great smokes too. But I'm not sure you'd fit with their life, the women have it hardest. One of the girls I worked with in that bar, just over there, was married to a roma. I think he gave her a tough time.'

Barb looked back again and gave him a wave. 'Better keep in with him then, and so handy, just on the doorstep.'

Nervously I approached the door and rang the doorbell. It was the middle of the day; maybe they were at work. We waited for a minute of two, looking up, listening at the door, but no one answered, no friendly face peered at us from over the balcony. This was not the big welcome I'd anticipated.

As we dragged our suitcases through the gate back on to the pavement another voice called me. 'Hey, Frankie. Is that you?' I looked up and saw Antonio coming towards me, arms open wide. He kissed me on both cheeks then held my chin with his thumb and forefinger. 'You look good.' His smile was genuine. 'And Tonk?' his voice lifted at the end, loaded with hope.

I shook my head and looked to my feet before looking him in the face again. 'No. We lost him a little while back.'

Antonio rested his hands on my shoulders, crestfallen to lose his friend. 'Lo Siento, Frankie. He was a good guy.' After a moment he regained his composure and asked, 'And who's this?' as he turned towards Barb.

'This is Barb, a good friend of mine and Tonks. Barb this is Antonio, he owns that bar there.'

'You want your job back? I have work for you both if you want it. Just let me know.'

'Thanks Antonio, we'll let you know. I've got some things to sort out first.'

'Ta luego entonces.'

'Luego.' I watched as Antonio walked back towards the bar.

'Okay, so now what? I'm starving and I'd like to ditch this suitcase sometime soon.'

'Well, we have two choices. Plan A: we go and get a burger from down the road or we go with plan B.'

'What's Plan B?'

'We head round to Angie's place a couple of blocks away and figure out what's happening, leave the suitcases there if needs be and go and get food and beer, in that order.'

'Now that sounds like a plan,' Barb smacked her lips. 'Will she know you're coming?'

'Hope so. I'd written to say I was coming back but hadn't been clear about the date. Let's just hope she's in. Come on.'

Angie's face lit up with sheer delight. She kept looking at me, shaking her head and smiling. 'Demasiado,' she kept saying, then she would grab me by the cheeks and hug me.

'What is that she keeps saying?' asked Barb.

I laughed, 'She's saying *too much*.'

'Si,' chimed Angie, 'Too much!'

Her family welcomed us in, fed us tostados and hot tea as Angie fussed round us laughing at our travel tales.

'You back for Gary? He know you're here?'

'Not a clue. I called at their apartment but there was no one in. He must be on base.'

'No problem, tia, I go on the base now and tell him you're here. Wait here. I'll be back in twenty minutes.'

It felt like the longest twenty minutes I'd ever had to endure. My head in two camps. The conversation before me was other worldly, as if the words came from another room and were washed with filmy water. I'd flick back and forth from deep thought to making polite conversation with Angie's family and Barb. All the while wondering how long it would be 'til I saw him again.

Chapter Twenty

Angie, her family, and Barb had cleared out of the house to allow us our time together. I sat and waited, overthinking what I was going to say, how the reunion would unfold.

I locked my fingers together and placed them in my lap, I could hardly breathe for the excitement of it all. Forcing myself to take in deep breaths. The last thing I wanted was to pass out before he'd even reached me. A puff of air brought the scent of jasmine and a few idle petals through the window. They twisted and spun, like white spears softly coming to rest in my lap.

I was so nervous I didn't trust my legs to hold me. I was sitting in the alcove when I heard the hinge of the gate rasp, then steady footsteps on the path. I didn't dare look out, I couldn't. A few quick adjustments, smoothing my skirt, my hair, smacking my lips. Did I look good enough? Would he still find me attractive?

I looked up. His shadow appeared at the doorway, stretching long into the house; an arm leaning on the doorframe, one hand resting on the door, his head cocked to one side.

'Frankie?'

I tried to move but my legs shook so hard I could hardly stand. 'In here. I'm in here.' My voice faltered as though all the breath had gone from me.

And suddenly there he was standing before me, tanned, toned in his t-shirt and shorts. That crooked smile on his face.

It felt as though everything within me short-circuited. I functioned like a giddy teenager, my mouth moving but no words coming out, hands flailing unsure where they wanted to start first.

He was taller and broader than I remembered. Crossing the floor in three strides, as if in slow motion - he lifted me up and into his arms as though I was light as a feather. I held on tight, burying my head in his neck, inhaling his musky scent, touching the smoothness his skin, warm and recently washed. Wrapping my legs around him I lost myself in the intensity of the embrace.

We held on to each other for an age. His hands rediscovering me, running his fingers through my hair, my face, my neck, my lips. We breathed each other in, our lips meeting like it was a primal thing, reacquainting ourselves with an urgency that only time apart creates.

Finally, I pulled my head back and looked at him. Our eyes meeting, steady, drinking each other in, committing every curve and shadow to memory. It felt like every fibre of our being was radiating joy. Everything about us was smiling, bathed in an untouchable golden glow. I was exhilarated.

'Come, we have things to do we can't do here.' His hand drifted tantalisingly between my breasts, reaching up to hold the back of my head and pull me in for another tender embrace.

'Let's grab a taxi. I've got a new apartment just waiting for us to put our own stamp on it.' And there it was, that lopsided smile that I would have travelled to the ends of the earth and back for.

The new flat was across the other side of Rota, in an area unfamiliar to me. We climbed the three flights of stairs and stopped at the middle door on a landing that smelled of disinfectant and vaguely-masked cooking smells, from somewhere above. Loud music played and a dog barked. Gary put my suitcase down, opened the door, then swept me up in his arms and carried me across the threshold.

Hours later we emerged from the flat, blinking in the late afternoon sunlight. We hadn't stopped to really talk about things, attending to our physical needs after such a long time apart seemed the natural thing to do.

We met Barb, Angie and her husband at Benny's bar, a popular establishment situated on the sea front with spectacular views. That night was no exception, marbled pinks and yellows wove across the sky as the spinning evening sun disappeared beneath the waves. We stayed there a short while then moved on for something to eat as the bar numbers swelled and the music got louder.

At every point Gary and I sat close, knees touching, his arm around my neck or stroking me in some way. I was purring with happiness, smiling from the inside out. What a thing it is to feel claimed and desired, like a drug, totally intoxicating. I was hooked.

I could see Barb watching us closely, making her mental notes with her sideways glances. Knowing her, it was all being recorded for future reference. She was not one for being easily duped. I wondered what she made of him but no doubt she would tell me at some point. I could rely on her for that.

After the meal, we parted ways. I left Barb engrossed in learning Angie's Spanish drinking salutations 'Ariba, abajo, el centro, el dentro,' she was trying to follow her words, but the alcohol had taken over her capacity to control her lips. I knew she would be well taken care of. Angie promised to look after her while Gary and I got reacquainted.

We walked along the sea front hand in hand, pausing at the pier to look out at the low-slung black sky weighed down by a carpet of jewels. We smoked a number as we listened to the water lapping at the pier's wooden stakes. I didn't feel there was a need for words. This was too perfect.

Back at the flat Gary and I lay in bed nestled into each other, finding the places where we fit best, my head on his chest, listening to his heartbeat, the gentle rise and fall, my hand tracing the smoothness of his chest. Under a crisp white sheet we made love, slowly this time and lay entwined watching the flecks of moonlight dance on the dark moving sea beyond our window. As I lay there secure in his arms words gathered in my mouth, suddenly impatient, bursting from me like bubbles of champagne.

'I love you. I love you with all my heart. I've missed you so much. This is where I want to be, right by your side. Always. It's you that's kept me going throughout all these months. Just the thought of us being back together ... '

As I whispered into the darkness, he remained silent, the antithesis of what he'd written in his letters telling me there was so much he wanted to talk about, that he missed me, couldn't wait for me to be back in his arms.

I snuggled into his chest, waiting to hear those words repeated back at me. But they never came.

I felt exposed and strangely betrayed.

A silence followed, building, with every second that passed, a void between us.

He shifted slightly, loosening his hold. From somewhere, perhaps outside in the street, I heard voices raised in anger, a woman crying.

'You want a smoke?' He sat up, tipping me onto the pillow. I watched him reach across to the nightstand, pull a cigarette from the pack and light it in a fluid movement. It was an action I'd seen before, one that reminded me of Dad, the way he lit his smokes, particularly when he was going to say something awkward.

Gary's face, although in shadow, showed furrowed lines on his brow.

Here it is, I thought, the black shadow catching up.

Finally, he spoke. 'Frankie, we need to talk,' there was a finality in his tone. 'There's things I need to explain.'

I wanted to cover my ears, curl up, blot out whatever he had to say. It was the way he had started the sentence; I knew it wasn't going to be good.

'This girl on base, the one I told you about. She's due to give birth very soon. What can I say? I'm involved, I have to be around for that. It's why I'm distracted. Everything has gotten so complicated. I ...'

'So are you telling me you've changed your mind? That you're with her now?'

'No. I don't know. It's not like that – it's her first, my first child.'

How I hated her in that moment for having what I wanted, something that bound us together, ours, made by love – but instead, she was the one driving a wedge between us. 'Is that why you got this flat, so you could move her in when the baby's born?'

'No, I didn't say that. The timing is awful.' He pulled hard on his cigarette, then exhaled slowly, allowing time to gather his thoughts. 'I'm due to fly back Stateside for a month in three days' time. My sister's graduating, Dad's been ill. I've not been home in over two years. I can't get out of it, not now. You understand?'

I listened, my body tensing and curling like some animal skin pegged out to dry in the sun. I felt flayed. In the darkness fat tears rolled down my cheeks. I turned my head and buried it into the pillow, not knowing how to respond. All those months of waiting, the trouble I'd taken to get to him, the total high earlier in the day where I felt loved and secure ... to this.

This complete crashing down.

We'd had our physical climax earlier that day but this, this was a signal, the warning shot to say it wasn't going to be the happy-ever-after I'd hoped for. The excuses seemed stacked against me. Were they excuses, or genuinely bad timing? What would I have done in his situation? I knew it wouldn't be this.

My thinking started going on a downhill slide, dragging every ounce of self-worth with it. It had to be something I'd done. That was my go-to mantra, my internal programming. I would always put the blame on me. It was always my fault. But what was it that convinced me that this was the beginning of the end? Then I realised, it wasn't what he'd said, but what he hadn't said.

There were no words professing undying love.

He didn't ask me to stay.

Who was I kidding? Was it that I'd mistaken his well-practised moments of tenderness for love? Was it just sex to him with a few carefully placed platitudes? Oh, how easily I'd been duped. What did I know about love? Barb had directly asked me that before we came. She had warned me.

I found it hard to fathom, to unravel the real from the perceived. There were cultural boundaries after all, not to mention those subtle differences between males and females.

My head was spinning, darting from one argument to the other. One minute I'd convinced myself it was over, it wasn't worth it and the next I'd rallied again, throwing my heart back in the ring, finding excuses to pin my hopes on him. For months I'd brain-washed myself, convinced myself that this was the real deal. I'd cut that mental groove so deep I didn't know how to jump off it, even if I'd wanted to.

I drifted off to sleep with the yes, no, battle raging. How was I to cope with rejection when I'd built my world around him? I had but three days, three days to change his mind.

At 7am I heard the latch of the door click. He'd left a note at the side of the bed.

> *See you at 7pm tonight.*
> *Smokes on top of the dresser.*
> *G. x.*

I rolled over and shut my eyes. I was tired and emotional. Dragging myself out of bed I stood beneath the shower for an age trying to wash away the dread. He was slipping through my fingers before we'd even given it a chance. I toyed with the idea of staying on after he'd gone back to the States but then the insecure part of me considered what would happen if he'd decided to get the apartment so he could accommodate her and his child. How would that play out? I'd be the unwanted guest listening to them making love from the other room or worse still left to do the babysitting. I tortured myself just thinking about it.

Barb and Angie appeared at the door. Laughing and making rude comments. I let them in. Barb took one look at me and folded me into her arms. I wept on her shoulder. Angie went to get a glass of water.

'What the bloody hell has he done?' Barb wiped my eyes tenderly and kissed me on the forehead.

'Nothing, not really.'

'I knew it would be too much. Especially after Tonk ...'

'No,' I gulped at the water Angie handed me. 'It's not that. It's just that he's going back to the States on Wednesday, for a month. He has to because his sister's graduating and his dad's been ill.' Then I started to really sob and hitch, 'And that woman on base is due his baby any time soon.'

'Is he still with her?'

'No. I don't know.'

'Then what is it?

'He hasn't asked me to stay. He didn't tell me he loves me. He didn't really do or say anything.'

'So he just fucked you and that's it?'

'Yes. No. I ...'

All that was running through my head was his response after I'd asked him if he'd changed his mind ... I don't know. Surely to God he'd had enough time to consider things? Perhaps that was the nub of it, if he couldn't decide for sure then this wasn't right. But why was I feeling so strongly that we could make this work? Why was my heart taking over my head?

'Frankie, listen to me. If you have any doubts, any at all, then this isn't right. Remember what Tonk said, live your life.'

'But what did he know about life?' I spat. 'He went and left us, left me.'

Barb eyed me patiently. 'He knew and did a lot more than you give him credit. You know he had his own way of looking at things.'

We both nodded.

'He hated mediocrity, remember how he used to rail against being incorporated, the 2.4 kids, mortgage and 9-5 shit?'

I smiled remembering one of his rants, could see him, sunlight making his spiked hair glow fire-red, his eyes lined black, blazing with passion as he urged us to fight back against the system.

'You know he was wholly against settling down precisely because he was too young, had more life to live. You know that was why he finished with ...'

'He never told me that!' The thought of him not telling me felt like a betrayal, tantamount to being wounded. I thought we shared everything.

'We spoke about it at length. He really cared for her but didn't think he could commit to settling down – and I think that that was what he recognised might happen with you and Gary.'

'But that doesn't mean I have to follow his ideals. I'm driven by different needs.'

'And that's the nub of it. Men and women are made up differently. I'm just saying ...' Barb's words faded into the background.

In my head I was still fighting for my heart's desire, reasoning why Gary seemed to be distancing himself. I told myself he was tired when he came home that night. We both were. It had been harder on him having to put in a full day's work on top of staying up virtually all-night fooling around with me. I reminded myself that he was distracted, having to consider what to do next given the impending birth, going home and then there was me in the mix.

I started to analyse everything – every moment – to see where I might have gone wrong. When we'd gone for something to eat at one of the local eateries, nothing fancy, I had felt nervous and awkward and waved my hands around far too much as I spoke. Then I spoiled it all by knocking over my drink spilling it all over the table.

'God damned clutz!' He barked as he reached for a napkin to mop it up.

His comment threw me. It was harsh and impatient. I froze, noting my own physical withdrawal. I told myself I was being sensitive, but his reaction wasn't the response I'd expected, not from someone who was supposed to be delighted to see me and welcoming me back.

As we made our way back to the flat, I found myself struggling to think of something to say, the silence felt awkward, like a line had been drawn that was not to be crossed. At the flat I tried to nestle up close, rekindle what I thought we had but the feeling hadn't been the same. I put it down to both of us being tired.

When I woke up the next day I felt hollow, aware that some huge emotional storm clouds were heading my way. I knew it wasn't working but didn't want to accept it, kept pushing it to the back of my mind. I didn't want to admit that for whatever reason, there was a huge bank of eggshells before me that no doubt I would soon find myself walking on.

Every time I had tried to broach it he'd change the subject, fidget, light a cigarette, get a beer from the fridge. Evasive tactics. I got so frustrated at one point I blurted out, 'You remind me of my dad, always avoiding discussing things at any level. Christ, you even wear the same aftershave as him.' It all came out wrong, rather than setting us up to talk, I'd thrown another obstacle in our path.

Having Barb and Angie around in the daytime proved to be a life saver, a good distraction to stop myself becoming maudlin.

On the third night Matt – the chap who had taken me to the Marine Corps Ball - called by unexpectedly. Said he just wanted to say hi, see how I was doing.

Gary invited him in, but stood woodenly, arms folded. We all went through to the living room and sat chatting politely. Gary subtly steering the conversation. Then Matt produced some pictures of us at the ball. He thrust one in front of me and Gary, 'She's beautiful isn't she,' he pointed at the picture. 'You're one damned lucky guy!'

I sensed an instant tension. There in the background was Gary, his arm around what I presume was her. They looked happy together. She had that love-struck look about her, looking up at him, smiling. Just the mere glimpse of it made me seethe, set my teeth on edge.

Gary deftly picked up the picture and handed it back to Matt. 'Well Matt, thanks for stopping by but it's our last night together so I'm sure you'll understand …' Matt stood up. 'Why sure. I'll leave you guys to it.'

I walked him to the door. 'I'm thinking of coming to England at Christmas, if it's okay with you, would you mind if I looked you up if you're there?'

His words stung me with such a force I was momentarily stunned. What was it that made him assume I was going home? Nothing had been said. Then it occurred to me that he knew more than I was party to.

'Sure Matt, I'd love that. Gary has my address.' As I said the words, it struck me that I would indeed be going home. That, in reality this - whatever it was - was over.

Gary came to the door and looked over my shoulder, 'See you tomorrow, Matt.'

'Yes Sir,' and then he was gone. The sound of his footsteps clattered down the stairs.

I shut the door after him and leaned my back on it. 'How come he called you Sir?'

'I'm a higher rank than him, he's just a corporal.'

'Oh, now I see why Willy didn't call you sir,' I watched Gary visibly bridle, a sharp intake of breath, a hint of a flinch that made him stand just that little bit straighter.

'Don't mention that mother in my presence.'

I'd hit a nerve; no doubt Willy had said something to him he didn't like and I knew that at some point I would find out.

The time left with Gary was miserable. I tried to make the best of it, tried to change his mind in a gentle unassuming way. Not be clingy or too needy. Maybe I performed that part too well because on the day he left I couldn't cry. Everything just stopped at the back of my throat, like it did at Tonk's funeral. I was wailing inside but on the outside I was frozen. I didn't put up a fight, I needed to hold on to some semblance of dignity, perhaps he would remember and respect at least that about me.

He was wearing his uniform when he left, kit bag hoisted on his back, cigarette in his mouth, his body half turned at the door, eager to get away. There was no long anguished goodbye, no lingering kisses.

He didn't say I'll see you soon or don't forget to write, just 'Bye, Frankie.'

It seemed perfunctory, like he hardly knew me. I could have been a checkout girl who'd just bagged his groceries for all it mattered. It left me confused, struggling to figure out what to make of it.

I watched him disappear into the blackness of the stairwell, the sound of his heels echoing off the walls, shrinking into quiet the further he went. When I heard the front door slam the finality hit me. There wasn't going to be any last-minute reprise, no charging back up the stairs saying 'Frankie what was I thinking, I could never leave you.'

I felt numb, emotionally anaesthetised – automatically playing to a stereotype, that typical English stiff upper lip approach. I tried to brush it off, make out it didn't matter but inside I felt as though I'd been smashed to pieces; that nothing could put me back together again. I had been so convinced we were going to waltz off, hand in hand, like love's young dream. It felt as though I'd been turned inside out, then dipped in salt for good measure.

Chapter Twenty One

Barb arrived minutes after he'd left. She might have passed him on the stair. She let herself in only to find me sitting at the table in the virtually empty flat staring out across the sea. Noisily rummaging in her pockets, she produced a box of matches.

'You alright?

My swollen eyes, unkempt hair and sagging shoulders told their own story.

'Here, try this. It's from the Commissioner.' She put a joint to my lips and lit it. It was strong. As I smoked, she made tea in the kitchen humming a little tune as she crashed about washing the heap of dirty dishes that lay in the sink. I found her cheeriness irritating; how could she be in such good spirits when my life's plan had just crashed and burned? Returning ten minutes later with a steaming mug of tea, she placed it before me, took a seat and studied me closely. Her gaze was kind, one born of understanding.

'He wasn't worth it Frankie. One day you'll look back on this and thank your lucky stars that you didn't get bogged down with it.'

I held up the flat of my hand to her. 'Stop. Not now, please. I can't hear it right now.'

'Okay,' she sighed, 'but you only get the morning to mope, this is still my holiday. And I don't intend to spend it minding a grizzle-guts.'

The airplane took off from the base, its white fuselage arching upwards into the Mediterranean blue sky leaving a small white trail of smoke in its wake. I imagined Gary strapped into his seat, already thinking about the things to come, his family, his hometown friends, his sister's high school graduation. I was now something he left behind, just another chapter in his book. This time he was doing the leaving and it was final.

In the kitchen Barb busied herself, wiping the cupboards, cleaning out the fridge. Then she swept the floor and put her things in the second bedroom. When finished she bounced back into the sitting room. 'Right, that's enough of that.' She checked her watch. 'We have to go and meet Angie at two, she's taking us to a bodega.'

I groaned, 'Are you sure you want to do that to yourself? That stuff's lethal. And how come you're so chirpy today?'

'Since when did you get all conservative?'

I shook my head and drained my cup.

'Come on, lighten up, he's gone, end of story. Forget him, Frankie. Let's go out, it'll be a laugh.' Putting on her pretty-please pout she grabbed me by the hand and pulled me to my feet. 'A smile would be nice.' She softened her voice and raising its pitch put her face close to mine and lightly, using thumb and forefinger, stretched my lips into a pseudo smile. 'Now say after Auntie Barb, Gary. Is. A. Wanker.'

'Gary is a wanker.' A smile tripped my lips as I repeated the words with increasing levels of loudness. 'Gary is a WANKER!' It reminded me of a time when I was a kid, me and my then best friend Patsy, screaming bloody bollocks down at the park. I was low then, trying to swim my way through the soup of grief, although I didn't understand that what I was experiencing was grief back then. Patsy's friendship and laughter hauled me through. I wondered what she was up to and where she was – probably still in that council estate just up the road from Mum's. She never was one for straying far, not like me, Thursday's child. I made a mental note to look her up when I got home.

'There now, doesn't that feel better? Now, go get your eyeliner on and let's go, we're late already. We clattered down the stairs and out into the bright sunshine, the heat lightened my mood. Looking sideways at Barb I noted a bouyancy in her stride.

'So, what's with all this chirpiness?'

'Me chirpy? Now that would be telling.' She sashayed in an exaggerated fashion across the pavement and turned dramatically.

'Let's just say I'm now acquainted with the Commissioner.'

'No.' I stopped mid-stride. 'You can't just leave it at that. Tell me more!'

Barb grinned. 'He was very much the gentleman. We went for a drink to like a local bar; live Spanish music and impromptu flamenco.' She twisted an arm up into the air flamenco style and lifting her chin up looked at me, all haughty. 'Ole.' I laughed and bumped her with my shoulder.

'Nutter. Come on, spill the beans.'

She looked at me, barely masking a smile, 'A lady never tells.' Her hands danced, drawing animated shadows along the pavement. 'I'll tell you later, okay? Just cool your jets man, tranquillo.'

I rolled my eyes feigning disappointment. 'Honestly Barb, you'd think you'd been here a year the way you're acting. You crack me up. So, what else did you get up to?' Her expression was resolutely closed. 'You didn't go and spend the night with the Commissioner did you?'

'No,' she mock slapped my arm. 'On the way home, we met Angie and your old flatmate Willy, and we all went to a party on the beach. Someone made a fire out of driftwood; we ate burgers and drank beer and had some smokes. I don't think we got back to Angie's 'til 3am.'

'Bloody hell, that's amazing Barb, you don't hang around, do you?'

'Nope.'

'So, tell me, what did you make of Willy?'

'He's really good people. He gave me a good insight into Ga...'

'Don't mention his name,' I snapped.

My stomach lurched. It was still very raw; I noticed a new emotion surfacing. Humiliation rose like one big black cloud, reminding me of what an idiot I'd made of myself, how I'd allowed myself to be used. I'd even told everyone back home I was going off to Spain to get back to 'The One.' How was I going to face everyone, hold my head up? Embarrasment was waltzing with my disappointment, and I couldn't figure out which one was taking the lead.

'I wasn't going to talk about him, I was going to talk about Willy and his take on things.'

'Really? How?'

'He really cares about you. He had hopes you two would … He's hurting too, but in a different way. In that buttoned-up way guys have for expressing their feelings. You know he had your back all along don't you?'

'Yes, but … I was stupid, what can I say?'

'No Frankie, you weren't stupid, gullible more like. Gary fed you the bullshit that you wanted to hear. He didn't value or respect your feelings. You can't be held responsible for that.'

'But I should have worked it out. Not gone in there all gung-ho like some lovesick teenager. It felt so real when I was here last time.'

'Maybe it was then. But this guy is led by what's in here,' she pointed to her crotch. 'You were duped. Tripped up by your own naivete. I bet you thought you two would just swan off into the sunset and live happily ever after.' She clocked the look on my face, where the full realisation that I'd been such a mug was beginning to show. 'Wake up Frankie, this isn't bloody Disney. Now you're having to learn the hard way. It happens to the best of us.'

'Did it happen to you?'

'Yeah, sort of …'

'What's sort of?'

She let out a long sigh, blowing out her cheeks as she did so. 'God, it seems so long ago now. We were childhood sweethearts, even got engaged the year after I left school. A cheap little emerald the size of a pin head but I was so chuffed with it. Yep, I even got fitted out for the big meringue, the whole shebang. At the time he was my everything.'

'So what happened?'

'My sister.'

'What?' I stopped in my tracks, mouth agape. 'I didn't know you had a sister!'

'That's probably because I've never told you I had one.' Barb's whole demeanour changed, she held her head a little higher, her chin jutted out, that mask of defiance fully applied. But she wasn't fooling me, her eyes spoke a different story.

'Shit, that must have hurt.'

'I was devastated. Even more so when they got married. It was a bloody mess and caused all sorts of upset. Can you believe it, she asked me to be maid of fucking honour!'

'Barb, I'm so sorry. That must have been awful for you.'

She nodded. 'It's done now.'

'Really?'

'Yes, really, but it was a close-run thing for a while. It's not something I like to talk about but …'

'But?'

'Okay, I kind of went off the rails. Life was really black for a while. I struggled with drink, anything to numb the pain. I think if I could have got hold of hard drugs then I would have just gone for it.'

'So what stopped you?'

'A couple of things really. I got caught shoplifting when I was drunk, stupid really. I didn't have any need for a lamp or the bloody table mats, that was humiliating. My parents were mortified. Then I moved into the Derry Ann Guest House and squatted for a while. Got pregnant, don't even remember who knocked me up. I lost it pretty early on and I think my hormones took over. I went on a complete downer and that's when my cousin stepped in.'

Barb's revelation rather shocked me. I'd always thought of her as grounded and steady and here she was telling me that she was fallible, complete with flaws and a history to show it.

'I'm not proud of what I did or how I acted but that's what can happen when your heart is broken and you don't have the wherewithal to deal with it.'

'Is that why you insisted on coming with me to Spain?'

'Yeah, I didn't want to see you going the same way I went. It's easy to end up the wrong way up, let me tell you.'

'Thanks Barb, I really appreciate it. I couldn't ask for a better friend.'

She smiled and inclined her head to one side.

'But on the bright side, if it hadn't happened, I'd never have met you and you'd be all tied down and bored shitless up to your ears in middle-class wifedom.' I grinned at her.

'Yeah, what a drag,' she pulled a face. 'Weird to think though that here you were running towards what you thought in that stubborn little head of yours was love and marriage and then there's me, always running away from it.'

I stopped mid-stride. 'So is that why you broke up with Sam?'

'He was getting too serious and I don't think I can handle that grownup stuff, wedding cakes, families coming together …' her voice trailed off.

'You're still into him though aren't you?'

She grimaced, 'We all have our ones that got away. He'll get over it. I'll get over it.'

'Hmmn, I'm not so sure. You and Sam were perfect together. And why should you get over it?'

Moments passed as we walked along in silence.

'Have you seen him since?' I asked.

'Who, Sam?'

'No, the one your sister nicked.'

'No,' her response was instant, like a punch. 'Neither him or my sister since they got married four and a half years ago.'

I looped my arm over Barb's shoulder, 'C'mon, fuck it, life's too short to waste on the what-ifs and could-have-beens, let's get on with the now shall we and go and get riotously pissed.'

Angie was waiting at her gate, sitting on top of its concrete pillar, legs swinging, smoking a cigarette. She jumped down when she saw us, greeting us Spanish style. I was amazed to see how Barb had assimilated this custom so quickly and readily. She was much more reserved at home.

'Vamo,s tias. We have some partying to do.'

We headed down the street walking three abreast. It was quiet in the winding backstreets, no mopeds or vans speeding past at regular intervals. Just the background lull of TVs and radios, children playing kick-the-can mingled with the sounds of our heels and voices bouncing off the houses. I imagined people sleepy in their beds, all tranquillo, unhurried, there was always mañana afterall. The stillness had an intimacy about it, something grounded and ancient. I loved the way the heat of the sun slow-cooked the tilting yellow walled houses, how it poached the red geraniums trailing from balconies, their woody sweet perfume hanging in the air. All that, against the backdrop of cooking smells, flavours of garlic, herbs, and heated oil from meals eaten before the siesta.

The drink was cheap at the bodega. First, we ate tapas on Barb's insistence. 'We can't drink without first lining our stomachs and neither of us have had breakfast yet – or lunch for that matter.'

Not that I minded, the walk had given me an appetite. After the tapas we ordered bocadillos and more tapas, then the drinking began.

Initially I drank to drown my sorrows, but the liquid gold substance I poured down my throat wasn't allowing me that. Instead, it brought out the laughter, the nonsense, the joy of just being. Thoughts of Gary floated into my mind at times, but I was determined to push them away. There would be plenty of time to mull over that later. Now was the time to be with friends, sod the upset.

We drank into the early evening. Willy stopped by, sidling quietly into the pub. I acknowledged him with a nod and a wave but was preoccupied with attempting to teach Angie and Goodie a rather rude rugby song, complete with actions. Some of the patrons had joined in too which was making for lively and raucous entertainment. When next I looked for him, I saw he was deep in conversation with Barb at the other end of the bar.

The shenanigans continued for a while until Goodie and Angie went home leaving me sitting alone trying hard to remain upright. Barb was nowhere to be seen, probably disappeared to the bathroom. As I waited, trying to liberate a cigarette from its packet, Willy sat down heavily opposite me. He looked weary, his face set to disappointment. He didn't speak, didn't need to because his expression said it all and I was not so drunk that I couldn't read it.

Groggy, I eyed him, the alcohol had mined my regrets and brought them to the surface – he was such a good friend to me, especially when I first arrived. He gave me somewhere to stay, fed me, took Tonk to the airport, even made sure I had female friends. We hung out together, took awesome trips out on the bike. I'd even told him some of my deepest secrets, things I never normally divulged. I considered him to be one of my closest friends and yet I'd hardly seen him, spending all my time with Gary. And here he was, checking in, making sure I was okay. I didn't deserve that.

Emotion bubbled up, riding on a crest of alcohol and a wave of self-loathing, tears cascaded down my cheeks. 'I'm sorry Willy, I really messed up this time didn't I?'

He rose and sat beside me, placing an arm around my shoulder and drew me in. 'Frankie, it's okay, I get it. You can't help who you fall in love with.'

I cried harder, 'You are so lovely Willy, I really don't deserve you as a friend and I'm so sorry if I've hurt you.'

'It's okay. I just want to see you alright. Gary is a prize idiot, and he will live to regret this – damn, I'd give my eye teeth to have a woman like you hitch across continents to see me. Now that's a keeper. If truth be told Frankie, you were always far too good for him. I think he knew that deep down.'

'It still hurts though. I don't know if I'll ever get over it. Ever. I'm going home and I'm never coming back.' I banged the table with my fists trying to emphasise the point, but my hands were uncoordinated making weak impressions.

'Are you going to be alright going home – with that Blake guy hanging about?'

'I will be. He's on remand at the moment,' I swallowed down a hiccup, 'for attempted murder, so I'm the least of his worries.'

'You never told me that.'

'No. It's a bit mortifying to be honest,' I looked at him unsteady. 'Me, being tangled up with a killer. Who knew, eh.' I waved my hand dismissively.

'How did you get into that state?'

'Naiveté. I was too frightened to tell him to piss off and then got in way too deep. It was a crappy situation that just kept giving. Tonk came up with the idea of taking off. He was like you, always looking out for me and now he's gone too.' I bit my lip, determined not to cry but my eyes leaked involuntarily.

'Come on, I'm going to get you a coffee then I think it's time you went home. I'm going to have to go soon as I'm at work tomorrow, but I promise I'll come and see you off okay.'

By the time he'd returned from the bar with the coffee Barb was back with her cigarettes. After Willy left, she rather noisily voiced her contempt that I should even contemplate sobering up. 'We are coming to the end of our Spanish holiday,' she held up her hand in a flamenco-like flourish. 'We need to do it in a manner to which we are accustomed,' then, as an afterthought floated across her synaptic processes she leant forward, 'and we're celebrating you not disappearing into the Spanish sunset with GI Joe. Mr Arsey-hole.' She thumped the table, 'Marriage is very overrated these days anyway. This calls for a little celebration.' She promptly raised her hand and called the barman's attention. 'Dos brandies mas por favor,' she turned and smiled at me, her eyes straying in different directions.

'Bloody hell Barb, you've really got your head around the lingo haven't you.'

'I know, I'm impressive aren't I?'

'Very. Very impressive indeed.' I patted her on the shoulder.

When the brandies arrived she tipped mine in my coffee and slammed the empty cup on the table.

'There, here's to us, young, free and single and not giving a fuck.' She patted my mug. 'Alrighty?'

'Yeah, alrighty!'

We left the bodega leaning on each other as we staggered home. I didn't remember much of it, only that getting back into the flat caused a bit of a problem. The key didn't seem to fit, but a good bump on the door made the lock give way. I had a bruised hip to prove it. The late evening Sun poured in through the small balcony window, leaving a pool of light in the sitting room. Barb opened the balcony door and there the two of us sat on the seats we found. Either the drink or tiredness or a bit of both meant that we succumbed to falling fast asleep.

The next thing I knew a hand shook me roughly awake.

'What the goddam fuck? ... Who the hell are you'

I opened a bleary eye, half disoriented. Inches away from my face was that of a huge black man and he was looking none-too-pleased. I sat up, looked around then shook Barb. 'Wake up I hissed,' I turned to the guy and in my politest English accent said. 'I am terribly sorry ... we seem to have ... ' It was dawning upon me that this wasn't Gary's flat. His didn't have a balcony, nor lots of furniture in the front room, or a big blue rug on the floor.

Barb sat up and yawned.

'Oh Lord, looks like Goldilocks has got the wrong bloody bed! What's the number of this flat?'

'Flat?' The man's nostrils flared in and out, they were all I could look at.

'She means apartment.'

'Oh! 402.'

'Yep. Thought so. We've come to the wrong flat! We're guests on the floor below yours.' Then Barb stood up and brushed herself down. 'Easily done.' She leant forward and helped me up. 'Come on.'

I grabbed her hand and struggled to my feet. My tongue had swollen in my mouth to what felt like gigantic proportions. I was parched and had difficulty following what was going on.

'Were so sorry to have troubled you. It won't happen again.' Barb pushed me in the direction of the door and got us out into the corridor pulling the door too after us. We went gingerly down the next flight of stairs to Gary's flat. Managed to open the door midst stifled giggles and fell through. We remained lying on the floor laughing till our stomachs hurt and faces ached, regaling little clips of the incident.

'Did you see his face?'

'Yeah, If I hadn't been so shocked and hungover, I would have cracked up there and then.'

'And there you were lying there, feet up the wall, knickers showing and dribble coming down your cheek.'

'Where did those bottles of beer come from?'

'What beer?'

'You know, those bottles that were strewn at our feet.'

'Oh God. Now it's coming back to me now. I got them from the fridge.' We both clamped our hands over our mouths, eyes wide.

I had a vague recollection of Barb insisting that lying in the Sun without something to drink was bad for us, her words, *it doesn't pay to be dehydrated*, ringing in my ears.

'When you opened your eyes I'd swear you rubber-necked it, like that time when we got so stoned and got on the wrong bus and woke up stranded in Worcester.'

'Well, at least we didn't trash the place or throw up everywhere.'

Barb suddenly sat bolt upright.

'What? Oh no, please don't tell me ...'

She looked sheepish. 'I might have been a little sick over the balcony.'

I sat up. Should we go and look?

She lay back down. 'Nah. We're leaving tomorrow. Why cause us the distress?'

Chapter Twenty Two

We didn't go out until much later that night having had copious amounts of tea and a good dose of paracetamol each. Barb fussed about making sure that we'd packed the bulk of our things, got our flight tickets and passports put away in a safe place. All we had to do was find our way back to Faro.

We ate in Benny's bar, just regular chips and burger and washed it down with cold tins of coke. We didn't have the stomach for anything stronger. As we sat there a familiar face, one of the old patrons of Paul's Bar crossed over to say hello. His friend joined him and they sat confidently at our table.

He reached his hand across the table to Barb, 'Hi, I'm Wayne and this here is my friend Joel.' Then he directed his conversation to me. 'I heard you'd left. Is this you back for good?'

'Nah, we stopped by for a little holiday after a stint in Portugal.'

'That's interesting, how did you find Portugal? We're heading out that way tomorrow.'

I looked at Barb, she looked at me. She sat forward, leaning into the conversation. 'Well, I can thoroughly recommend Faro, all those quaint little cobbled streets and houses almost leaning into each other. They've got some great restaurants there too – some amazing sea food. There's one I could thoroughly recommend.'

I kicked her under the table. Her smirk virtually purred back.

'I love sea food. I hear they have a specialty that I'm just dying to try. Did you try the bacalhau or the cataplana.' Wayne asked me.

I shrugged. 'I have no clue, but the bacalhau sort of rings a bell. Barb, isn't that one you said was too salty?'

'Might have been, but we were so wasted at the time,' she laughed then fixed her gaze on Wayne. 'So, tell me Wayne, how are you planning to get to Portugal?'

'Oh, we've hired a car. We're picking it up tomorrow morning from the garage across the road.' He nodded his head at the garage visible through the bar window.

'How marvellous,' said Barb, her beady eyes gleaming. I could almost hear what she was thinking, it was as though the two of us were working like lionesses hunting our prey.

I chipped in, 'Wayne, I hope you don't mind me asking, but you wouldn't happen to have room for two hitchhikers looking for a lift to Faro would you?' I beamed my biggest, beguiling smile.

He eyes flicked to his friend; a look passed between them then he settled his brown eyes on me. 'Of course, we'd be glad to have you aboard.'

We were up early the next morning drinking black tea at the table before leaving. The sun was fierce. You could almost smell the heat in the air. We trundled our suitcases along the uneven pavements and across the cobbled streets to the other side of town. Semi-feral cats languished in sunlit doorways, yellow eyes watching us as we passed by.

We waited outside the car hire and would have wilted had it not been for a breeze blowing in from the sea. It dislodged petals of jasmine from the nearby bush. As the petals fluttered, I thought of how they were at the whim of the wind, travelling where ever it took them, subject to fate. I had felt like that for so long I'd considered it normal, just how things should be. Things happened to me, it was never me directing my fate.

Looking at my reflection in the window and the two men within, Wayne and Joel, sorting out the paperwork, I decided that it was time for me to take charge. From here on in I vowed to live my life on my own terms. Although I hadn't quite figured out what my terms were. It seemed like a good plan though.

Willy turned up, coffee in hand, his face still creased from slumber. He hugged me to him. 'You don't need me to tell you what an idiot Gary is. I'd have kept you in a heartbeat. You'll be okay won't you?'

'I will now Willy.'

'You'll keep in touch?'

'Always. You've been a good friend. Our paths will cross again, I promise you that.'

'I'll hold you to it. Love you, girl.'

'Love you too, Willy.'

Wayne and Joel stepped into the light, smiling, brandishing the keys. We dumped our things in the boot and started making our goodbyes. I was about to get into the car when I happened to look over my shoulder, one last look at the place.

'Wait!' A voice hollered from the other end of the street. I squinted looking towards the direction of the shout. Sheilding my eyes I could see it was Angie, shouting and waving.

'Wait!' She bent down and took off her shoes, running barefoot towards us, her raven hair fanning out behind her as she pumped her arms, a spiked shoe in each hand. She arrived all flustered and out of breath.

'Couldn't let you go without saying goodbye.' She flung her arms around me. Angie, Barb and I gathered together in a hug, promising to keep in touch, take care, write and all the things you do when a big goodbye is on the cards. We waited for our soon-to-be chauffeurs to finish their final preparations, load in their things, adjust their seats, the mirrors. They placed a large cooler bag into the footwell at the back. I heard the chink of bottles and caught a look on Joel's face.

'We'll need something to make the journey go with a zing wont we! Take a look.'

I leaned in and opened the bag. In it were a number of beers and on top was a lump of hash the size of my fist. My jaw dropped.

'What?,' I snapped my head back to look at him. 'I thought you were only going away for four days.' He nodded, 'Yup, we figured we'd best come prepared.' There was a mirth in his slow southern drawl. He pulled his baseball cap down over his brow putting his eyes in shadow, only a dimpled smile on view.

'Best prepared? Comatose more like!'

Barb was still caught up with saying her goodbyes to Angie so I decided not to say anything to her until we were on our way. It would make for an interesting surprise.

Wayne started the car and backed out of the garage forecourt. I knew it was going to be the last time I'd see us all together in Rota. My time there was done, but I was leaving with mixed emotions. My limbs felt heavy as lead, as though a sadness had lodged there and extended right to the tips of my toes and the ends of my fingers, wanting to peg themselves into the ground and root me there expecting - no demanding - a response. Some form of validation for their steadfastness. I shuddered, trying to dislodge the feeling. I had to get a grip on this new reality, pick myself up and start again.

It was hard. My head kept reflexively re-setting back to Gary. It was as though I was living life along parallel lines. There was the Frankie I showed to the world, this person, who smiled, went through the motions, made out all was well. Then there was the Frankie whose inner world was tortured, oscillating between rejection and self doubt. A maelstrom of hurt, disappointment, and abandonment. These were feelings I'd known before, they were almost old friends, I'd known them so well. They were feelings I could adjust to quite readily albeit uncomfortably, a bit like wearing a pair of old, familiar shoes that had become too tight.

There was also something else lurking, hiding among the spaces of despair. A seething. I was so bloody angry and outraged I could hardly comprehend how to let it out. How dare he do this to me? How dare he treat me this way! This thought went round and round in my head until I slipped back into the question. Why? Why did he treat me so? What did I do to deserve it? Why wasn't I good enough?

Throughout my childhood my mother continually reinforced the notion I wasn't good enough in both word and deed. I tried - oh God I tried - to appease, please, get her approval. When my little brother died, her favourite, I thought that perhaps things might have changed, that she would transfer her affections to me, but it just made it worse. I reminded her of dad. I was the product of all the things that were wrong with her life, and she took every opportunity she could to remind me of it. I lived with the mantle of guilt and shame but with no understanding as to why – at least not until I was older.

My parents were forced into a shotgun wedding. I was the product of their first foray into sex. It wasn't love, just too much alcohol and rampaging hormones that resulted in a lifetime sentence of being stuck with the wrong person. A situation possibly repeating itself with Gary's unwanted pregnancy that they were going to live with – I had a pang of sorrow for their baby.

And so, my inner and outer worlds raged with each other, and I tipped between feeling okay to wallowing in the depths of despair. It seemed no matter how I tried, I couldn't shake my addiction because that's what it was, an addiction, obsession, call it what you will. I'd built him up into some kind of demigod. Made him perfect in spite of his flaws. He was unreachable, unobtainable, just like my dad. That was the territory that I knew. That was where I felt safe.

Willy slapped the car playfully as we moved off. Wayne beeped the horn as Barb and I waved frantically, heads and arms hanging out the windows as the sounds of our goodbyes echoed down the street. It didn't take long for us to hit the major road taking us back to Portugal.

It was hot, the sun was at its zenith, even resting a hand on the car door outside risked a superficial burn. Our bodies were sticking to the vinyl seats leaving little sweat marks despite the open window and the warm air funnelling around the car.

The road picked up red dust from the fields and sloping hills and left rising clouds of it in our wake. I forced myself to think of the great arching maya blue sky that dominated the view through the windscreen.

Presently Joel twisted round and said, 'Aint it time we broke out the beers? And while you're there, roll up a doobie too.' I left it to Barb to open the cooler. All eyes were on her just to witness her reaction and it didn't disappoint.

With some difficulty several doobies were rolled, although a lot of the contents, particularly hash, got spilt on the seat and floor. It proved to be pretty strong stuff and left Barb and I shrieking with laughter from the back seat, over what I couldn't even begin to explain. The lads soon joined in and we found ourselves driving along what appeared to be an empty road rocking the car with laughter.

Bang! The car came to a quick standstill, our bodies snapped back and forth. It happened so quickly there was hardly time to see, let alone process. We had followed a sharp bend in the road with little heed to the speed we were travelling, only to drive smack dab right into the back of a Mercedes that had stopped to allow a small herd of goats to pass.

Our car began to hiss and steam rose from the bonnet. After a moment of frozen shock, Barb and I frantically made to grab all the drug and beer paraphernalia and stuff it into the cooler out of sight. Wayne and Joel sat up rubbing their eyes mumbling a stream of expletives.

I watched, breathless as the red-faced owner of the Mercedes climbed out of his car and slammed the door shut. It took him four swift strides to reach the driver's window. He was built like a bull and a raging one at that.

Wayne jumped out of the car, no doubt anxious not to let Mr Mercedes get a whiff of what we had been consuming. He steered Mr Mercedes to the point of the accident where a small jet of red-hot steam was now spouting. Joel jumped out too inspecting the damage while Wayne was deep in broken Spanish negotiations. Mr Mercedes was waving his arms like he was directing an orchestra, his voice raised and peppered with lots of Spanish expletives, especially the word joder.

Barb and I watched as Wayne leaned down, his face creased with concern. We heard him loudly announce, 'Looks like the car's totalled.'

'Oh what?' Barb began to laugh, partly because of the absurdity of the situation and mostly because we were all stoned out of our tiny minds. It was evident, our eyes were bloodshot and slitted.

Grasping the situation a little better than Barb I stifled the urge to laugh, holding my breath and rubbing my eyes. 'Barb, this is serious!'

She laughed even harder, arms crossed, holding on to her sides bent double, utterly helpless. The more I tried to dissuade her from laughing the harder and louder she laughed. Eventually I cracked too, the two of us rocking the car we were laughing so hard. At one point even the men stopped haggling to look at us through a steady cloud of radiator steam squawking in the back seat.

I leaned my head out of the window, 'It's okay, we're just a bit hysterical from shock!' Barb was now hiding her head behind the passenger's front seat trying to stuff her mouth with a knuckle. She was beyond help.

'How the hell are we going to get home? Our flight leaves in less than three hours?' I said to no one in particular. Outside, Wayne and Mr Mercedes were exchanging details. Mr Mercedes had the only working transport to be seen for miles around and was probably about to get into it and drive off.

I jumped out of the car, the heat of the tarmac burning the soles of my feet, setting me off hopping from foot-to-foot lively fashion. 'Aeroport!' I squawked, hopping, flapping my arms and tapping my watch trying to grab Mr Mercedes attention. 'Aeroport!' I shrieked more insistently, my voice rising in volume and octave while simultaneously trying to do my best impression of a plane. Finally, I got Mr Mercedes' attention in spite of Barb's raucous laughter.

'You go aeroport?'

I was still hopping up and down on the spot like some rare extravagant bird caught up in a strange mating ritual.

'Yes, aeroport. Yes. Yes.' I nodded my head frantically.

'Okay. Aeroport,' Mr Mercedes shrugged as though worn down by the situation. Then he opened his boot and Barb and I quickly loaded our luggage into the back. It all happened so quickly, as though in some form of surreal dream and lets face it, the drugs had a lot to do with it. Next thing we knew, there we were sitting in the back seat of the Mercedes watching Wayne and Joel recede into the distance, half wondering how they were going to get out of that dilemma.

'Well, at least they've got a bunch of beer and smokes to keep them going,' said Barb, a chuckle rising from her throat.

The Mercedes proved to be a far better lift; air conditioning, seats that weren't scorching hot and didn't stick to your sweaty legs. Classical music played in crackle-free stereo as we sped our way to the airport. Mr Mercedes even kept a tin of boiled sweets in his glove compartment that he passed round. So classy.

He dropped us right at the departures area at the airport. We trundled in, utterly unflustered and, by some miracle, arrived in time, including the hour we should have been there for the international flight - a point that had somehow been completely overlooked by us.

Our plane touched down on a rainswept runway at Heathrow airport. We queued at passport control shuffling alongside rows of travel weary passengers, screaming children and leathery looking seniors who looked as though they'd spent too long in the sun. We waited for our suitcases to appear at the luggage carousel for what seemed like an age. As we waited Barb asked what I planned to do next.

'I have no clue Barb, just take each day as it comes. What about you?'

'I've been thinking. In fact I've been doing a lot of thinking. I don't think I am ready to let Sam go. He's a good guy, a really good guy.'

'Are you saying what I think you're saying?'

'What, the 'L' word?'

Well, is he 'L' word material?'

'Yes, I think he is.'

I beamed, 'That's wonderful. Does that mean I have to get a hat then?'

'Steady on. Let's not go that far. I've got to see if he'll take me back first.'

'Mrs Barbara ... '

'Enough!' she punched me on the arm. 'Look, there's our cases.'

We leapt up to rescue them from the carousel, diving our way between the other passengers clogging up our access. Having retrieved them we forged our way through the hundreds of passengers all in a hurry to get somewhere until we finally arrived at the bus terminal to take us home. I had that sense of being ambushed with all the rushing, the noise, the hordes of people, so much so that my shoulders felt as though they had hitched several inches higher than they should have been. The laughter had been leached out of us with all the preoccupations of catching the right tube, being at the right terminal, being on the right bus at the right time.

I sat on the nearside of the window looking out as the countryside sped by. Barb and I hardly spoke. My mind was trying to gather the fortnight's events, grapple them into some semblance of order and understanding. Here I was, unexpectedly back home again. My happily ever after had gone the way all mediocre breakfast cereals go. Things hadn't turned out as I planned. Was it love? I still couldn't quite decide, perhaps it was on my part. One thing was for sure, I needed to re-examine my understanding of what love, and being loved, meant. My recent experiences had changed me irrevocably. I was emotionally bruised, my pride dented, but I was still intact. I had learned what love wasn't, the hard way. And, as Barb tactfully pointed out, 'Sometimes things just don't work out, not because of something you did or didn't do, but because of what's going on for someone else.'

The thought turned over like some kind of balm in my head then I turned to my friend and said, 'Thank for being there, Barb.'

She looked up from her tabloid and smiled. 'De nada. I've had a blast. I don't think I'd have done this on my own and if I had I certainly wouldn't have had as much fun as I did with you Frankie.'

And I knew, even though my heart was still raw, that eventually things would work out right, that perhaps one day, real love would find me, but not quite yet.

Our bus rounded the corner and headed into Cheltenham's National Coach depot, passing a row of cherry trees. I craned my neck to look, noticing that the blossom phase had finished, new leaves were emerging and buds beginning to swell. It struck me that I had come full circle. I was back where I started - but there was a change. I was different somehow. Something had shifted. Despite it being such a monumental year I felt girded, stronger, more able to stand in my own shoes and I knew, in that moment, that perhaps things were going to be alright afterall.

About the Author – Lea Taylor

Lea Taylor is an author and professional storyteller and as such has written and performed both nationally and internationally. She has a fondness for the ridiculous and an eye for a story. Known for stopping double decker buses on the Royal Mile in Edinburgh as part of her art, she has a penchant for dressing up (driving with crinolines can prove bothersome) and always has a toffee hammer to hand which she claims is a left over from her Suffragette days!

Lea graduated from Edinburgh University as a mature student and lives in Scotland with her husband, son and two crazy rescue dogs. She is the Creative Director of The Book Whisperers CIC – a social enterprise that helps people write, edit, and publish their books. Her own books are eclectic, ranging from contemporary folklore to books for children and novels for adults. She is also an avid tea drinker with a fondness tea cakes.

Twitter: Lea Taylor – Author @Leataylor5783

Other books by Lea Taylor
- The House Beside The Cherry Tree
- Animals, Beasties and Monsters of Scotland
- Midlothian Folk Tales
- Malaky Midge and the Loch Ness Monster

Printed in Great Britain
by Amazon